MEET THE FORCE RECON TEAM .

JACK SWAYNE
The leader of the team. A brilliant tactician and superb soldier. For him, failure is not an option . . . ever.

GUNNY POTTS
A giant of a man. Loyalty to his team comes first, the mission comes second . . . and nothing else comes close.

NIGHT RUNNER
A full-blooded American Indian. Even with the cutting-edge technology used by the team, the deadliest thing about him is his senses.

FRIEL
An ex-street thug turned disciplined Marine. A natural-born killer with no remorse. Possibly the deadliest shot in the world.

FORCE RECON
The first novel in the explosive new series by
James V. Smith, Jr.

FORCE RECON

James V. Smith, Jr.

BERKLEY BOOKS, NEW YORK

FORCE RECON

A Berkley Book / published by arrangement with
the author

PRINTING HISTORY
Berkley edition / August 1999

All rights reserved.
Copyright © 1999 by James V. Smith, Jr.
This book may not be reproduced in whole
or in part, by mimeograph or any other means,
without permission. For information address:
The Berkley Publishing Group, a division of Penguin Putnam Inc.,
375 Hudson Street, New York, New York 10014.

The Penguin Putnam Inc. World Wide Web site address is
http://www.penguinputnam.com

ISBN: 0-425-16975-8

BERKLEY®
Berkley Books are published by The Berkley Publishing Group,
a division of Penguin Putnam Inc.,
375 Hudson Street, New York, New York 10014.
BERKLEY and the "B" logo are trademarks
belonging to Penguin Putnam Inc.

PRINTED IN THE UNITED STATES OF AMERICA

10 9 8 7 6 5 4 3 2 1

DEDICATION

To the best of the Few, the Proud

EVENT SCENARIO 12—DAY 1

"CAP THE SECOND Mook first?" said Friel, squinting through the electronic scope of his 20-millimeter sniper gun at the Cubans in the longboat four hundred meters offshore. "You seen enough, Number One? I seen enough."

Friel's staccato accent came off like a string of damp firecrackers in Jack Swayne's earpiece, all fizzles and pops. Swayne recognized the tone well enough. Friel being Friel. Working up to make a kill. Venting homicidal hostility, the kid's dominant emotion.

"Affirm," Swayne said, keeping his voice flat. "On my order."

Even as Swayne pronounced the death sentence on him, the Cuban whipped his pistol barrel across the face of his captive, one of two Marine pilots who had been forced to punch out of their trainer over

Cuban territorial waters. The pilot tried to lean away, but the Cuban jerked his head back and continued working him over.

Friel let loose a stream of street curses, ending with, "Dammit, let me take his ass out right now, Boss."

"This is Spartan One. I *said,* on my command."

"Spartan Four, roger, out," Friel snapped. Not enough to be considered insubordination. Just enough to be considered.

Swayne made a mental note for the after-action debriefing. Call Friel down on freelance comments over the radio. Not that foul language bothered him. Even with Operational Mission Control monitoring their radio traffic via uplink to satellite and downlink to two hundred feet below the sacred, secret ground at Quantico, Virginia. Trouble was, useless chatter wasted time, and right now every second was precious. At any instant, the calculations cycloning through Swayne's head might flash a result, maybe a call to bore a 20-millimeter tunnel through the Cuban's head, maybe with only a half-second window of opportunity. So, he didn't appreciate gratuitous commentary. Couldn't afford it. Wouldn't stand for it. Friel had joined the team three missions ago. Time he got with the program.

Not that Swayne disagreed with the Boston hoodlum-turned-Marine. No way did he feel as flat as his voice. Friel's Mook definitely would be the first of the three to die. And soon.

• • •

FRIEL CHAFED AT the tone of reprimand in the captain's voice. *What was it with officers anyways? Always looking for the fly shit in the pepper.* He liked Swayne well enough—as well as he could like any officer. But why the hell couldn't he lighten up once in a while? Weren't they a team? Wasn't that what they were called—a Force Recon *Team*? Hell, they were just like the Celtics, except that they only had four players and shot bad guys instead of hoops. And that they were up against Castro's Mooks and Khadaffy's Kripps instead of the Indiana Pacers and Chicago Bulls. *What about that, Captain?*

He took a deep breath and held it. It helped him chill whenever an officer came on with the hassle. A technique right out of his sniping ritual. He put the infrared laser dot on the right temple of the second Mook, feeling an immediate calm. The motion of the sea caused the longboat to bob in the chop, but that invisible IR laser spot stuck to the Cuban like a tattoo. It would stay put until Friel made it move. Until after he launched one of his miniature fire-and-forget missiles at the dot. Until the projectile made its self-guided flight and merged with the laser spot, passing through the skull, sucking out the gray matter through the vacuum trail, emptying the Commie Mook bastard's head like an enema. His sense of humor restored, Friel finally exhaled. He permitted himself a smile. Nice thing about Communists these days—nobody much gave a shit when you capped one of them off.

He practiced his shift from the first Mook to the second, then to the third. He had them all drilled. He reviewed his ordnance: One six-pack of inert sabot shot locked and loaded. The titanium-alloy slug could pierce nine inches of hardened armor steel at 55 degrees. Five rounds in the hopper, one in the chamber. All he needed now was the captain's *Dominus vobiscum*.

"What do you think, Number One?" he transmitted through the discrete, voice-activated boom mike at the corner of his mouth. "The medieval Mook first? Then the bastard at the tiller?"

SWAYNE SMILED AT the octave shift in Friel's voice. No matter how pissed Friel got, he cooled off in seconds. Never pouted. Always tended to business. A rough-cut Marine—one of the few and proud who had taken a four-year hitch in lieu of five to fifteen at Massachusetts Central Correctional Facility. Swayne liked him. A lot. He was tough and spirited and maybe the best shooter in the Corps, if not the entire DoD. Plus, he had that raggedy-assed accent Swayne found so amusing. *The bastid at the tillah?* And that erratic vocabulary. What words he didn't borrow from Oprah, *Star Trek*, and the cop shows, he made up on the spot, inventing his own brand of Beavis and Butthead.

"Negative," Swayne said, getting down to business. "Take the target in the bow on the second shot."

Swayne had checked and rechecked the situation

in the boat. In contrast to the maniac beating on the pilot, the Cuban in front with the AK-50 was alert. Too alert. He kept scanning the beach where Swayne's team awaited them instead of gawking at the light show that had been arranged astern. On the horizon, the Navy and Coast Guard were putting on a display of pyrotechnics and searchlights worthy of a rock concert. The idea was to create the impression that all the effort had gone into searching for the downed Harrier crew in international waters. A complete ruse. All for the benefit of the Cubans.

And the press, of course. When the inevitable news helicopters showed up, they would get their precious pictures for the early morning news cycle. Meanwhile, Castro's boys were supposed to be lulled into a false sense of security, so Swayne's Force Recon unit, Team 2400—called Team Midnight for the obvious reason, radio call sign Spartan—could do its work.

But the guy in the bow of the boat wasn't buying into the eye-candy offshore, wasn't letting down his guard. Because of his vigilance and all that firepower, he'd be second to die. The third Cuban, the one manning the longboat's tiller, was no factor. As soon as he beached the tossing boat, he'd see the other two fold and drop in place, the way head-shot men always dropped. He'd abandon ship and take off running, all asshole and elbows.

He'd be found back-shot. His unit would know he'd died a coward. His family too, if Fidel saw fit to order the body returned to them for burial. Which he wouldn't. The guy would be left to the crabs and gulls. Week later, an official military condolences delegation would show up at the family's shanty with a bushel of crabs, compliments of El Presidente. The family would cherish the dearly departed in a way they had never enjoyed him in life. Best crab cakes they'd ever eaten. Amused CIA insiders had described the ghoulish practice to Guantanamo Bay Force Recon units as Fidel's remedy for cowards and deserters.

Swayne recalculated the equation. No need to be cruel about it, he supposed. Maybe they could cut the third guy some slack, maybe shoot him in the face.

WHITLASH, MONTANA—2042 HOURS LOCAL (0342 ZULU)

THE MATTE-BLACK DODGE Durango rolled through Whitlash from the north at thirty miles an hour and continued into the Sweet Grass Hills. Elapsed time in town: less than five seconds.

Two miles north lay the U.S.-Canada border. Left and right of the Dodge lay the Hills, a string of three volcanic buttes called the Broken Mountains in 1806 by Meriwether Lewis, co-commander of the Corps of Discovery.

The figure in the passenger seat pulled back the sleeve of his camouflage-pattern utilities jacket and checked his washtub of a watch.

"Might as well slow down," he said to his driver in French. "We're not going to arrive at the Gold Butte on time."

"My apologies, General Pareto. Who could have known the Border Patrol would have repaired the broken fence since our reconnaissance?"

Pareto gave a smile that would have been anemic even if his mouth weren't so pinched into his broad face—a smile that said: *Why, you, in fact. You could have known. It was, after all, your job to know. Idiot.* He pointed at the windshield. "Ahead there. Turn off the road and put the vehicle in defilade. I'll make the calls from here."

The driver turned onto the prairie, but jammed on the brakes right away, struck by the raucous flashing of red, white, and blue lights reflected in all his mirrors. "Border Patrol," he stammered. "We are finished." A siren yelped twice. "Quick, my general, make the calls before he catches up."

Pareto adjusted the rearview mirror and blew a kiss at the reflection. He lit a cigarette and sucked the smoke deep into his lungs, holding it so it could be absorbed. On the exhale he opened the passenger door.

A loudspeaker crackled as the interior lights came on. "Stay in the *vee*-hicle," ordered the amplified voice.

"Good advice," the general said to his driver. "Stay. Two men will make him wary." He stepped to the ground, feeling the crunch of frosty grass under his boot soles. Pareto calmly checked the skies.

His people at The Fortress had told him of a sudden blizzard blowing up in the southwest of the state. That would complicate things, for certain.

"I repeat: Stay—in—the—*vee*-hicle."

Pareto might as well have been deaf. He walked alongside the Dodge, shielding his eyes with his both hands. When he reached the rear bumper, a spotlight hit him full in the face. Beneath his fingers the general glimpsed a Montana exempt plate that told him this was not a Border Patrol officer. He stumbled, then stood still, grinning broadly, trying to look as stupid as the stupidest American he had known. *A difficult task,* he thought.

The truck door opened.

"Don't move, sir," said a voice—now unamplified—from beside the left front fender. "Officer Windsor, Montana Fish, Wildlife, and Parks. You boys are out late for hunting today. Or else early for tomorrow."

"*Oui.*" *A game warden.* The dumb smile grew dumber.

"*We,* what? Which is it, early or late?"

The general shrugged in his best *aw-shucks* imitation.

"We been getting tips about poaching. You just drove off the road onto posted land. You got permission to be driving across private land?"

"*Oui.*"

"We again. How come it is that your brand-new vehicle is squeaky clean but the license plate is cov-

•

ered with mud? You wouldn't object to a search of your vee-hicle, would you?"

"*Oui.*" Pareto brushed at the mud on the plate, then inspected the soiled goatskin of his glove.

"*Oui?*" After a pause the warden said, "Ah, I get it. You're speaking French, aren't you?"

"*Oui.*" In French, Pareto told the officer that he was from Montreal. And that he was going to shoot him in the face.

"Ah." The voice lost its edge. "I got part of that. *Canadian.* And *Montreal.* Sorry, but I don't speak French. You speak any English?"

The general manufactured a smile so broad it hurt his small mouth. Nodding and smiling, he began speaking French in torrents, spewing obscenities like water from a fire hose—but in a high pitch, as if he were afraid of this twit.

When the general went silent, the game warden stepped toward him and said, "May I see your hunting license and permission, sir?"

"*Oui.*" The general had closed his eyes. Now he opened them to slits. He saw the boots, the officer's right hand on the butt of his pistol, his left hand held out.

The general reached behind his right hip, as if to get his wallet. Instead he unlatched the rear hatch of the Dodge.

"Hey!" The general saw the warden's hand tighten on his pistol grip, the flap open on his holster. "How come it is that you can understand English so well but don't speak it."

"Ironic, no?" the general said in English.

Instead of holding out a wallet, he came up with a .45-caliber pistol. "Here is my license." With his free hand, he pulled open the rear of the Durango, and three black forms spilled into the night, three broad-chested Rottweilers.

The game warden convulsed, first in shock at seeing every cop's worst nightmare coming true, then at the sight of the dogs—or rather, their rows of fangs.

Pareto uttered a command in French. Before the combined 350 pounds of attack dog hit the warden, the man felt the impact of a low-velocity, hollowpoint slug entering his body under the chin, blooming into a copper rose inside his head, and exiting with a chunk of skull and brain matter the size of half a grapefruit.

The general called the dogs off to keep them clear of his line of fire. "Here is my permission." A second bullet tore into the officer's right temple. Already dead, the game warden flinched, shooting a .38-caliber bullet into his own thigh. On the frozen grass, he twitched once and lay still. The general inserted a fresh clip and let the slide ram home just as his driver appeared at the rear bumper.

Pareto handed him the old clip. "Reload this."

"He is dead," the driver pronounced, his voice trembling, keeping a wary eye on the dogs.

"It would seem." Pareto felt mild disappointment that he had no time to let his Rottweilers finish the business with the warden.

"I think I might be sick."

Pareto sniffed and checked the inside of his wrist. "Be sick then. But don't vomit on the truck. I must make the calls." He murmured to the dogs, and they vanished inside the Dodge without a sound.

He produced a cell phone and tapped out the first of four preset numbers. He made his calls to a pair of units at sites farther south inside Montana, a third unit at Naval Base San Diego, and a fourth at Fort Benning, Georgia.

Inside Cuba—2253 hours (0353 Zulu)

As the boat approached to within three hundred meters of shore, the scenario played out in Swayne's head all over again: the sudden deaths of the Cubans. Followed by the rescue of the two pilots—he hoped like hell the lump under the tarp in the bow was the second. Gunny Potts and Sergeant Night Runner would each snatch a pilot out of the longboat, calm him (and if he wouldn't be calmed, incapacitate him with a forearm shiver to the point of the chin), and leading (or carrying) a man apiece, haul ass. Swayne would run point, clearing the egress route to the cove a quarter mile away, dive into the black water, blow the ballast on their DRACULA craft moored at neutral buoyancy on the bottom, and surface to stand ready with covering fire for the others. Friel would bring up the rear, watching everybody's six with his 20-millimeter cannon, accurate to a thousand meters at night, three times that under ideal day conditions.

Swayne might become impatient with Friel once in a while, but he felt utter confidence in his ability as a shooter. He'd watched the lance corporal touch off a full six-round load at a squad of watermelons at a mile and a half in training, splattering a dozen in under ten seconds. Friel's shooting was even more remarkable than the fire-and-forget technology of his 20-millimeter weapon, state of the art in sniper weaponry, replacing the single-shot 50-caliber McMillan sniper gun the SEALs still used. The laser spot of his scope would barely illuminate a target before he would touch off one of the self-propelled rounds and move to the next watermelon, his aim as steady as if his body operated on the same NASA-developed stabilizing gyroscopes that each round carried. As the last three rounds of the first load were homing on their individually designated targets, Friel could be up and running to a secondary position, reloading on the move to select another group of targets. On two previous live missions, Friel had proved that what could be done with watermelons could also be accomplished to the turbaned heads of Libyans and Iranians. Friel was, in short, the most efficient—not to mention most enthusiastic—killer Swayne had ever met.

After Friel had covered their trail, there'd be the surface dash at fifty-five knots on the DRACULA craft, built on the principles of an oversized Jet Ski but capable of underwater operation like the Swimmer Delivery Systems of the Navy. They'd reach the safety of the blacked-out cruiser loitering not entirely in international waters, and hand off their precious cargo to the Navy. Wrapping up Team Event 12. Leaving the Cubans nothing but crab bait. End of story, end of mission.

He checked in with the remaining two Spartans, Gunnery Sergeant Delmont Potts and Sergeant Robert Night Runner, his voice activating the boom microphone suspended at the corner of his mouth.

Potts came back. "Acme kit out and set to seismic, remote, and self-destruct," he reported in his mild, even tone. "Negative contact, Cap."

POTTS SWEPT THE tall grass and low scrub in overlapping arcs with his night-vision goggles, clearing the closest areas first. In successive, sweeping motions, he looked farther outward from his position, gazing over the top of his XM-80 machine gun, called the Brat for the sound it made when fired in short bursts on automatic. Force Recon Marines themselves had taken the concept of the Brat to the top-secret R&D team at Colt. The M-60, a proven combat weapon from Vietnam to Desert Storm, had only one liability, the weight of the weapon and the ammunition a team had to carry. The mission was to design exactly the same weapon as the 7.62-millimeter M-60, but scaled down to 5.56, the same ammunition as the M-16. Using composite materials like graphite, and light but durable metals. Adding a variable rate of fire on automatic. And some electronic gingerbread. The result was the XM-80, already combat-tested by Team 2400 on four previous missions. Potts found he could carry 2,500 rounds plus the gun and still pack less of a load than when he toted his M-60E3 and only a thousand rounds. Potts had pronounced the weapon fit for duty, calling it "fine as the frog hair on a baby's behind."

His teammates didn't even mind carrying five hundred to one thousand extra rounds either. In an emergency, they could always de-link the ammunition and fire it in their own weapons.

Potts cleared his sector carefully, stopping his head, moving his eyes in a jerk-stop-jerk-stop pattern that helped him pick up movement and unusual shapes. In only ten minutes, he had reconned the roads leading into the rear of the team at the beachhead three times over, from three different positions. And he had already positioned an ambush kit at a road intersection, its components easily carried inside a briefcase but capable of enough explosive firepower to simulate a platoon-size attack. *That Friel,* thought Potts. *He could be a funny little infantile delinquent when he wasn't so busy being a painus in the anus. He had been the one to name it the Acme kit. Said it reminded him of one of the gadgets that Wile E. Coyote was always ordering to bust the Roadrunner's balls.*

In his sparse transmission to his captain, Potts had reported that he had selected a variety of triggering devices. A vehicle rolling by would shake the device and explode a seismic detonator. Or Potts could set it off himself by remote control from more than a mile away. Finally, a timing device would self-destruct the kit after the team had departed, so the enemy could not recover the technology. The kit had built-in fail-safes too—anybody who touched one of its components before disarming it with an electronic code would have an arm blown off.

Potts never like that part. Always worried that some curious kids might stumble onto one of the devices. So he always blew the things himself on the way out of an Event.

By the way, did birds have balls?

NIGHT RUNNER, OBSERVING the men in the longboat through the night scope on his own specially modified carbine, the CAR-15XE2, simply said, "Three is set."

He had long since swept his sector of the tiny beachhead a hundred meters beyond the position where he and Friel now lay. He'd cleared the area with both his electronic night-vision sight and his own ultra-sensitive devices, the eyes of a Blackfeet warrior. He had declared the sector free of enemy. No sight, no sound, no track, no smell. No Cubans— no nothing (of the human species anyway)—had been in the area anytime today.

THE MISSION UNFOLDED as it always did—in Swayne's mind.

The know-it-alls and big shots had it wrong. Forever blowing smoke about how coolheaded he was under fire, packing sand in his skivvies about his tactical battlefield leadership. Buying him drinks. Slapping his back. Wanting to get close to him. Thinking they could experience combat vicariously by standing at his shoulder. Hoping to learn something about leading a Force Recon Team. If only he'd reveal the secrets about leading Team Midnight into eleven combat operations—tonight was twelve—they might be as good as the Spartans.

What they didn't know, and what Swayne couldn't teach them, was that any poor dumb bastard who waited until somebody popped a cap was already behind the eight ball. Planning and training? Yeah, sure, good stuff. But what Marine didn't train? Hell, even USAF bluebonnets trained. And if planning alone could get the job done, the Navy already would have planned warfare right out of existence.

No, preparation, quick wits, and bravery by themselves didn't feed the feline. Just ask the Army Rangers that had taken the rectal ram in Somalia, or the SEALs that had endured back-to-back disasters in Grenada and Panama.

What the wannabe combat leaders needed to cultivate more than anything was the ability to fight and win a hundred variations of the battle beforehand. In their heads. That was Swayne's gift. Not luck or magic. No psychic hotline. Just the uncanny capacity to calculate the possibilities and—so far—to select the best odds, and come out on top.

He'd survey the situation, gather data, and factor

in the variables. Refigure. Refactor. Replay. Again
and again, never assuming he'd figured a situation
pat. Just when you'd calculated a problem right into
a corner and mentally maneuvered it to a standstill,
it could go south as fast as—

The pitch of the longboat's outboard engine sputtered, and the wake of the boat caught up to its
outboard motor.

See?

THE MISSOURI BREAKS, MONTANA—2056 HOURS (0356 ZULU)

A FIVE-TON GMC rolled on the command spoken in
French over the cell phone. The diesel truck rum-
bled along the very route Lewis and Clark were fol-
lowing when they first heard the thunder of the
Great Falls of the Missouri in June 1805. East of
Great Falls, Montana's second largest city. Home of
Malmstrom Air Base.

The GMC turned off the asphalt onto a well-
groomed gravel approach to the two-acre area en-
closed by cyclone fencing.

Inside the windswept compound of the Minuteman III Missile Sector Command and Control Center, motion detectors picked up the truck.
Surveillance cameras showed three views of it to the
duty NCO sixty feet underground. The technical sergeant nudged the Staff Duty Officer, a newby right
out of the Academy, to get his attention. The two

of them watched the truck accelerate down the quarter-mile access road to the compound.

"Mac Attack, sir."

The butter-bar, hearing only the one heart-stopping word, squealed, "We're under *attack*?"

The sergeant laughed. "Relax. *Mac* Attack. Mac is short for Old MacDonald. It's probably a drunk farmer. Sometimes they get tanked up after selling a load of grain. On the way back to the farm they make a wrong turn and pull up to—"

"He's not slowing down. I'd better roust the SPs. You think?"

"He'll stop."

"What if he damages the fence?"

"SPs'll take his keys and call the Highway Patrol. We'll make an entry in the log, and—*Shit!*"

The GMC plowed through the locked, reinforced fencing, setting off intruder alarms all over the compound. A second camera, a bird's-eye view from a communications tower above, showed the truck aiming for the reinforced concrete blockhouse. No need to alert the Security Police now. The duty sentries would see the danger for themselves. A head-on shot of the truck showed it barreling toward the guardhouse.

The butter-bar snatched up the secure blue telephone dedicated to non-nuclear emergencies and fumbled for a set of keys belted to his waist. "I'm calling this in," he shouted, his voice pitched higher than ever. He found the right key, inserted it into the transceiver box. Turning it activated a direct, underground landline to Malmstrom.

A voice in the receiver of the blue phone said: "Malmstrom CACC. Major Sharp, Duty Officer. What is it, Sector November 25 Bravo?"

"We have a physical intrusion. A drunk farmer—"

The sergeant interrupted. "Those guys ain't farmers."

The snowy black and white security camera images showed the battle unfold like a poorly made home video. An intruder's assault rifle sparkled. Answering flashes from the blockhouse washed out the image of the ground-level camera, but the overhead view showed the gunman go down, writhing. The second intruder ran behind the truck, out of the direct line of fire, heading for the gate.

Four SPs ran out of the blockhouse, two to each side of the truck.

Suddenly, the video image flashed over. The interior lights flickered as the site's self-contained power units took over from downed electrical lines. The explosion set off a second set of alarms—calibrated for nuclear blasts or earthquakes 3.5 or higher on the Richter Scale. Most of the ground disturbance was moderated by the facility's seismic-shock-absorption system, but the men in the control center could still feel it.

A voice barked through the receiver: "What's your SitRep?"

The butter-bar, mesmerized by the security camera images, hadn't said a word since reporting the drunk farmer. He might be a newby, but he'd seen enough CNN coverage of Desert Storm to know what that last flash and dead screen meant.

"A bomb," he said into the blue phone, his lips trembling. "We've just been hit by a truck bomb."

INSIDE CUBA—2259 HOURS (0359 ZULU)

SWAYNE STUDIED THE Cuban longboat through his laser-designating, laser-ranging night-vision binoculars, an improvement on the technology that came out of Desert Storm. But they were heavy and bulky besides, hanging like a goiter from his neck. He'd never have brought them, except for Colonel Zavello, who not only insisted they be tested on an operational mission, but also demanded a full report on them within twenty-four hours of returning, hand-carried to the OMCC.

Colonel Z. Swayne visualized the hard, square face, his eyes—one good, one glass—usually hidden behind wraparound shades black and opaque as a pay phone. *The Z-Man.* Easygoing as a bucket of acid. *The Killer Z.* Compassionate as Saddam Hussein. *Zorro.* Reasonable as—

Swayne checked his thoughts. He could not afford to visit the part of him haunted by Colonel Zavello. Not at a time like this.

His left forefinger probed for the ranging toggle, but found the zoom instead. The binocular motor whined like a mosquito, increasing the magnification power to 20X. Too much too fast. *Damn things.* He reversed, dropping back to 10X, found the other switch, and ranged, working the toggle until the longboat settled into a workable magnification.

He murmured into the boom mike in front of his lips. "They've started a right turn." He reported the digital readout in the binoculars to his shooters: Friel, the primary, and Runner. "Range, two-eight-zero." *283.492 meters if you wanted to get anal about it,* he thought.

"You think we been tagged? Want me to go dental on him?"

"Negative." *Dental.* Swayne shook his head. Friel. Talking about giving the guy a 20-millimeter root canal. Street talk. Another thing they were going to address on the post-event de-brief. "Range, three-one-five."

"They running out to sea? Want me to fire them up?"

"Negative." He gave a sigh of relief as the longboat continued turning, coming around first to a head-on view, then slowly broadside—ranging out at a steady 272.373. The Cubans had made a tight circle. The man at the tiller fiddled with the engine, working at it with both hands. The longboat settled into its own wake. The motor sputtered and died.

They lay offshore, bobbing just beyond the shelf where the surf began building. Waiting. To Swayne that could only mean two things, both of them bad. Either the enemy knew the team had come ashore and were afraid to land. Or they were playing it safe, waiting for reinforcements to secure the beach before coming ashore. Or both.

New variables, either way. Lying amid the sigh of a breeze in the sea oats, Swayne began calculating a fresh set of solutions.

FORT BENNING, GEORGIA—2301 HOURS LOCAL (0401 ZULU)

AN E-Z HAUL rental truck, a twenty-two-foot Isuzu diesel four-door, sat perfectly camouflaged—in plain sight. On the street, parked at the curb in front of a vacant duplex in the Field Grade Officers Family Housing Area. Anybody who noticed the truck would simply think that yet another major or colonel and his (or her) family would be moving into the neighborhood tomorrow. Nobody paid much attention to one more blip in the never-ending turnover rate at the sprawling post.

When his cell phone warbled, the driver sat up in the backseat where he'd been napping fitfully, and grunted into the mouthpiece.

"Alo."

He listened, grunted again, folded the phone, and climbed over the front seat, awakening his partner by stepping on his head, not altogether by accident.

The man started the engine and chugged the Isuzu away from the curb, checking his mirror to see that the sixteen-foot trailer followed. A sketch map and instructions lay on the seat beside him, wrapped in a case of double-weave Nomex fabric. He picked up the map case and slapped the kid across the chest with it.

The kid gave him a narrowed glare, like some enforcer on a junior-level hockey team. The driver showed a wide-eyed look of fear, and turned his attention to the road. The kid snorted in satisfaction, too stupid to know he was being mocked. Smiling, he began to open the map case.

The driver said, "Tuck that into your jacket. So we don't leave it behind by accident."

He said this in French, thinking all the while, also in French, that leaving it behind was exactly what he intended to do.

INSIDE CUBA—2309 HOURS LOCAL (0409 ZULU)

SONOFABITCH!

The realization hit Swayne harder than the occasional pistol-whipping being laid on the pilot in the longboat. He'd blown it. Big time.

Oh, yeah. For all his cocksureness about his computer-like brain cranking out fail-safe solutions, he'd screwed up to the max, and the Marine Corps was about to lose two good men because of him. Not to mention the embarrassment the country would suffer when Castro paraded his captives down the main streets of Havana.

To confirm his blunder, he trained the too-

bulky, too-heavy, too-many-functions-crammed-into-
one-case binoculars on the Cuban with the AK-50,
the carbine version of the AK-47. He jammed at the
zoom toggle, running the power out to 48X digital.
At that magnification, the combination of his pulse,
his hands trembling, the sea breeze, and the rising
and settling of the longboat in the chop made it difficult to pick out detail. But not impossible. Swayne
saw the unmistakable glimmer of a wire draped over
the side of the boat.

And the AK-50. He should have noticed earlier
that it wasn't standard issue. Okay, the folding metal
stock was standard, but not the muzzle end. It was
too short and it had no hinged bayonet. The barrel
had been cut down, making it the loudest, most in-
accurate, hardest-to-control assault gun in the world.
Sexy-looking but practically useless for aimed fire.
The kind of weapon the machismo Navy of Fidel
Castro would prefer. The men in the longboat
weren't fishermen or irregulars or militia. They
weren't even soldiers.

The wire was a low-frequency antenna. SEALs
used them all the time to communicate underwater.
No wonder the AWACS hadn't intercepted any radio traffic between the longboat and another station.

He projected the navigation charts for this area
onto his mind's eye. Two hundred meters offshore
the seabed dropped away sharply. At three hundred
meters—where the longboat drifted—the depth fell
away to four hundred feet.

"Rally on me," he growled into his mike. "ASAP. Those guys are Cuban sailors, and they're waiting on a submarine."

NAVAL BASE SAN DIEGO—2012 HOURS LOCAL (0412 ZULU)

EYEWITNESSES DESCRIBED THE hit on the light cruiser *Thomas Jefferson* as something right out of a World War II movie. First reports said a dive bomber must have hit the ship, sending up vertical spikes of flame, as in films of the Japanese attack on Pearl Harbor. Close behind those narratives came descriptions of the cruiser's fantail lifting right out of the water and breaking in two à la *Titanic*.

But nobody could conclusively establish that an aircraft had overflown the cruiser, so one enterprising duty officer phoned military and civilian towers. A night supervisor at the ATCC confirmed that no aircraft had been painted by radar in the area of the explosion for at least half an hour. Harried Navy watch officers began to probe witnesses about the possibility of a submarine. Sure enough, as soon as the question was asked, half-a-dozen excited witnesses came up with an entire fleet of submarines, which proved to be nothing more than a pack of sea lions feeding in the bay.

Nobody even considered the possibility that a measly nine-pound mine with magnetic framing, a clumsy East-European knockoff of the U.S. Limpit

mine, delivered by a swimmer in off-the-shelf sport
SCUBA gear, could have caused so much damage.

Except for the rescue crews on site and the inevitable swarm of news helicopters, everybody
seemed more concerned with the lapse of security
than with the loss of life—and the news crews
didn't care all *that* much. They had their smoke and
fire. Ambulances and the bandages. Flesh and blood
and screams. Pictures and audio to die for.

INSIDE CUBA—2313 HOURS LOCAL (0413 ZULU)

IN SECONDS, FRIEL and Night Runner found Swayne
and took up positions to provide all-round security
while they waited for Potts.

But Gunny did not close up right away. Instead
he reported, "I got trucks and tactical cat-eye lights
to the northwest. Maybe five miles. Driving under
blackout. A reception committee, maybe?"

Swayne rogered, cranking the report of the new
factor into his equation. His scenario was fast becoming worse than worst-case.

Potts asked, "You still want me to rally on
you?"

"Arm your Acme kit and come on in."

In minutes, Potts materialized out of the night.
Swayne never quite could get over how swiftly the
three-hundred-pounder could move. And so silently,
quieter even than his low voice.

They literally put their four heads together on
Swayne's hand signal, a snipping motion with the

first two fingers of one hand. They switched off their mikes. Every member of the team wore a miniature secure radio strapped his body with headphones and a voice-activated boom microphone. The age of technology had simplified the special operations combat leader's role in so many ways. No longer did a Force Recon Team require a host of discrete frequencies, one for communicating with his team and another for reporting to headquarters.

Everybody transmitted on the same frequency, their microphones operated by individual voice recognition, every transmission electronically scrambled. If headquarters wanted to know what was going on, all somebody on the OMCC staff had to do was listen. Each space-age radio had been given a priority for transmission precedence as well. So that when two people tried to talk at once, the higher-priority radio would override. And miracle of miracles, the top precedence rested with the Force Recon Team leader on the ground rather than at headquarters. In this way, a unit under fire could tell the staff weenies a thousand miles away to stay out of his hair until the shrapnel rain had subsided.

What's more, the man on the ground never had to worry about reporting his position to some desk jockey. Every man carried a personal locator beacon, PERLOBE, that constantly transmitted his location, accurate to within three meters. Since PERLOBEs had been issued, the incidence of friendly aircraft accidentally bombing their own special warfare troops on the ground had been reduced to zero. Naturally, each team member carried an elaborate military version of a personal data assistant, a GPS device that allowed him to navigate using the Global Positioning System.

Still, sometimes, after long formal silences, it was a relief to carry on a conventional conversation. Not to mention the secret satisfaction of knowing they would not be overheard in the OMCC below Quantico.

In a low voice, Swayne asked his team members for their reactions to the likely existence of a submarine.

Friel's was predictable. "No matter if there's a sub or not." He hefted his sniper gun. "I can take out all three cane-eaters—" Remembering that he was not the only sharpshooter on the team, he nodded toward Night Runner. "Well, me and the chief can. You can fire up the DRACULA, pick up our boys, and get the hell out of Dodge."

"I thought about that," said Swayne. "One of the good guys is in the bottom of the boat with the tarp over him. Both of them are probably tied up. If the Cubans capsize the boat, our pilots might drown before we can get to them."

"Oh." Friel was out of ideas. He seldom looked for an alternative to the direct approach, most often involving bloodletting.

Swayne couldn't blame him. The Marine culture told him that a Marine must act honorably and decisively in the face of danger. It was the Marine prayer: *God, grant me patience—ASAP, dammit!* At moments of doubt, you were supposed to do something.

Naturally, the testosterone coursing in his own blood, along with an excess of adrenaline, seconded that message. Charging was the right thing to do. Somewhere, deep in the back of his head, the voice of a patriotic firebrand lived and glowed. It said things like liberty, death, honor, glory. An inner voice reminded him: *The hero dies once, while the coward dies a thousand times a day.*

Finally there was the other thing, the words of his grandfather: *Face it, son, you don't have it. Your daddy didn't have it, and that's what got him killed. And you're just like your daddy. So give it up. Choose life, son. If you feel like you gotta wear a uniform, let me put in a word for you with the Postal Service.*

More than anything else, that was what made Swayne lean toward the frontal attack. Prove the old man's bogus down-home wisdom wrong. Shove it in his face. Take that finger he was always waving under somebody's nose and break it off, leaving nothing but a stump so short it couldn't even by used for nose-picking.

But he did not give in to the impulse to hasty action over thoughtful calculation. Nothing good could come of engaging an enemy in a state of high emotion. Especially at this range with the target tossing on the sea. Not that he lacked confidence in the shooting ability of either Friel or Night Runner. Somebody needed to worry about the safety of the pilots. The Spartans were here for them and not for the sake of their own egos.

Calculation. Caution. Logic. Patience. Measured responses. These things had never let him down. And yet, he hated those qualities in himself. Perhaps because rather than possessing them, they possessed him. Just once, he would like to fly into a Friel-like homicidal rage. Kill somebody now and sort the corpses later.

Swayne became aware that the silence in his little huddle had grown awkward.

He could see the hulk of Potts shrugging against the night sky.

"What is it, Gunny?"

"If they's a submarine out there, why send in a convoy besides?"

"I can't say. It could be a backup. Maybe they've been tipped off to our landing. Or maybe just co-incidence. How many trucks?"

"Six, maybe seven. Hard to tell through the trees."

"A company-minus," said Swayne, thinking aloud.

That much infantry would complicate everything. Swayne dared not risk ordering his snipers to open fire, revealing their positions. They might be well trained in the skills of escape and evasion, but that didn't justify recklessness.

"Gunny," he said, "go raise DRACULA. Give your Acme detonator to Night Runner. You and I will try to get beneath the Cubans before the submarine. If the convoy doesn't trigger the ambush, Night Runner will set it off and cause a distraction. You and I will come up on them from seaward. Sergeant Night Runner, you and Friel find covered firing positions in the rocks off to the west. On my command, take out the Cubans. Gunny and I will pick up the Americans and take them out to one of the ships offshore. You two go to ground and wait for us to come back for you at Rally Point Charlie. Any questions?"

"Cap'n?"

"Stow the smart-ass, Henry," Potts told Friel.

Potts hadn't raised his voice, but he'd hissed the esses just enough to sound dangerous to Friel. "No smart-ass, Gunny," Friel said. "I got a legitimate question is all."

"Make it quick," said Swayne.

"What about the Geneva Conventions Alternative? In case something goes wrong? You want me and Night Runner to execute it?"

"Negative on that," Swayne snarled, not because Friel asked the question, but because such an abomination as the GCA even existed.

FORT BENNING, GEORGIA—2315 HOURS LOCAL (0415 ZULU)

THE ISUZU IDLED beneath the yellow arch: U.S. Army Ranger School, the word "Ranger" a huge replica of the Ranger tab sewn at the top of the left

sleeve of soldiers who earned it. A block from the
first set of barracks, the driver pulled to the curb.
As they had rehearsed, he and the kid hit the ground
and unhitched the trailer in twenty seconds.

The kid ran to the curb side of the trailer, pulling
a stiletto blade from his boot. He poked the side-
walls on both tires and bent to listen for the escaping
air—it was essential to the plan that the trailer look
as if it had been abandoned with flat tires.

As he stood up, he sensed a movement in the air
by his head. *"C'est—?"* Before he finished giving
voice to the question, his left temple caved in beneath the impact of a brass hammer head.

The driver arranged the limp body behind a
nearby dumpster, hidden in the shadows so it would
not be spotted. He patted the kid's chest to be sure
the map case was still there. *Perfect.*

At the front of the trailer, he felt for the triggering
device, a wire that ran into the trailer through a nail
hole, ending at a timer, everything spring-loaded.
He put his head to the trailer wall and yanked the
wire half an inch. A metallic snap told him the
safety had been broken. He used his Leatherman
pliers to cut the wire, and the running end zipped
through the hole, disappearing inside. A second metallic snap told him the detonator had been armed.
Twenty minutes after the main blast, this one would
go. About the time gawkers had collected at a safe
distance—this distance, to be precise.

Meanwhile, if anybody tried to open the doors of
the trailer, a secondary circuit would be closed and

detonate the explosives sandwiched between sand-bags and surrounded by cartons in the trailer. If anybody jostled the trailer—say, in trying to move it—a bead of mercury would spill, closing a ten-millimeter gap in a tertiary circuit. In every case it would be the same result: A quarter ton of C-4 would scatter fourteen cartons of roofing nails at belly-button level, killing and maiming to a radius of a hundred meters.

He ran to his truck and drove it to the far end of the barracks and down the street between buildings—far enough away so that the main blast would not set off the secondary explosion by sympathetic detonation. He looked around for the brown Buick that was to pick him up. Where was it? He parked in the center of the street and ran around the grille of the Isuzu. On the curb side of the van box, he found the wire, put his head to the truck, pulled hard, and heard the first metallic snap. He looked around again and felt a stab of apprehension. What if they weren't coming for him? What if they planned to double-cross him the way they'd arranged for him to screw the kid? Hell with that. He wasn't about to cut this wire until—

The sweep of headlights turning at the next corner assured him his getaway car had arrived. He put the side-cutter blades of the Leatherman tool to the wire and pressed his ear against the truck.

The instant he squeezed the wire-cutters he saw in the glow of the streetlight that the vehicle at the corner was a marked military police van. In the first nanosecond after the wire separated, he realized he wouldn't be hearing a second metallic snap. In the final nanosecond of his life—before he was particalized—he concluded bitterly in French: *The double-crossing bastards probably won't be sending the Buick either.*

INSIDE CUBA—2322 HOURS LOCAL (0422 ZULU)

SWAYNE RECOVERED TO DRACULA just as Potts's head broke the surface in the submersible. He took up a position in the assistant-operator position as Potts turned the craft seaward and began motoring toward the longboat at five knots, submerging at a shallow dive angle. Potts would level off at about ten feet below the surface. At that depth, the wake reaching the surface would be minimal.

Swayne put on the full-face mask, equipped with an onboard microphone and regulator. The closed breathing system prevented bubbles from rising to the surface. DRACULA's system contained scrubbers that removed the carbon dioxide and pumps that recompressed the recycled air, enriching the mix with oxygen so it could be rebreathed, storing the carbon dioxide for later release on the surface.

Although the craft's electric motors barely made a vibration in the water, Swayne doubted they could escape electronic detection. Just the drag of their wind- and watershields pulling through the water would create a sound signature that could be picked up by signalmen listening on board the Cuban submarine. They might not be able to identify the unique Force Recon craft, but they could certainly alert the longboat crew on the surface and the reaction force, by now closing to within two miles.

When he thought the DRACULA might be about a hundred meters from the longboat's position, Swayne worked a series of controls at his position. The first sent up a short periscope—barely an inch in diameter and only 5.2 feet long, but equipped with a low-light television lens that fed an eight-inch screen on the console. It took some delicate handling to put the periscope high enough out of the water to see over the swells while keeping the craft quiet, avoiding the noises of water slapping against its surface. But Potts was up to the task.

Swayne rotated the periscope until he located the longboat. It was still dead in the water, and the Cubans had not been alerted. The one the middle was pounding on the pilot again. Ordering Friel to kill that guy was not going to give Swayne a single moment of sleeplessness.

Swayne retracted the periscope, and Potts steered DRACULA down a few feet, adjusting his course to sweep around and come at the Cubans from offshore. Swayne turned on a second scope, a digital metallic resonance imager. DIMRIM had been invented to let Force Recon Teams locate metal objects on the seabed and to approach enemy shipping in zero-visibility waters to plant explosive charges.

The DIMRIM's max effective range was a hundred meters, and Swayne hoped that it would not pick up anything now. They needed time to shoot the Cubans, grab the pilots, and make their run. Before the submarine could react.

No such luck. Dead ahead at fifty-four meters, submerged no more than fifty feet beneath the longboat, lay the submarine. No, he realized. It wasn't lying steady at all, but rising toward the surface.

Swayne, a longtime believer in the visualization techniques of world-class athletes, could no longer visualize his team snatching the pilots to safety. Instead, his mind's eye pictured a submarine breaching at the surface. An armed squad of Cuban sailors rushed on deck, hauling the occupants of the longboat into the sub.

As if to emphasize the accuracy of this vision, DRACULA was hit by an audible sonar ping.

Yet again, Swayne recalculated his conclusions about how the operation would go off. It required him no more than a second to realize that, with or without his influence, things were going to begin happening on their own. If he did not act now, his Force Recon Team, touted as the best in the Marine Corps, was going to become about as useless as a crew of United Nations observers. What little initiative remained on this mission was going to belong to the Cubans.

While he still had a limited ability to influence the action, Swayne knew he must act. Into his underwater microphone, he ordered, ''Take her to the surface.'' As soon his head cleared the water, he transmitted, "Night Runner, blow the ambush. Don't anybody watch the detonation," he added unnecessarily, chiding himself for wasting words. None of these seasoned professionals would be so stupid as to ruin their night vision by staring at explosive flashes.

No sooner had he spoken the command when an explosion rocked the night a hundred meters inland.

Swayne trained his eyes on the spot eighty meters away where the Cubans were floating. As he had expected—as anyone might expect—the Cubans turned toward the first explosion just in time to have their vision dazzled by a series of successive blasts. He visualized a chain of explosions going off on one side of road, followed by a second set of explosions on the opposite side. Simulators would touch off decoy machine guns from three positions—he heard them now. A trail of small-arms-fire simulators would eventually lead away from the site. Anybody caught in the killing zone of this automated ambush could not help but believe a force of guerrillas had struck them. The sounds of fire tapering off would lead them to believe the force was now fleeing by fire-and-maneuver techniques.

The kit could be lethal, blowing shrapnel from high-tech Claymore mines and shooting actual slugs. But more than anything, it was designed to make authentic noises of combat. Any casually trained military unit would be paralyzed into inaction. Elite soldiers would not be able to resist pursuing the phantom force. Either way, the Acme kit would buy him time he needed to pull off an adjusted plan of attack. The nearness of the submarine permitted no time for calculations. What was needed now was fast, direct action. Something straight out of Hollywood. As much as he disliked having his options diminished, Swayne relished the idea that he'd be able to vent his frustrations on the enemy.

"Full throttle," he ordered. "Approach on the surface."

Potts pushed the throttle lever full to the stop. "Want me to ram the boat?"

"No. Stop just short." He pulled his 9-millimeter, shaking it once to clear the bore of water and looping its lanyard around his left wrist. "But make it look as if you're going to ram them. I want anybody who isn't already head-spammed to jump ship."

By the time they had closed to fifty meters, the Cubans in the longboat were still cooperating with Swayne's renewed vision of how the attack should unfold—it was as it if he were directing them by some psychic power that kept them staring toward the beach.

DRACULA had reached twenty knots, and the only sound was of a squishing of water. At that speed DRACULA came clear of the surface and rode on hydrofoils, its propeller dipped into the water like the tail of a dragonfly. Swayne thought they might just pull it off. He adjusted his mask and saw the Cubans jabbering to each other. Friel's Mook had even become too distracted to pound on the Marine in his custody.

At forty meters, as he ripped off his regulator mask and gave the command for his snipers to shoot, control of Event Scenario 12 slipped out of Swayne's grasp entirely.

The sea boiled ahead of DRACULA, and a mass of steel blocked his view of the longboat. The Cuban submarine broke the surface like a gray whale breaching. The nose of the craft rose out of the water between DRACULA and the longboat, continued diagonally into the air as if in slow motion, then began toppling toward the sea.

Sparks blossomed three times on the hull in quick succession, and Swayne was momentarily confused. Then his mental recalculator went into overdrive, and he realized the sub had come up between the snipers and their targets as well. The blossoms were the rounds of Night Runner and Friel smacking the steel hull.

"Do you want me to go around the bow or the stern?" Potts shouted.

"Neither." There wasn't time. In only seconds, those armed sailors in Swayne's vision would be pouring onto the decks, scanning the surface and alerting the crew of the longboat. "Take her down."

"Under the keel?"

"Right under the belly." Swayne crouched and braced himself against DRACULA's framework as Potts cantilevered the controls forward, putting the craft into a dive. Swayne held on, waiting for the impact of the water. They were traveling too fast for a safe dive, and he knew it. But this was no time to be worrying about playing it safe. This was time to do. Or else to die.

BLACK BUTTE, MONTANA—2129 HOURS LOCAL (0429 ZULU)

THE ONLY SOUNDS inside the hunting cabin were the snap of coals and the quiet snoring of the guide tangled in his mummy bag on the top bunk.

Outside, a blizzard raged, winds driving snow against the roof, trying to force Arctic air down the chimney. A second man, the hunter who had hired the guide, sat awake, rereading *King Lear* by the fire, occasionally adding a split log to ward off the downdrafts.

Before going to sleep, the guide had complained about the storm ruining the hunting. The elk, he'd said, would wait out the blizzard in the densest possible deadfall of the forest. After the storm, they would migrate from the mountains and take up winter residence on the ranches and resorts. *But who knows?* he had complained. *Storm like this might not end for a week. We gonna get skunked, certain.*

All the guide's fuss meant little to the hunter. Personally, he might like to see an elk, but he sure as hell wasn't going to go to pieces if he didn't get a chance to shoot one. He had come to these mountains to decompress. If the storm trapped them there for a week, it wouldn't matter all that much. It just meant less opportunity for somebody to disturb him. In person anyway. They could still nag on him electronically. But they wouldn't dare unless—

He thought he heard a sound on the porch of the cabin. The first thing that came to mind was a grizzly bear—everybody had wanted to warn him about Montana's grizzly bears. But no, even bears would have more sense than to be out in this weather. More likely, it was his imagination, or perhaps a chunk of ice falling from the roof.

No. Not his imagination. The sound came again, this time heavier. Still the hunter was not alarmed. In all probability, one of the horses had strayed from the corral and was seeking shelter. He stood up to get his parka, debating whether to awaken the guide. He knew enough about survival to know that it was not safe to go out into a storm alone in unfamiliar territory.

Before he could arouse the guide, bootsteps outside the door told him to forget about horses. Impossible as it seemed, somebody was out tonight. The hunter's internal alarms sounded, not for his own safety but for that of other hunters. Nobody would be out on this night except on a matter of life and death. Somebody had shot himself and needed medical attention. Or else somebody in a hunting party had gotten lost in this sudden storm.

Before he could get to the door to see which, the planking shattered, letting in the storm and half a dozen men in camouflage.

The guide sat up. "What the hell? Close the damned door, you morons. And quit pointing those guns at people."

Another half-dozen men crowded inside.

The hunter could see that the masked intruders were not morons. For that matter, they were not hunters either. They carried military weapons, M-16's, AR-15's, and pistols, both 9-millimeter and .45s. Their eyes were not friendly, and they showed no inclination to lower their artillery. He manufactured a smile, and casually putting his hands into his pockets, asked, "You boys want me to put on the coffeepot?"

In answer, one man flicked the muzzle of a nine-mill his way and said in a thick accent, "Are you Masterson?" A thick *French* accent.

The hunter put on an expression of dismay, intentionally widening his eyes. "Why, no, I'm not Masterson." With his right hand, he worked the three-button combination on the PERLOBE in his pocket, transmitting a top-priority distress alarm. He gave the guide a knowing look. "I don't know any Masterson. Do you know anybody by that name?"

The guide, still groggy, took too much time on the uptake. He stared at the hunter for a full three seconds, as if he were as crazy as the intruders. Then his eyes revealed that danger had begun to dawn in his understanding.

"I'm not General Masterson either, and I never heard the name."

The hunter sagged at the guide's blunder.

"Then how would you know he's a general?" the intruder demanded, raising his pistol at the guide.

The guide glanced at Masterson, but looked away quickly. Clearly he was ashamed to be giving up the hunter, but not so ashamed he would sacrifice himself. "I'm sorry, General," he said, pointing at the hunter. "He's Masterson."

"No," Masterson said, but he was too late.

Two slugs splattered the guide's brains against the wall.

Inside Cuba—2331 hours local (0431 Zulu)

Dracula smashed into the sea, decelerating by half on impact. Before he could even recover against being thrown forward into the watershield, Swayne felt himself being dragged aft by the current.

He fought to clasp his mouth to the regulator for underwater breathing, holding on as the water tore at him, trying to rip him from DRACULA.

The sure hand of Gunny Potts began leveling off DRACULA's descent even as he relaxed the throttle. Swayne found his regulator and took care of the immediate priority, catching his breath. Then he cleared his mask. As he did so, he checked the metallic resonance imager and saw that they were on a dive angle to pass beneath the submarine, clearing the hull by a full ten feet. Try as he might, though, he could not see the sub in the utter blackness. The two-hundred-foot hulk looming above and ahead of them, now a scant seventeen meters away, lay there, all but invisible.

"When we come up on the other side," he articulated into his underwater mike, formulating a new plan even as he was speaking it, "try to hit the longboat from below. Swamp it, and we'll try to pick the pilots out of the sea—"

Before he could get out the rest of the plan, Potts interrupted him, his voice warbling through the underwater commo apparatus. "Not going to happen, Boss. Take a look at the DIMRIM."

Swayne began to interpret what his imaging scope was telling him, even as his mind tried to persuade him that what he was seeing was not happening. The Cuban submarine had already begun submerging. The nearby hissing could only be the sound of flooding ballast tanks. Whether that meant the Cubans had already picked up the Americans, he could not know. The only certainty was that the submarine had begun settling in front of them like a steel curtain.

Potts decelerated and began a turn to starboard. "Circle on station or pass behind the screws?"

"Dive steeper. Pass below the keel. I still want to come up on the other side." Maybe, he thought, the sub's skipper had simply ordered the submarine a few feet deeper so it would be easier to take on the crew and captives on the longboat.

DRACULA's dive angle increased on his order,

and Swayne felt that tug of the sea as Potts accelerated.

Nothing in logic or experience could tell him that the Cubans submarine would stop its descent, giving them the necessary seconds to pass beneath its hull. He was guessing. Nothing in the arduous training program of Force Recon Marines had ever addressed this possibility.

As if things weren't complicated enough, the radio crackled. They were too deep to hear the transmission, but Swayne thought he recognized Zavello's voice and one word.

Abort? Swayne was stunned. That couldn't be. They were far too deep to decipher the message, let alone transmit. Besides, he was too occupied with the submarine sinking toward them.

WHEN SWAYNE DID not respond to Zavello's escalating fury to abort the mission and acknowledge at once, Sergeant Robert Night Runner waited for Gunny Potts to jump in and take the call. Hoped like hell that Gunny would jump in. He, Night Runner, Spartan Three, was third in line for the command of this team. And he did not want it. Not now.

Finally, after Friel cursed and pulled the receiver off his head to clear his ears of the intrusive yammering, Night Runner knew that he must respond.

"Mission Command, this is Spartan Three."

"Where the hell have you been?"

"One and Two are both out-of-pocket right

now.'' Night Runner tried to think of a way to explain about the submarine without wasting a lot of words. It wasn't necessary. Zavello was going to do all the talking.

The colonel repeated his order to abort the mission and demanded, ''Acknowledge the following message code.''

Night Runner entered the code into his own personal data assistant. In seconds, the computer gave him a response to send to Zavello, which he did by pressing ENTER on his machine rather than waste words and risk pissing off the colonel.

Beside him, Friel let out an exclamation, and Night Runner understood why the captain would sometimes get impatient with the Bostonian. He could create distractions out of thin air.

''Look, Chief. We might get another chance.''

Night Runner obliged by looking through the scope on his rifle, and saw the hulk of the submarine submerging, allowing the longboat to come into view over the curvature of the forward hull.

''Stand by,'' he said.

Zavello came back, his tone no longer frantic. No more yelling, no more commentary. He gave Night Runner a series of letters and numbers, six in all, and demanded an immediate acknowledgment. ''Both in voice and by electronic message,'' Zavello asserted.

As Night Runner entered the code, Friel lowered his sniper gun and stared at him.

''Get back on target, Hank. The captain gives the

word, you be ready to start shooting again."

"I gotta bad feeling, Chief," said Friel. "When you finish key-diddling around, that computer is going to tell us to do a GCA number on them."

"Bull—"

The computer flashed a blinking command:

EXECUTE GENEVA CONVENTIONS ALTERNATIVE

The machine produced the acknowledgment code that he was to send back. That was all. No explanation, no amplification. Never one to use a lot of words and not appreciative of those who did, Night Runner wished for something else now. Wasn't there a loophole in this deal? Wasn't there any room for slippage? Discretion? Who in hell made up such a contingency as this anyway?

He had some other questions, pertinent questions, but Zavello was already on the line, demanding a response.

Entirely boxed in, Night Runner gave the only response he could, transmitting the code the computer had given him. Next, the computer gave him a blinking reminder to repeat the code as a voice transmission. He did, and pushed the ENTER key once more as the computer instructed. Zavello answered with one more code, which matched the combination blinking on Night Runner's screen. It was the final confirmation of his authorization, the order to act.

Of all the times to be left in command.

Zavello couldn't just get on the horn to get a simple SitRep. No. He had to issue the most dreadful order imaginable to the senior member of the team available. And that member happened to be Night Runner.

And he, Night Runner, had just been ordered to kill the Americans in the longboat.

FRIEL BARELY TWITCHED, and the thermal spot in his scope swept the submarine from bow to stern, from target to target.

Friel knew damned well that he didn't have the education of a Night Runner or the captain, but that didn't mean he did not know what was what. Superwarrior could read animals and tracks and even smells on the wind. But not even an Ivy-Leaguer like Runner could read people like Friel could. His degree was from USC, the University of the Street Corner. He *knew* things most citizens never even suspected.

The chief might debate it a while, but Friel already *knew* what the result was going to be. He *knew* the chief was going to ask him—

"Henry, can you do it?"

"Hell, yes, Chief. But that's not the question, is it?"

"Will you?"

That was the question. Friel watched as a pair of lines were tossed over the side of the submarine. To the Cubans in the boat, he assumed. The lines went taut, and the boat was drawn alongside. Where the hell were Potts and Swayne? They should have gotten Zavello's message. They were closer to the action. They were the ones with the big pay vouchers. They should be doing this.

But no, everybody expected Friel to do the dirty work for the Spartans. He was low man on the totem pole, for one thing. For another, everybody assumed that he was a natural-born killer, that he even liked it. Who in hell could like shooting one of your own? Even if it had to be done?

He heard Night Runner draw a deep breath. "Hank, the sub is submerging. One of our guys is on deck now."

"I can see that."

"We have our orders—"

Friel picked up on the hesitation. "But what?"

"But what if you were to miss?"

"I never miss, and everybody in Force Recon knows it. Nobody is going to buy it if I don't cap off the flyboy."

"What if *I* do it?"

"You ain't got the gastros for it, Chief."

"I mean miss on purpose."

"You got a rep as a fair shooter too."

The Cubans had put a rope around the pilot's chest and hauled him up to the deck of the submarine as the trio of Cubans scrambled over the slope of the hull. One of the deckhands tossed the pilot's rope to another hand on top of the conning tower. Already water had begun sloshing over the deck as the submarine accelerated its dive.

Friel worked the lever on the side of the 20-

millimeter, ejecting the clip. He cracked the bolt, throwing the sabot round clear of the chamber.

"What are you doing?"

Friel didn't answer. He reached into his pack for a second magazine, five rounds of APIT, Armor Piercing Incendiary Tracer. This was a move he had practiced a hundred times a month while blindfolded so he would not have to fumble in a real situation. Never had he tried it under such stressful conditions, though, and his hand wanted to tremble. As with a surgeon, unsteadiness was not an option for a sniper, so Friel held his breath, willed away the feeling, and inserted the magazine. He chambered a round of fresh ordnance.

His legs flailing, the pilot was being dragged up the vertical side of the cupola as sailors poured down the top hatch ahead of him in a file. The sea washed over the foredeck of the sub.

"What's it going to be, Henry?"

Friel felt a hand on his shoulder as Runner said, "Whatever you decide, I'll back you up."

"You do that, Sergeant." Friel squeezed the trigger of the 20-millimeter, sending the first of three self-propelled missiles unerringly on the way to the targets he had designated. *The nice sergeant's going to back me up,* thought Friel. *Like that means something to somebody.*

BELOW THE SURFACE, Swayne had no clue to the drama being played out above. He did not hear the impacts of the 20-millimeter rounds. Not that it mattered. He had enough concerns to deal with.

A check of the DIMRIM confirmed the extent of Swayne's first miscalculation. The submarine had not leveled off at the surface after all. It settled deeper, cutting into their dive angle so DRACULA would intercept the hull. He felt the dive angle sharpening again.

"Can you pull out?"

"Negative, sir. We're committed to the max."

Swayne never detected even a hint of complaint in Potts's tone. The ultimate noncom, Gunny never second-guessed his calls or groused once a decision had been made. They might be crushed between the hull and the seabed, but Potts, the consummate Marine, would never be heard bitching about it, not even with his last breath.

The dive accelerated, and the tug of the sea redoubled. For a moment it occurred to Swayne that he ought to give the command to abandon ship, such as it was. He checked his imager scope again. No, as Potts had said, they were past the point of no return, at the keel line. If they bailed from DRACULA now, the drag of the submarine—it had begun moving forward at perhaps five knots now—might sweep them along the hull and suck them into the screws. However bad things were now, it was probably better to rely on DRACULA's thrust to pull them clear.

Swayne reinterpreted the DIMRIM scope, trying to make the result come out in favor of DRACULA. Intellect overpowered emotion, and he realized that the geometry made it impossible to clear the submarine.

"Stand by for a ram, Captain," Potts murmured so matter-of-factly, he might have been reporting that the black-eyed peas were underdone.

DRACULA's watershield struck steel and glanced off, shooting downward at a vertical angle. Potts used the rebound to advantage, accelerating. The hull struck them a second time. This time they did not bounce off. The squeal of DRACULA's graphite composite against the submarine all but deafened Swayne. Through the scratching sound of DRACULA dragging across the barnacles, paint, and rivets, he thought he heard more radio traffic in his earpiece.

Again Potts increased the thrust of DRACULA's propellers, and the two craft separated. Swayne saw by the images on the scope that they would be hitting again—he reasoned that the slipstream of the submarine was sucking them against the hull. An image of the submarine's screws appeared to him again, stainless steel, glittering in crystalline waters. It was an easy image to dismiss. Should he contact those propellers tonight, he would never see them coming—or going.

DRACULA rammed the hull again. This time the smaller craft stuck to the larger for a moment, like a vacuum-mouthed remora fish to a streaking shark. The DRACULA yawed in the direction of the submarine's travel. The contact spun the amphibious craft like an underwater top. Swayne's grip was torn clear of DRACULA's handholds, and the onboard regulator ripped away from his mouth, robbing him of his air supply. He too began spinning underwater, striking the side of the submarine as he rotated, his mask torn from his face. Once, when he was facing the hull, he tried to push off, stroking to swim clear. Although the submarine seemed to be moving at a snail's pace through the water, it exerted a tremendous pressure on him, drawing him to the metal as if he were magnetized. Three times in succession he smashed into the steel, once flat on his back, a second time with his left shoulder, and the third time with the backs of both legs. It felt like falling down a mountain.

Swayne rolled himself into a cannonball position and waited for the right moment. He felt himself being carried back along the side of the craft, bouncing first on his left side, then against his buttocks. Not knowing when he might have another, better opportunity, he straightened his legs, launching himself away from the submarine as hard as he could thrust.

It wasn't enough. The slipstream sucked him back, slamming him chest-first against the metal, scraping against his gear, turning him to strike another blow against his right elbow. A sudden anger coursed through Swayne's veins. The anger came in an echo of his grandfather's words: *You're not up to it, son, just like your daddy.*

• • •

GENEVA CONVENTIONS ALTERNATIVE. *What bull-shit,* thought Friel, as the first and second rounds struck the conning tower of the sub. Two-dollar words made up by the fat-ass brass in the Pentagon so they wouldn't have to feel like they ordered one of their own to be killed.

But those college-educated words didn't mean squat when you had to be the one to touch off the slugs.

Friel had sent two rounds rocketing at the sub, aimed a meter or so over the pilot's head as he dangled at the end of the rope. They struck the steel tower just a second apart. Right at belly level of the first sailor hauling on the rope from inside. The APIT rounds carried a charge of white phosphorus. The white-hot willie-pete rounds were deadly sparklers designed to touch off ammunition and panic inside armored vehicles.

The glow of a fire escaped the sub's open hatches. As Friel had intended, the Mooks hauling at that rope found themselves preoccupied with the more serious matter of being burned to death inside a diving submarine. They released the rope, and the pilot fell to the deck, bounced twice over the curved hull, and slid into the sea, bobbed to the surface, and vanished.

"Pick him up, Captain," Friel murmured more to himself than to Swayne and Potts. "Pick up the stupid bastard, Gunny, before he drinks the big gulp."

The third APIT he touched off went at the back

of the Cuban who had been doing all the beating in the boat. The man had been scrambling across the deck in ankle-deep water, now stepping up on a steel ladder to climb up the conning tower, now—

The APIT struck him between the shoulder blades, the brilliantly hot tracer cauterizing the hole left by the slug. Such was the velocity of the round, the Cuban likely did not feel the impact. It did not even throw him against the sub. Rather, the explosion of titanium against steel in front of his gaping chest, accompanied by the tracer bursting into a phosphorus shower, blew him backward off the ladder. He fell into the sea, chunks of willie-pete still burning so hot that the water could not extinguish them, and sank slowly, his body illuminated by the chemical volcano gushing from his chest.

Friel smiled. Everything else on this pissant mission might be a waste of breath and energy. But at least he had the satisfaction of the sight of that burning bastard tattooed on his memory so he could recall it at any time he needed a chuckle.

HIS GRANDFATHER'S VENOMOUS words in his head gave Swayne the strength he needed. He rolled himself into a cannonball again, marshaled every particle of strength, and lunged out, breast-stroking toward the bow of the submarine, angling away, turning his body into a kid's hand held outside the window of a speeding car. The maneuver worked. He felt himself peeling away from the submarine's slipstream and into undisturbed water. The mechan-

ical part of him, the Marine Corps officer, instructed
him to make a mental note of his maneuver for the
after-action report. This would be a technique to
pass along to other teams who might get into a sim-
ilar situation. Although he doubted anybody could
duplicate a debacle of this sort.

His human side struck out for the surface immediately, needing air desperately, and even more
desperately needing to know which way was up so
he could get to it. Panic rose in his chest. But rather
than struggle, Swayne relaxed, allowing the natural
buoyancy of his body to tell him which direction to
swim. Intense training, begun as an interservice student in the Navy's Basic Underwater Training and
finished in the Corps' version of grad school for
Force Recon Marines, had hammered it into his
head that the body could not be trusted implicitly.
Sometimes, under the influence of vertigo, the body
would lie—nothing in the evolutionary experience
could prepare a man's system for what had just happened to him. To test for the truth, he pulled his
knife from its sleeve scabbard and released it. Feeling gingerly with his left hand, he found the floating
handle. His equilibrium, upset by being tossed about
underwater, contradicted what the floating handle
was telling him. He knew he must trust the knife
and the laws of physics, and so began to swim away
from the direction the blade pointed.

He tried calculating the distance he would have
to swim, subtracting three feet for every stroke from
the seventy-nine feet he last remembered seeing on

the depth gauge of DRACULA. He found he didn't like doing the math, didn't think he had enough air in him to handle the number of required strokes.

Everything in his world had been reduced to one all-consuming issue. He needed a fresh breath, even if it were to be his last. He could hardly care about anything else.

If the Cubans in the longboat had not yet boarded the submarine, they would shoot at the first ripple. If they even suspected that they were dealing with a team of Force Recon Marines, the Cubans would make no attempt whatever to capture them. For they knew no Force Recon Marine had ever surrendered—or ever would. They would know that in every encounter with such Marines, everybody on one side or the other died.

When he had traveled as far as his muscle power and the scant supply of air in his lungs would take him, Swayne called upon his grandfather to arouse his anger once again. The recollection bought him a few more strokes, but still he did not break clear into the night air.

Swayne felt a desperate scream rise to his throat. Just this side of panic, he imagined his grandfather sitting in the longboat. When he surfaced he would leap on board and wring the old man's turkey neck. That used up the last bit of adrenaline that he could muster, and the issue of whether he could find strength to continue stroking in slo-mo to the surface passed out of his hands and into the realm of consciousness beyond willpower. All that powered him now was an undifferentiated anger. Anger at his grandfather for being there. Anger at his father for *not* being there—and for not being here, now that he needed him most. Anger at Potts, a noncom senior enough to know better, for not talking him out of his reckless attempt to navigate beneath the hull of a submarine. Anger at himself for being so weak as to blame his predicament on Potts.

His hatred for everything imaginable had surpassed all reason when Swayne finally felt a sudden change in the water temperature. He'd found a warmer level. But how thick was the layer?

He doubted he would survive even ten strokes more. The buzzing in his ears had become the roar of a waterfall.

At a dozen strokes, he knew he was finished, his muscles cramping with lactic acid, refusing to answer the helm. In his head he screamed at himself to find just ten more strokes. At eight, he broke the surface like a Polaris missile launched from below.

He felt a chill from his head to below his waist, so far did he shoot out of the sea. Still, nothing mattered. Not the Cubans, not Zavello, and not his grandfather. For an instant he did not even devote a thought to his team or the pilots he was supposed to rescue. All he ever needed and wanted in life, he sucked into his lungs, expelled, and gasped back into his chest. It was oxygen, it was free, and it was delicious.

"Captain Swayne."

Swayne caught a glimpse of the long, low boat

against the glowing skyline to seaward. Somehow the Cubans had learned his name. He ducked underwater and began swimming at them, his arms numb. He stopped a moment to search for his pistol, but found it had been torn from its lanyard—and he hadn't even felt that. He reached for his knife once more, and remembered that he had released it. Finally, he realized that it made no sense for anybody but the members of his own team to know his name. And certainly they could not mimic the soft, melodic voice of a Georgia grizzly bear by the name of Delmont Potts. He resurfaced, swimming in a comfortable crawl stroke.

Once at the longboat, he held onto the side, too spent to throw himself on board. "The Cubans?" he gasped.

"Gone as yesterday. Probably on the sub," said Potts. "With one of the pilots, I reckon."

"Where's the other one?"

"Dead as innocence," he said, pointing. "Right there in the bottom of the boat. Lost a leg and bled to white. Maybe when he punched out."

Swayne rested his forehead on the side of the boat and rolled his head from side to side.

"Colonel Z," said Potts, "he's going to croak like a horny toad when he finds out they got away with our boy. But it ain't your fault, Cap. You did the best you could. We all did."

Swayne raised his head. "Gunny, I thought I heard him telling us to abort. Did you pick up anything like that?"

Potts shrugged. "I lost my radio a long time ago, maybe the second time we hit the boat. Lost my headset, lost my weapons, lost my gear—damn near lost everything." Gunny shuddered, shaking the longboat. "I almost went through those screws, Captain Swayne. I don't know how they missed me. To top it all off, I got tangled in a rope."

"A rope? Out here?"

"I know. What's a rope doing out here is exactly what I was thinking. But not for too long. I had to get topside for air."

Swayne could tell he wasn't alone in feeling lucky to be alive.

Potts's hulking body shifted in the boat. "Maybe it was part of a fishing net or something."

Swayne shuddered.

"Give a hand up, Cap."

Once inside the boat, Potts set about starting the outboard motor. Swayne fumbled around for his boom mike, finding that it had been pulled to the top of his head. He adjusted it, kissed it, and touched the secondary transmitter key of his vest radio.

Letting Colonel Zavello know that he still existed did little more than give the colonel somebody to bitch at. And bitch he did, demanding to know why Swayne had not responded immediately to his calls. Swayne tried to explain the situation.

Zavello wasn't entertaining explanations. "When I tell you to break contact with the enemy, that's what I expect you to do. I don't expect you to be thinking about it. I don't expect you to be advancing for one meter more. I expect you to break it off.''

The terrifying experience of being forced toward the sea bottom with the full expectation of being crushed between the submarine and the sand flashed through Swayne's head. It would have taken too long to explain that, or Potts's brushes with both the propellers and a fishing net. Besides, Zavello would not have let him finish the first sentence. So he simply said, ''Wilco.''

Still, Zavello wasn't through with him. He ranted a while longer, until he began repeating his complaints. Finally, he growled, ''An extraction bird is en route to pull you and DRACULA out. You and your team are being shipped out of Gitmo tonight. I want a full report when you get here.''

Swayne saw little point in reporting that DRACULA was a combat loss. Along with some pretty fancy equipment and weapons, including the experimental binoculars, the XM-80 Brat, and the rest. As far as he knew, they had not even inflicted any casualties on the Cubans, who had gotten away clean with the living pilot. When the extraction helicopter came to pick them up, it would be humiliating enough. That humiliation would be geometrically increased at the mission debriefing. Still, it would be nothing compared to the fiasco created if Fidel should parade the captured pilot down the streets of Havana tomorrow for the benefit of the international media. The American government might never acknowledge the existence of his Force Recon Team and its failed mission—certainly not to announce that the team had rescued part of a dead pilot and requisitioned a beat-up Cuban fishing boat in trade for a four-million-dollar watercraft. But people in the know would know. The Spartans had found the enemy but had failed to engage them, leaving the team, the Corps, and the country open to extraordinary criticism.

ABOARD A NIGHT SHADOW HELICOPTER—2357 HOURS LOCAL (0457 ZULU)

ONCE ON THE extraction bird, and soon after on final approach to Naval Air Station Guantanamo, where they would pick up a jet to Virginia, Potts touched him on the shoulder, and Swayne winced, reminded of the battering he had taken under the sea.

"Sorry. You think we'll be fired when we get to Quantico?"

Swayne shook his head. He might still be puzzled about the issue in general, but one specific aspect of the fiasco had become the certainty: "We're not going to get fired over that. They were calling off the operation even before they knew it was falling apart. They'll be pissed about losing the pilot, all right, but—"

Friel's hand shot up. "Permission to interrupt."

Swayne's first instinct was to shoot back: *You already did interrupt, Henry.* But a vague intuition kept his tongue in check. Chewing out Friel for transmitting when he ought to have been receiving had fallen in priority to the back burner. He had no right to take out the frustration of his personal failures on the junior member of the team.

"What is it, Lance Corporal Friel?"

"Begging your pardon, sir, we—the team—didn't lose the pilot. Not in the way you think anyways."

Friel was displaying an uncommon discomfort. Something had shaken his customary confidence. Swayne realized Friel had been as reticent as Sergeant Night Runner from the moment the stealth-equipped Night Shadow had picked them up from Rally Point Charlie moments after they'd arrived. This was their first chance to debrief, and Swayne knew he'd better be listening.

"What do you mean, didn't lose the pilot?" he said.

"I mean, we lost him, but the Cubans didn't get him."

Swayne felt his blood congeal. "What do you mean?"

Friel looked to Night Runner. "You better tell him, Chief."

The Indian's face was slacker than normal, Swayne now could see. Preoccupied before, he had missed the troubled expression.

"I was waiting for the right time to tell you."

Swayne shook his head. "You didn't—they didn't order a GCA?"

He had his answer in the hangdog look on the two men's faces.

"Yes, sir. They did order it," Night Runner said. "When you were underwater. We—I had to handle it." Night Runner recounted the conversations with Zavello.

As he explained, his style even more halting and telegraphic than usual, anger swelled up inside Swayne, making him forget his aches and fatigue. Night Runner explained how Friel had tried to handle the situation. How they had not dared to make radio calls to tell Swayne and Potts to pick up the helpless man who had fallen into the sea. "Colonel Zavello would have known we didn't carry out the order."

Swayne shook his head. He'd heard rumors of missions in Vietnam to track down American deserters and defectors to North Vietnam, units that even deployed nerve gas to wipe out traitors. But this? This couldn't be classified as anything worse than a political embarrassment to the Administration. Could cynical politicians really condemn American fighting men to death just to save face and manipulate public opinion? He gazed absently at the pilot they had recovered, still wrapped in a tarp at the back of the helicopter's cargo deck.

Friel brightened, injecting a hopeful thought into the sterile moment. "But at least we didn't do him, Captain. Not directly anyways."

Night Runner recounted the incident's outcome.

Swayne exchanged glances with Potts.

"I must have got tangled in the rope," said Potts, barely audible above the drone of the helicopter.

The remainder of the flight went off in silence, each man of Team Midnight left to contemplate his horror of the night, each Marine trying to make sense of the personal hell inflicted on him in Event 12.

Except for Swayne. Onto his own shoulders he took the burden from each of his men in turn. Night Runner had been forced to give the order to kill another Marine. Swayne felt guilty because that should have been his responsibility. And angry that he had not been given the chance to carry the freight. That was what he was being paid for.

Friel, clearly not the psychotic he had pretended to be, had been compelled to pull the trigger. He'd had a double burden. First he had tried to fudge an order that might be legitimate in the court of Special Ops but would have no standing whatever under the Constitution. Second, in trying to save the pilot's life, he had consigned him to a slower, perhaps even more horrible, death.

And Potts. Poor Gunny. He had survived an encounter with a lethal propeller, only to be entangled in a dead man's tether. The garrulous, folksy Potts was already superstitious enough. How would ever reconcile the intrusive notion that he might have been dragged to his death on the sea bottom by a corpse?

All in all, thought Swayne, what could possibly be more bizarre than Event Scenario 12?

EVENT SCENARIO 13—DAY 1

"SOMEBODY'S KIDNAPPED THE Commandant of the Marine Corps, and your team has been pulled out of Cuba so you can go snatch him back."

They were the first words out of Zavello's mouth. Swayne had expected the colonel to chew him up and spit him out for all that had gone wrong on Event 12. But no. He had to go one better, blowing him away with this bombshell.

The Commandant of the Marine Corps has been kidnapped?

How could that be? They didn't have security for somebody as important as General Harley V. Masterson?

The Mastermun of the Marines had been kidnapped?

Zavello often wore an eye patch over his war

wound from the last days of Khe San. But sometimes he didn't. Depending on his mood, the grape-
vine had it. When the glass eye was in and the
socket was dry, as it seldom was, the Z-man could
be predicted to be in a rare good humor. When the
eye wept, word had it you'd better stay out of his
way. When the good eye was inflamed besides,
don't even pass by his office. When he wore the
black wraparound sunglasses, stay out of sight. To
stand before the satin patch required uncommon
valor; to confront the leather patch, suicidal recklessness.

Tonight was the wraparounds, but Zavello was
acting cordial, which made Swayne all the more
cautious.

''That's the reason you were pulled out of action.
I regret the intervention. And that I came down on
you over the radio.''

The apologies were pure bullshit, and Swayne
knew it.

"Bat" Masterson had been kidnapped.

He realized he had to overcome his astonishment.
Zavello was telling him other things, worse things,
even to a Marine who had just been told that the
God of the Corps had just been snatched by the
enemy.

Swayne tallied up the damages as Zavello ticked
them off. A training barracks at Fort Benning? A
Navy cruiser? A Minuteman missile site? All this
and the Commandant? In one night? What the hell
was the country coming to? Wasn't anybody in the

conventional forces standing watch anymore?

Zavello put the red dot of his laser pointing stick on Swayne's chest. "You and your team are on the spot for this one. Not because of the little catastrophe in Cuba but because you're supposed to be the best Force Recon Team in the Marines." Emphasis on *supposed*.

"Four incidents. You think the Cubans shoot-down—"

"Forget the Cuban thing. That was the only co-incidence of the evening. Castro was damned lucky to have a submarine that was able to get on station before you could save those boys."

Although Zavello wasn't saying it outright—and he never would—with that admission, he was telling him that he had forgiven Swayne's team.

"Altogether, we can account for five incidents. On the Minuteman Missile attack, the bastards waited around for an Air Force special operations team to react by helicopter. Two helicopters lost." He tossed his pointer down. "Everybody on board killed."

Swayne's mind, recovered from the shock of hearing about the loss of the Commandant, had begun making the first calculations concerning the next mission of Team Midnight. Event Scenario 13 hardly seemed like a traditional undertaking for such a small special operations team.

"What kind of conventional forces are going to be involved? And how are we going to support them?"

Zavello shook his head. "No conventional forces. This much we already know from documents taken from the body of one of the terrorists at the scene in Fort Benning. We're dealing with Canadians."

Swayne's mouth fell open.

"Yes, Canadians. A separatist group that's come in under the radar screen of the CIA.". He turned his head and made the sound of spitting. "Goddamned CIA. Can't find nukes in India. Can't find an army of terrorists on our doorstep." The colonel yanked off his wraparounds and spat on the floor for real.

Shocked as he was at that, Swayne felt a sudden revulsion that Zavello had revealed his barren eye socket. Nobody had ever told him what *that* meant. He glimpsed a moist, gray-pink mound of matter in the hole, and hoped it wasn't part of the man's brain leaking out in fury. He didn't know where to look, but he didn't want to be looking at that. So he found a sudden interest in the scrapes on the backs of his hands.

Zavello was oblivious to his discomfort. "Goddamn CIA. Can't find their asses with both hands." He repositioned and adjusted his sunglasses, collecting himself with visible effort, and continued. "Conventional forces have gotten the word through the chain of command to stay put. This is from the highest authority. Every military installation in the world will be on full alert. But there is to be no attempt at military retaliation. Can you even think of a circumstance under which we would put military forces on the border between the U.S. and Canada?'' He answered his own rhetorical question. "Of course not.''

Swayne's stomach had settled down, but he wasn't getting this. Or if he was getting it, he certainly didn't like the idea of taking on an outlaw operation. Before he could reason the issue, Zavello hit him between the eyes again, this time not with his laser pointer.

"One more similarity between these attacks. You should be aware of it. The attack on Fort Benning destroyed most of the Ranger school. I already told you the Air Force lost a Special Operations Group reaction force. The Navy cruiser—''

Swayne got it all at once and beat Zavello to the punch. "SEALs were on board?''

"That's right. An entire platoon lost. Somebody's got a hard-on for Special Ops. We're assuming that anybody who took the Commandant would realize that every Marine, active or retired, would want to retaliate. And that Force Recon would be leading the charge.''

Swayne took a turn shaking his head. "Colonel, you already told me that the National Command Authority won't allow military intervention against Canada—''

"That's not what I said. I said the President has issued an executive order forbidding in the deployment of conventional forces that might look like saber-rattling against Canada.''

"I can't believe what I'm hearing. You're telling

me that I might have to take my team on an operation that could turn out to be illegal.''

"There's no *might* to it. You're taking the mission. And don't use that *I*-word again. It's perfectly legal. A training mission.''

Zavello didn't specify the *or else* implied in his tone, and Swayne didn't want to know. He had no doubt about Zavello's power to destroy his career in the Marines. They both understood that to pursue this issue any further would mean the second catastrophe of Swayne's day.

"It's settled then,'' Zavello said. "Now let me give you the rest of the bad news.''

SWAYNE FOUND THE members of his team where he had left them, draped in all manner of uncomfortable positions over the chrome and plastic furniture of a ready room on the flight line.

"This is a training exercise,'' he began without conviction. "The scenario is this. The Commandant of the Marine Corps was elk hunting in place called Black Butte, Montana, when he disappeared.'' He handed a list to Potts. "This is the list of requirements I gave to the logistics people, so they can put together our combat package and load it aboard an aircraft. Check it out, Gunny, and add to it as you see fit.'' Swayne checked his wristwatch. Somehow, it had gotten to be 0335 hours. It seemed like such a short time ago that they had been launched right after sunset to pick up the Marine pilots.

"Our flight departs at 0700 sharp from Hangar D-27. We have an appointment to be kicked out of a C-141 in the mountains of Montana later today."

Night Runner visibly brightened. Montana was his homeland. He had been brought up in Heart Butte, in the foothills of the Rockies. Friel just shook his head. Swayne knew that he was questioning the wisdom of successive operations—one night rappelling into the Caribbean, and the next day parachuting into the mountains.

Potts studied him so hard Swayne had to restrain himself from squirming.

"Captain, this list . . ." Potts's mouth worked but no words came out.

"What about it?"

"This is a combat load. We've never gone on a training mission stateside with enough live ammo to sink a fleet."

The others inclined their heads toward him. Swayne could see another, more brutal question forming before it was asked.

Potts said, "Isn't there some law against military forces carrying out combat operations in the States? The *posse*-something-something?"

"*Posse comitatus*," Swayne said. He weighed the truth against the cover story he'd been ordered to tell them. He began relating the lie.

"Yes. Combat ops would be illegal. But our mission is a training exercise. The Commandant himself is involved. He's the target we'll be seeking. For the purpose of the exercise, he wasn't kidnapped in Montana, but in a mythical country called Paragonia."

Swayne struggled to maintain eye contact, but found he could not go through with the deception. He couldn't bring himself to stare into their eyes any more than he could meet the gaze of Zavello's gushing hole in the head. "That's bullshit, of course, but if anybody should ask, you know the cover story. The Commandant really has been kidnapped."

Friel yelped in astonishment. "Somebody copped the Batman? No way—" He caught Potts's stink-eye expression and shut up.

Swayne went on. "We're going to drop in on the heads of some Canadian hockey-school dropouts, and were going to kick their asses all over North America if we have to. We're going to rescue the Commandant of the Marine Corps."

The three men of his team nodded in unison, giving him back the same wry grin he was giving them. Friel sighed. "We're gonna rescue the Batman. Who'da believed it?"

Not Swayne. But he wasn't thinking about that. He was relieved that he had regained the confidence of his team. These men, like all Marines, understood honesty, fair play, and directness. And they distrusted evasions of any kind. When would the brass ever learn that?

"We meet our plane in just over three hours." He gave a time hack, and they synchronized watches. "I don't care how you spend all your time," he said with a wry grin. "Just don't miss the flight."

OUTSIDE HIS APARTMENT, Swayne made a rare mistake for him, the mistake that a fatigued soldier always makes—relaxing his sensitivity to the external world. He had allowed himself to be sucked into the maelstrom of his throbbing muscles and turbulent emotions. Swamped by disappointment at the failures in Cuba. Torn between obligatory respect for Zavello and his anger at being humiliated by the man. It was as if he were near drowning again, this time in guilt for taking on a mission that could not possibly be rationalized as lawful. Combine that with the shame he felt for his lack of moral courage to refuse the mission. Compound that with the haunting thoughts of having dragged three fine Marines into a quagmire of some politician's questionable ethics. Whether from a sense of duty or of machismo, they had agreed to a man and without questioning the legitimacy of the mission. Every one of them knew that for one to refuse would disqualify the rest of the team—some other Force Recon bunch would get the mission rather than try to substitute a new man at the eleventh hour on such a critical mission.

No matter that some group of psychopaths had kidnapped the Commandant. To his mind, there seemed to be little justification to do a bad thing for good reasons.

These competing thoughts cycled through Swayne's head as he pulled out his apartment key. And of course, his scrapes and bruises had begun to assert themselves too, stinging and aching in turn. The new mission would be hell, hitting the ground after a half-day plane ride and a forty-second parachute drop, his muscles stiff as beef jerky.

Inundated by these thoughts and sensations, Swayne didn't react to the sounds of rushing feet behind him until he felt a body hitting his back, arms wrapping around his throat. But it didn't take long for his instincts to kick in. A flick of his right wrist, sharp and well practiced, stretched the band of his watch, releasing a catch. The haft of a five-inch combat dagger flicked out of his sleeve and into the cupped palm of his right hand. He lurched left, putting his attacker on his right hip. The dagger blade he swung backward toward the spot where the kidney of his attacker would be.

In the instant before his blade struck home, the fragrance of her distinctive perfume hit him, combining with his realization that the body on his back was too light to present a realistic hazard.

"Nina," he said, redirecting his blow, slapping her on the butt with the blade.

"Ouch!" she squealed, taking his right ear into her mouth.

Shudders ran up and down his spine. She let herself be turned in his grasp until they were mouth-to-mouth. With both arms behind her back, he released a catch, sheathing the dagger, freeing his hands to clutch her to him.

Swayne felt her lips melding to his, becoming part of his own body. He willed all his tensions and anxiety—selfish though it might be—to burst through the floodgates of his body and into hers. The kisses, long and deep and wet, might have gone on for mere minutes. Or maybe it was hours. He did not know. Did not care. For this was where he wanted to be. Anyplace than where he had been. Or where he had been ordered to be—he lifted his arms and pressed the button on his wristwatch so he could read the illuminated dial—so damn soon.

She was the first to pull free. "Jack, you take my breath away."

"I'll bet you say that to all the guys. Anything to get an interview. What the hell are you doing out at this hour anyhow?"

"Stalking you. What does it look like?"

"Inside, lady."

Once behind closed doors, they spoke not at all, except in the language of the body. Each greedy touch was answered in kind. Each ragged breath of one accelerated the breathing of the other. They tried undressing each other, but that proved too awkward, so they resorted to the more efficient alternative—she ripping off her own clothes, he stripping himself.

She went for his naked body but froze, her arms outstretched. "My God, what happened to you?"

She probed gently at the scratches and welts covering his six-foot, three-inch frame.

"Nothing."

She grasped his hand and led him to a full-length mirror. "That's nothing? You look like you've been devoured by wolves and shit over a cliff."

If only, he thought, remembering the submarine's hull. To be honest about it, though, the bruises did not look as bad as they felt.

Realizing how moronic *nothing* sounded, he said, "We got into a scrape. I can't talk about it."

Besides, nothing about his reflection in the mirror looked as good as hers. She had a runner's body, lithe and well-muscled in the legs. She did a quarter-turn, aware that he was staring, and willing to let him. She made a concave of her flat stomach and stood on tiptoe to emphasize the roundness of her ass. In that position, she looked like a dancer, tall, graceful, translucent white—especially her breasts. She might have been sculpted from alabaster, lovingly hand-polished until she had come to life. That thought made him want to touch her.

His gaze met the reflection of her dusky gray eyes. She inclined her head toward the mirror, lowering her face but not her eyes, holding him captive with her expression of many messages. He saw both submission and challenge in her look. Threat and promise. Hunger and surfeit. Question and answer. Her look granted him permission to touch.

Then they were at each other, stroking, clutching, pulling, nipping, cursing—growling obscenities of

sexual mock-violence—and finally bursting in relief—she first, then he an instant later, taken to his
peak by her satisfaction and the urgent curses she
had strung together, shrieking them in his ear.

Trembling, gasping, and sweating, they finally
rolled apart, each gasping the other's name. They
lay, spent, chests heaving like sprinters after a dash.

"Thanks, Bennie," she said after her breathing
had returned to normal. "I needed that."

"Bennie?"

"You're not Bennie? I must have the wrong
apartment."

"Funny."

"A pact," she murmured. "You must promise
me we'll never stop meeting like this."

"Fine." He closed his eyes and felt himself slipping toward the abyss of unconsciousness.

Like a driver realizing he was falling asleep at
the wheel, he bolted upright in bed, fearful that if
he lay there even for a minute, he might never make
the flight he'd warned everybody else not to miss.
Suddenly, everything that he had forgotten in the
last—he checked the alarm clock—ten minutes cas-
caded back to his consciousness.

*The bastards had kidnapped the Commandant of
the Marine Corps!*

And he was lying in bed with an investigative
newspaper reporter. There had to be something sac-
rilegious in that. "What do you want, Nina?"

"I've already gotten what I came for." She
propped herself on an elbow, completely unabashed

about her nakedness. He smiled at her, half wondering about the irony. Moments ago, she had seemed soft and moist and fleshy in all the right parts. Now, lying on the bed, she seemed as hard and angular in body as in spirit.

"Bullshit. That was only preliminary. It's always a preliminary and only that. I have a plane to catch. I have to shower. That will give you a moment or two to concoct a better story. But don't waste too much effort on it. I'm not going to tell you anything anyhow."

She gave him a playful sneer. "You've already told me volumes, Jack. Go on and take your shower and I'll see if I can get anything else out of you." Her smile told him that he might capitalize on the double meaning in her words, so he wasted no time hitting the shower.

In the few months he had known her, she had taught him the original, confident assurance of Adam, the ability to be blatantly naked around her. So he strode into the bedroom after his shower, still toweling himself dry. As he circled the bed, they studied each other, as if archenemies sizing each other up before the attack. He no longer felt as confident in reading her as before. What did she want from him? His body or his secrets? A single twitch of her lips gave him his answer: first his body, then his secrets. It was a deal he could live with, confident that he could not rest easy without her body, and just as sure that he could stave off her attempts to get at his secrets.

Their lovemaking this time was deliberate and unhurried. All the same sensations came into play again, except that they stole over them in phases, welling in intensity rather than tumbling over them like whitewater rapids. This time they took a full half hour with each other. She brought him to a climax first, her mouth at his ear, coaxing and cajoling, as if she were making a provocative phone call instead of sitting astride him gripping his hair for leverage to push against him. Although he protested that he needed rest, she insisted that he perform the same magic on her. Fifteen minutes later, he fulfilled her needs, and they lay locked together in an embrace.

After their breathing had returned to normal once again, she unstuck her damp body from his. She poked into her purse and came up with a cigarette and lighter. She pulled hard at the cigarette, drawing the smoke so deep into her lungs he half-expected it not to come out on the exhale. He toweled himself dry again, waiting for the inevitable.

She did not disappoint. "So. You've been in the ocean."

He raised an eyebrow.

"I tasted the salt on you, remember?"

He did remember the licking. With a shudder.

"It was not quite the same as body salt. Not as delicious." She wriggled her nose at him and flicked her tongue across her lower lip.

Involuntarily he glanced at the clock.

"We don't have time to do it again," she said.

"You've got to catch a plane, remember. Just give me a hint. You put your body at risk tonight. And I don't mean with me. What gives?"

"You know I can't say, Nina. Why do you even ask?"

"It wasn't that business in Cuba, was it? The shoot-down?"

"It wasn't a shoot-down," he blurted out before he realized what he had told her. "Damn you."

She smiled. "So you pulled a couple boys out of the drink. Word at the 'Gon is maybe a student pilot got disoriented and punched himself and his I.P. out of a perfectly good plane."

He had long ago stopped being surprised that she had sources of information equaling anything he had seen in the J-2 of the Defense Department. He yawned. "I don't know a thing about it."

She hosed his face with a stream of smoke. "Then you ought to hang around and read about it in the morning paper. I already wrote the story, and it's running on the front page."

She lit a second cigarette from the coal of the first and blew smoke at the ceiling. He saw she was getting ready for a frontal attack. More than anything else, he liked that quality in her. No faking, no dekes or subterfuges. When she wanted something from him, she got right in his face and said so. She would have made a helluva Marine. The next thing out of her mouth was going to be, *Let's be honest, Jack.*

"I'm going to level with you, Jack. The SecDef

himself called in the select few for a briefing a couple hours ago. He told us about the bombing of the Ranger barracks at Fort Benning, the Air Force ambush in Montana, and the sinking of that cruiser in San Diego, so I already know all about those things, and you don't have any responsibility for what I know. I just want to make that clear."

He shook his head—not at hcr, and she seemed to understand that he was thinking: *What the hell was the point of enforcing military secrecy on the front-line troops, when the bigwigs turned right around and called press conferences to fill in the blanks?*

"I wasn't sure if the SecDef was holding anything back in his backgrounder. Until I had this little encounter with you. Now I know that you're barely back from one mission before the Marines are sending you out on another." She held up a hand at him to keep him quiet. "Don't say anything. Don't confirm or deny. Just let me talk, and you will never have to admit to this conversation because it is no conversation. Got it?"

He shrugged. As usual, she was right. He had to trust that she knew how to play politics, even military politics, better than he did.

"Here's what I know. The Secretary of Defense has been given orders from the President himself. Orally only, of course. Other than an elevated alert status, there isn't going to be any military reaction to these provocations from the terrorists. He didn't say what kind of terrorists, so I'm going to have to assume that they are coming from one of our allies or near-allies—if Khadafy had pulled any crap like this, the bombers would already be airborne. So, what do we have?'' She held up that hand again to let him know the question was rhetorical.

''We have a Marine officer in charge of a small unit flying out of Virginia at dawn. No way in hell is he out there to avenge something that happened to one of the other armed forces. So, what the SecDef didn't say tonight is that something is amiss in the Marine Corps. Captain Jack Swayne and his little group of troops is going to make it all better.''

He shrugged. *Maybe, maybe not.*

She smirked at him. ''Don't get lame on me, Jack. Mind what I'm saying now. I'm not asking where you're going or what you're doing. Pretend you're the guy at the information booth in the Pentagon. All I'm asking you to do is tell me where *I* should go. Whom shall I talk to the get the answers I want? Give me a name or a job title. That's all.''

He wished she were not an investigative reporter in the hottest investigative town in the world. He wished he had met her in an earlier life. Barring that, he wished they had not met at all. If he didn't know her, he couldn't care about her. He might meet her in a future life. Maybe things there would be different.

He shook his head, knowing that in his world he had no business entertaining fantasies. Here they were in the here and now. She was his enemy, professionally speaking. She would not attack him per-

sonally, but neither would she protect him from the
hell that would break loose if ever he answered her
question.

She lay there, propped on an elbow, smoking in
his bed. She had made her request and now awaited
his answer. Ninety percent of the Marine officers he
had ever known could have learned something of
enormous value from Nina Chase, star reporter: *Say
what's on your mind and then shut up*.

When he did not take the bait and start shooting
off his mouth, she turned her back on him, got up,
and walked to the bedroom window. Unabashed as
ever, she pulled the drapes aside and looked out into
the city night. Waiting. No tricks and no seduction.
Just waiting, giving him time to grapple with his
conscience and speak his answer.

He knew that if he gave her nothing, she would
either kiss him and get dressed or get dressed and
kiss him, depending on her priorities of the moment.
Then she would leave without reproach or recrimi-
nations. Someday in the future, maybe a week from
now, maybe six months hence, she would ambush
him again. As she had so many times before. This
conversation would never be discussed again, just
as no previous such conversations had ever been
discussed.

For the first time since he had known Nina, he
wanted to give her the answer. Outside of the Marine Corps, he had no friends. She was no friend, of
course, and could never be, but she was the closest
thing to it in civilian clothes. The answer she wanted

rolled around his mouth as he tried it out on his inner ear.

She recoiled from the window. "Shit!"

He went for the nine-mill in his nightstand drawer. "What is it?"

"A limousine just pulled up to your building."

He laughed and flopped on the bed. "Don't worry, it's not for me. Lois Lane might rate a limo from the *Daily Planet*, but the Marine Corps doesn't send one for anybody less than flag rank."

She was already pulling at her clothes—not her underclothes, just a dress. Her scanties she crammed into an oversized handbag. As she stepped into her shoes and turned to find her coat, he couldn't help but admire the hard body showing through the fabric of her dress.

"You'd better get into your BDUs, buster."

"And why is that, missy?"

"Senator Jamison Swayne is about to pay a courtesy call."

He shot up from his bed at the very mention of the name. His startled response coincided exactly with the buzzer box by his door. He fumbled with his shorts and pants as he pushed the door release.

"No need to see me out," she said. "You'll pardon me if I use the back way. I don't want to embarrass you with Granddad. What would he think if he caught you consorting with the enemy?"

She leaned into him, puckering for a kiss.

He gave it to her, and she caught his lower lip between her teeth, biting until he groaned in protest.

"I want you to feel my kiss long after you catch that flight," she said, stepping into the hallway.

He checked his lips for blood. "That was no kiss."

She giggled, showing a girlish side that he rarely saw in her. "Don't be a woosie, Marine."

He shook his head urgently to show that he was serious, and said, "I'll remember this night all of its own, Nina. I've never forgotten any of our moments together."

She drew back in surprise. "Why Jack Swayne. Is the lean, mean, fighting Marine going romantic on me?"

The elevator cable down the hallway began rattling.

"Actually," he said, "I can't decide whether I really hate you or not," he said, a grin working its way across his face.

She batted her lashes. "Such an odd way of saying you love me."

He shook his head. "I can't confirm that," he said. It surprised him to see the involuntary flinch in her expression. Amazing. She was disappointed that he wouldn't come right out and say he loved her.

"Or deny it," he added, restoring her confidence. "But I can say something else you want to hear. If you need an honest answer to your question about why the Marine Corps is sending me out on a mission that seems only to involve the other services, I don't know where you could find it." Another flicker of disappointment. "But if you want a dishonest answer, I recommend you go directly to the Commandant of the Marine Corps himself. If you can find him, you'll have your answer."

She gazed into his eyes. The elevator car made a racket, bumping and grinding up the shaft to Swayne's floor. At any moment, Senator Swayne was going to step out of that car and give his grandson hell again. For that was the nature of their relationship—Jamison Swayne would dispense hellfire, and Jack Swayne would take it until the dam burst and he fired back.

She began nodding, smiling, almost on the verge of tearing up.

"What?" he asked.

"I'm touched. You really do love me. Do you want me to come back inside? Hide out and stay the night?"

"Yes, but this is no night for you to stay. I have to go."

Besides, if she would stay, he might have felt compelled to answer her accusation that he loved her. Fact was, he'd didn't know the answer himself. Didn't want to know it.

She gave him a look he had never seen from her before, one of fear. She might well be just as afraid of the word *love* as he was. She turned on her heel and marched away. The door to the stairwell went shut just as the doors to the elevator car slid open. Swayne left the apartment door open and finished dressing, throwing on a camouflaged undershirt and jacket, tearing at his socks. He had begun lacing his boots when the cranky old shit that nature had dictated to be his grandfather pushed his way into the room.

The junior senator from South Carolina—even at seventy-eight, he could not wrest seniority from the oldest living member of that elite club—stopped inside the doorway of Swayne's apartment and wrinkled his nose.

"Since when did you start smoking?" He shook his head in disgust, his trademark shock of white hair whipping the air.

Give the man a goatee and handlebar mustache and he could've taken up a new career peddling fried chicken.

Swayne knew damned well his grandfather's disgust had nothing to do with smoking. He gave the old man an expression that might be a smile, might be a sneer. "Senator. Isn't it a little late for you to be up and about town? They's all kinds of bad elements roaming the streets at this hour." Much as he disliked the man and all he stood for, Swayne could not stop himself from dropping back into the speech patterns of South Carolina. *Idn't* instead of *isn't*. *They is* instead of *there are*.

"The business of government knows no quitting time, son." *Bidness, gummint, quittin'*. Whereas Swayne had devoted himself to scouring the last trace of a Southern accent from his speech, the senator reveled in it. His down-home, good-old-boy trademark amplified the image of Southern aristocracy that his constituency relished.

Swayne made the motions of gathering his personal items, as if packing for a trip. But he realized
he was just engaging in pointless activity. Everything that he would be taking on the mission was
either already in his pockets or—he glanced at the
clock—already loaded aboard their transport. He
made a show of looking at his wristwatch, hoping
to give the old man the hint that he had somewhere
to be, anywhere else but here in this room.

Naturally, the old man did not take the hint. He
understood that he was unwelcome, all right. But he
would never acknowledge something so inhospitable. It went against the grain of the Southern-gentry
image he was perpetually cultivating. Maybe it was
politics. Or maybe it was just a family trait. None
of the Swaynes—his grandfather, whom he hated,
or even his uncle, whom he loved—seemed able to
confront an issue head-on. Come to think of it, that
was probably the reason he was so drawn to Nina
Chase—at least she would acknowledge it when she
was being insulted.

The moment turned awkward. Since the old man
refused the less direct approach, Swayne went right
at him. "Senator, is there a reason for your being
here? I have to leave."

The senator's complexion darkened. "You learn
your manners from your women friends? The kind
that stands buck-nekked in the window?"

He would not be baited. "Senator, this has noth-

ing to do with my women. It's me, my attitude, my
rudeness. If you have something to say, get to the
point. I have to be—I'm pulling duty officer tonight
at the Pentagon. If I don't leave now, I'll be late.''

"Don't you lie to me, son."

"And don't you call me son." This discussion
felt so familiar to Swayne. It seemed that they had
had it fully a dozen times, in almost these precise
words. Someday he would have to record one of
these segments on tape. He could offer to play back
to the old man next time so the senator could cut to
his point.

Jamison Swayne's jaws worked, creating knots in
his temples as he tried to control his anger. Swayne
couldn't help feeling the slightest bit satisfied that
he could still agitate the man.

"All right, then. I'll call you *grandson*. You cannot deny you are my *grandson*, and I demand a
token of respect. Don't treat me like a fool and don't
lie to me. *Grandson*."

Ironic, that. The senator had probably never made
as direct a bald-ass statement of fact in his life. It
was not in his nature.

"Senator, if you don't say what's on your mind
within the next ten seconds, I'm walking out of here.
I wouldn't want you to take it as a sign of rudeness.
You can turn off the lights and shut the door behind
you."

"All right then. The reason I'm here is to save
your precious military career."

"Don't do me any favors, Senator."

"Son—*grandson*, you know I have untold influence in Armed Services. You know I have sources everywhere in this town. I know what you are up to—what the United States Marine Corps, to be precise about it, is up to. I also know that what they are doing is illegal—the posse comitatus act forbids sending military forces into action on precious American soil. It goes against the very Constitution of the United States. What they're asking you to do, you can refuse. You can save yourself and your career. Not to mention your life."

Swayne shook his head throughout the entire speech, thinking: *Is there nobody in the country who hasn't been briefed on our mission?* "Senator, I don't know what you're talking about. Somebody is feeding you bad information."

"Is it bad information that General Bat Masterson, the Commandant of the United States Marine Corps, has been taken hostage by a group of Canadian terrorists?"

Swayne made a conscious effort to keep his head shaking. "Again, I don't know what you're talking about. I'm going down to the Pentagon to man the Middle East desk in the operations center. I'll drink a gallon of coffee, eat some bad military-concession food, come home with indigestion, and go to sleep. That's what I am going to be doing for the next twenty-four hours. I don't see where that is any concern of the junior United States senator from the great state of South Carolina—even if he is the second-ranking majority member on the Senate Armed Services Committee.''

Swayne could see the old man flinch at the words *junior* and *second-ranking*.

The senator barked at him. "That's hog slop, and you know it. The American people will not stand for lawless acts by the Armed Forces of the United States. If they hear of this illegal adventure, it will result in your court-martial. I would not be able to intervene. You will go to jail at Leavenworth. I am deeply saddened at the very prospect.''

Swayne sighed deeply himself. ''No need to filibuster, Senator. I tell you, I'm pulling a duty shift, like any other desk weenie in the Armed Forces. If that's against the law, the best thing you could do for me is to have them stop putting me on the duty roster. If you really want to help me, do that.''

The old man's face had taken on the color purple. ''Don't mess with me, boy. Have you ever stopped to consider that the biggest mistake here might not be a personal one, that the fatal error is not yours, but that of the very Marine Corps you're so *gott*-damned proud of?''

Swayne realized they had come to the point in the discussion where civility flew out the window. Jamison Swayne was one insult away from all-out rage.

It was all so predictable. Suddenly Swayne felt very tired, as if all the battering of the submarine and the demands of Nina had imploded on him all at once. He patted his pockets and picked up his utility cap.

"You'll have to excuse me, sir," he said with strained politeness.

The senator stamped his foot. "They *is* no excuse for you, *suh*."

Swayne had the sudden, hysterical feeling that if the senator were holding a pair of gloves, he would slap him across the face, challenging his own grandson to a duel.

The old man must have caught a glimpse of a smile, and took instant offense. The next words out of his mouth, just as they had always been at this point of the conversation, would be his idea of the extreme insult.

"You don't belong in the Marine Corps any more than your father did. You don't have the temperament. You don't have the backbone, the courage, the stamina—"

Swayne had already stopped listening. He brushed past the old man and strode down the hallway toward the elevator.

The elder Swayne, immobilized by his own rhetoric, stood in the doorway of the apartment, shouting his canned litany of insults.

When that had no effect, he shouted, "Don't come crying to me, son. When this sordid affair blows up in-your-face, don't come crying to me. *He-ah?*"

After this last word, coming as a two-syllable shriek, the elevator doors shut the senator out of

Swayne's hearing. Bad as it was, it was nowhere near the worst Swayne had ever heard from him. And he had not put down the senator as cruelly as he might have. Once the old man had shaken a finger under his nose, bellowing, "You're just like your daddy. You don't have the guts to be a Marine, It's not in your genes." And Swayne had blurted back, "Well, just ask yourself this, old man. Ask yourself where me and my father got our genes." After that, the junior senator from South Carolina had become a lot more careful in choosing his words during their arguments.

Swayne told himself that it was the best, most hurtful comeback in the history of the long-standing family argument. But he knew there was no way for him to hurt the old man as harshly as Jamison Swayne could hurt him by insulting his own son, Jack's father.

He told himself on the way to the air station that the ongoing feud with his grandfather meant nothing in the long-term scheme of things. What mattered now was for him and his team to carry out an operation so delicate that they would have to perform as meticulously as software writers. They had to recover the Commandant. And they had to do it in such a way that no citizen of the United States not involved in the operation would ever find out. The thought gave him a moment's prickling of shame. Considering the stakes, and the delicacy of what they were about to do, even if they succeeded, Nina

Chase might eventually ferret out the story because of the hint he had given her.

Later, as he and his team sorted supplies that were to drop with them into the freezing November skies of Montana, he realized that that moment of weakness in directing an investigative reporter to the office of the Commandant was the most reckless thing he'd ever done. In a sense, he was worse than a traitor to his country. For he had betrayed the Corps.

Maybe the old man had been right about him all along.

THE SWEET GRASS HILLS, MONTANA—0409 HOURS LOCAL (1109 ZULU)

PARETO CHECKED IN with his operating teams. The pair at Fort Benning was no problem. Both dead. The group that had attacked the reaction force at the missile site was riding security for him, having gotten away from the Missouri River breaks and traveled north to rendezvous in the Hills. The Scuba team out of California would be escaping by air, flying by day to central Washington, hiding the plane in a crop duster's hangar, and escaping over the border low-level the next night into British Columbia—if the damned blizzard ever loosened its grip on the Northwest.

Meanwhile, perhaps the most critical piece of the puzzle would be the most difficult to manipulate into position. The sudden blizzard had isolated Masterson and his kidnappers even more. Driving out of the mountains was proving impossible. Staying in position would be untenable. The team with the most important element of the plan in its hands was going to need a bit of old-fashioned luck to get out of Montana alive. Pareto began formulating an alternative plan. If necessary—that is, if his team didn't prove to have the requisite ingenuity—he would just have to find a way to precipitate a gun battle that would proved fatal to the good general.

BLACK BUTTE, MONTANA—0830 HOURS LOCAL (1530 ZULU)

AT FIRST LIGHT, General Harley Masterson found himself riding in the third of six sport utility vehicles, all matte-black and loaded with options—his captors were well bankrolled. Even so, the convoy didn't move very fast when it moved at all. The storm had kept up its fury through the night, building huge drifts across the road and reducing visibility to zero.

Last night, he had realized right away that he had been kidnapped by a professional force. In the first place, they possessed both modern weapons and a proven willingness to use them to kill. In the second place, they had access to an astounding intelligence source. They had found him in this remote area of Montana when only a handful of highly placed of-

ficers and civilian executives of the United States
government knew where he was. As any top executive must not, Masterson never publicized his
travel schedule unless he was going to be in the
safest company in the world, among Marines. Yet
these people had walked in on him, and identified
him. They had found his PERLOBE as they frisked
him, removing the device from his pocket, and bran-
dishing it as if it were the object of the search. One
of the group, obviously a technician, had exposed
the operating panel of the tiny experimental device
and, using the tip of a ballpoint pen, disabled his
distress alarm within seconds. No trial and error to
it. For all Masterson knew, the man might have been
the inventor of the device. Certainly he had had access to its highly classified operation manual.

Naturally, somebody in Masterson's position
could never remain entirely incommunicado, even
on furlough. So he had kept in touch with headquarters twice daily, using a wireless satellite uplink
in his notebook computer, now in the hands of his
captors. The technician among them had inspected
the computer and carefully packed it away in its
carrying case.

That was the professional side to his captors, and
it bothered him greatly.

On the other hand, they had not blindfolded him
as kidnappers normally would, leading him free to
gather intelligence about them.

This much he already knew. He had been taken
by a force of perhaps two dozen men. He hadn't

been able to get an exact head count, but he could count vehicles, and it appeared that most of the seats were occupied. The men spoke French to each other and English to him, brusquely but with little hostility. They felt confident in discussing their plans openly in French, apparently not knowing that he had taken a crash course at the Defense Language Institute before a short stint in Montreal as a liaison officer to the Canadian Armed Forces. If they were as professional as they seemed, they should have known that. If they did not know it, they might be dangerous for lack of preparation, and therefore act irrationally in a crisis, such as a rescue attempt by the Marine Corps. He had no doubt one had been launched the instant he had gotten off his distress signal.

However, if they were indeed aware that he spoke French, and still felt free to leave him without a blindfold and to discuss their plans, they were more than professional, and much less than desperate. They were zealots, so dedicated to their cause that they would be perfectly willing to sacrifice his life and their own to it.

AIRBORNE OVER MONTANA, ABOARD A C-141E2X— 1157 HOURS LOCAL (1857 ZULU)

THE TENSION INSIDE the fuselage of the Starlifter reached its peak when the pilots put the craft into its descent, submerging them in a sea of bumpy clouds the color pewter. Night Runner maintained his usual sober expression, but inside he grinned broadly. To him, parachuting—especially drops involving free fall—was a mystical communion with the birds of prey. He could soar like an eagle or swoop like a falcon, depending on the attitude of his arms and body. Night and bad weather did not diminish the mysticism. Rather it increased it, allowing him to feel he had been separated from all things earthly, that he was transitioning between this life and the next. Parachuting to Night Runner was nothing less than lucid dreaming taken to its zenith.

TO FRIEL, PARACHUTING was a dangerous thing that had to be done in getting from one combat action to another. A mere form of transportation, dangerous transportation at that. But kick-ass fun when he could see where he was going. Which had never happened since training. There had always been darkness or bad weather on operational missions. Just one more thing about the Marines that pissed him off.

POTTS HATED PARACHUTING because it felt out of control, leaving him at the mercy of the breezes. You never made a sharp ninety-degree turn. You swung into a gentle arc to make the corner. While floating in the air, the agenda was not your own, but that of the arbitrary forces of nature.

The only nightmare he ever remembered was seeing himself skewered on a splintered treetop like a weenie at a picnic. Cowardice had nothing to do with it. Potts simply hated jumping out of perfectly good airplanes.

SWAYNE BARELY GAVE jumping thought. Even when the pilots called him forward and recommended that he put off the maneuver until later in the day, when the storm was forecast to diminish, he didn't hesitate. Against their recommendation, he directed him and his men to continue flying and drop him and his men in the blind.

"How much time remaining until we hit the drop zone?" he asked.

"Twelve minutes and . . . thirty seconds— mark."

"Wind direction?"

The navigator consulted his charts. "North-northwest, 330 degrees, twenty knots, with gusts up to fifty-five. Piss-poor day to be snow-diving. Are you sure you don't want to postpone? We've got the fuel to loiter for four to six hours. We can get a tanker from Malmstrom for a drink. Stay up here all winter if you wanted us to."

That boast clinched it for Swayne. He was already antsy about the dozen minutes or so they had remaining. He'd rather jump without a chute and take a chance on the odds of landing in a snowbank than spend any more time up here, endlessly orbiting. He said, "Give us a heads-up at five minutes, one minute, and a countdown from ten, would you?"

"It's your ass." The pilot shook his head. "You

guys are crazy. But that doesn't mean we have to be. I'm not taking his plane down any closer to those mountains than I think is safe.''

''Wouldn't expect you to,'' said Swayne as he left the cockpit, hoping it sounded like an insult. *Bluebonnets.*

Back in the fuselage he waggled all his fingers to let the team know approximately how much time remained. They all knew what to do, standing up to check each other's jump gear and weapons one last time. Swayne went over Potts's massive body and oversized baggage—it must have taken enough fabric for two normal-sized men to manufacture his clothing and gear, including another XM-80 Brat to replace the one lost in Cuban waters. Distributed among the team would be five 1500-round drums of 5.56 ammo. The drums gave the weapon the look of the tommy gun of gangster movies. Except that the Brat was three or four times as lethal in firepower, not to mention range and accuracy.

At five minutes, the pilot directed the crew chief to prepare for the drop. The crew chief manipulated his cords and controls, opening the drop ramp of the Starlifter halfway. A rush of cold air reminded everybody on the team to adjust their gloves, face masks, and goggles.

At the two-minute call, the men lined up behind the cargo they would launch out the ramp of the airplane: three electric snowmobiles and a cargo trailer, each equipped with PERLOBEs so they could be located after the drop.

Night Runner would follow the cargo pack, swooping left into the teeth of the wind, diving for ten seconds in free fall. If a chute behind him did not open, he would not be floating beneath a load of humanity falling at terminal velocity.

Friel would follow Night Runner, his sniper cannon disassembled and carried in a white-painted case strapped to his back.

Potts would go third, Swayne last.

As American military forces always tended to be, even the Force Recon Team would be over-supplied for this mission. The weather and uncertainty demanded extra equipment to accommodate any contingency. Depending on the situation on the ground, they would cache or destroy any surplus.

At thirty seconds, the men tried to control their tension by stamping feet, rolling shoulders, and shaking arms. With the beginning of the countdown in their headsets, they bent to their cargo loads and tensed, shoving the entire pack out at the count of five.

Night Runner exploded out of a squat at the count of two, so he was in the full free fall at the instant the jump sequence lights changed from green to red. The other three shoved off at one-second intervals, so all were sailing into the frigid air of Montana within three seconds.

In his mind, Swayne kept up his count, even as he announced over his boom mike, "All clear."

When the numbers in his head hit six seconds, Swayne called out, "One-pull." In quick succession

Potts called, "Two-pull," Friel barked, "Three-pull," and Night Runner, reaching his ten seconds of free fall, sang out, "Four-pull." This low-visibility drop sequence prevented one of the following jumpers from dropping onto somebody's wing below.

Swayne's sense of direction came from knowing that when he turned his wing into the the wind, he was heading north-northwest. It was his only certainty.

The jump zone was to be a plateau west of Black Butte. He had been warned of trees, of course, but the ridge line he'd selected for landing had been relatively barren, according to reconnaissance photographs. Now, if only they could see something of it.

Swayne's mental countdown went on. By now, he should be hearing from Night Runner, who had the most dangerous situation of all to deal with, the first landing.

NIGHT RUNNER COUNTED himself lucky that only one lens of his goggles had cracked in the cold. One lens afforded him visibility enough to have the best chance of seeing the landing zone when it came up at him. Both hands gripped the brakes of his para-wing as he prepared to call out the landing for the benefit of the others. He swept his eyes from left to right, checking below and sweeping his gaze upward, to where the horizon should be. By now, even allowing for the wind keeping them aloft longer, he should be seeing something of the ground. He should be—

The blow came from behind, striking him below the right shoulder blade, piercing his back with a spear of pain, bringing a groan to his lips. As best he could, Night Runner formed his mouth around the escaping sound and air, trying to call out the words *"Four down,"* alerting the others to haul on their air brakes in two-second intervals. But no words came out.

FRIEL HEARD A sound, and knowing the possibilities, if not the certainties, that a man in a blind jump could well be injured, responded by applying his brakes, feeling the para-wing fill with air, bracing his body for impact. But contact with the ground did not come, and he feared his wing would stall out any second, dropping him out of the sky.

He felt a sudden anger at Night Runner for grunting or belching or whatever he was doing instead of calling out. But he put that out of his head, knowing he must alert the others. "Three is—" His feet hit a cushion of snow and, rather than reporting a disaster, he called out in relief, "Three is down," looking around for Night Runner so he could let him know how pissed he was. He couldn't see the chief. Or anything else in the driving snow.

SWAYNE MADE HIS call after Potts in sequence and landed uneventfully, softer than he had ever put down before anywhere, including in water.

He unbuckled his harness and struggled clear of the rigging, concentrating on getting his weapon free and switched off safe to full automatic. He looked around and saw nothing but nothingness. In this visibility, gathering and hiding the para-wing was no concern. Even security would not be a problem. Getting oriented in a raging blizzard on a mountain in Montana, collecting his men—all dressed in white camouflage—*that* was the problem. Time and again, Swayne had learned this lesson: The enemy, painted black and evil by a Marine's own imagination and clever and capable by military intelligence, was seldom the immediate danger. Too often the most innocuous circumstances got men killed before they could even get into rifle range of the enemy. And this was hardly an innocuous situation.

He lifted his goggles and turned full-circle, blinking away the snowflakes that kept clinging to his eyelashes. Except that his feet were on the ground and that the wind continued to blow, he had no sense of landmarks or direction. Black Butte, if it truly was black, should be dominating the horizon. Whether it was ten miles away, or he was standing on it, he could not see it.

If he could not find the mountain, maybe he could find his men. "Comm-check," he called out. Friel answered, "Four." Several seconds of silence ensued before Potts called out, "Two."

No Three, no Night Runner. Swayne had been right the first time. The sound in his earpiece had been an attempt to call out, an attempt that ended as a moan. Somewhere out there, Night Runner had hit hard. For an instant, Swayne forgot all about the Commandant, the terrorists, and the mission. One of his men—and in Force Recon a leader could ill afford do without any of them—was unaccounted for.

Swayne, who had always doubted the Marine Corps' increasing reliance on technology, preferring a good man to a nifty gimmick, hoped like hell that his new pair of experimental binoculars would do their job. Not only were they supposed to magnify the ambient light, forming images in the dimmest of starlight, as they had in Cuba. They were also designed to detect thermal images, using the infrared frequency range of light and heat. Running the automatic steps through his mind, he turned the device to IR function. He turned a circle, scanning for a thermal return. Nothing. He tried again, making barely a quarter sweep until a bright green blur morphed into the shape of the grizzly bear that was Gunny Potts.

"I have a fix on you, Two," he said to Gunny's profile. Potts's head came up, and he looked around.

"Negative visual on you," Potts said.

"I'm at your nine o'clock at fifty meters."

Potts began a pivot to the left. When he was head-on, Swayne said, "Stop turn. Start walking while I try to spot the others."

Swayne panned to the left of Potts's position and got another thermal hit. "Number Four, wave your arms." The faint green image of a man waving his arms took shape inside binoculars. Swayne could not tell whether he was looking at Friel's back or his front, so he directed him to wave the right arm only. Once he realized that he was all but looking Friel in the face, he gave the him the range and directed him to rally on his position as well.

Although he knew the two men were walking toward him at less than one hundred meters, he could not see them without the binoculars. Only when Potts was within ten feet could Swayne discern an outline with the naked eye. For his part, Potts did not see Swayne, and would have passed by within five feet. Swayne called out to him, and soon they were hunkered shoulder-to-shoulder, waiting for Friel in the driving whiteout.

Potts cupped a hand over his mike. "My jump goggles shattered like Momma's best china," he said.

Swayne grunted in agreement, but he was distracted, now aware of a far more serious problem. Although he could see Friel wandering his way—he gave him course corrections as the lance corporal kept trying to veer off downwind—the thermal image was growing fainter. Swayne reasoned that the frigid ambient temperatures had chilled everything, including their outer clothing. The insulation of their parkas would minimize heat loss from the men, rendering the IR binoculars useless before long. If they did not find him fast, they might never see Night Runner again.

He gave the binoculars to Potts. "Keep your eye

on Friel, so we don't lose another one.''

"I heard that, Cap'n," said Friel. "I never been lost yet.''

Potts put the binoculars to his eyes. "You're about to be as lost as a fart in this wind. Shut up and turn left. Stop turn. Keep walking." He covered his mike with one hand and said to Swayne, "Are you going to try to locate Runner's PERLOBE?''

Swayne nodded. From deep inside the layers of his clothing, he took his personal data assistant. He turned the PDA on, shielding it from the wind, and put up a small split-screen display, the left showing a digital readout of his compass heading in true, grid, and magnetic north. On the right-side display, he activated a directional finder, a small receiver that could identify and discriminate among as many as sixty PERLOBE transmitters. In turn, he called up the preset codes for Potts, Friel, and Night Runner.

"Shit," he said as his machine interrogated each PERLOBE.

"No Night Runner," said Potts.

Swayne shook his head. "His transmitter must have been damaged on landing.''

He tried two communications checks, knowing in advance that he would not get an answer. If Night Runner had heard anything at all of their concern for him, he would already have spoken up.

Potts handed the binoculars back to Swayne. He put them into his coat to keep them warm, now that he had found a new respect for them.

As Friel was about to stumble by their position, Potts stepped out, grasped his parka, and led him back to Swayne's position.

"I seen you, Gunny."

Potts snorted.

As much as he did not want to think about it, Swayne realized that the three of them might have to carry on Event Scenario 13 alone. He wished that notion out of his head and came up with the one solution—one very low-tech solution at that—that might help them locate the missing sergeant.

"I have a rough idea where I might find him. The three of us came down in roughly a straight line downwind, about thirty meters apart. By my calculation, he's out there." He pointed into the nothingness. "Maybe only thirty to fourty meters past Friel's landing spot on a heading of 330. Gunny, you get a fix on the PERLOBE transmitters for each of the snowmobiles and the cargo sled. Rally all the snowmobiles in one spot and give me a call."

Potts produced his own PDA. "What if you don't find him?"

Swayne, in turn, looked into the two sets of eyes, the only hints of humanity behind those snow masks, and gave them the answer they needed to hear.

"We will find him," he said with more conviction than he felt. If Night Runner, the quintessential Indian warrior and native tracker, had been in this group of three, Swayne would have no doubt about locating a missing man. Night Runner had instincts that transcended technology. All *they* had were their microprocessors and transistors, pitiful by comparison to Runner's eyes and ears.

"I have to move," Swayne said. "All I have of any value are my thermal binoculars, and wherever he is out there, Night Runner's clothing is chilling down to—" He pressed another button on his PDA and held it for moment into the shrieking wind. "Twenty below zero, wind-chill factor seventy below."

As Swayne took his bearings off his electronic compass and strode into the wind, he wished he had not checked the temperature. If Night Runner had landed on his face in six feet of snow, or was knocked out on a pile of boulders, he might smother in minutes. If he had landed hard on a tree and torn his clothing, he might already have bled out and frozen.

Swayne put such thoughts out of his head. *What trees?* Here he was in the Rocky Mountains, and he had yet to see his first one.

FOR HIS PART, Friel didn't think much about past missions. His existence was in the here and now. As to the future, he was concerned only about its immediate aspects. On the plus side, he and Potts were traveling with the wind at their backs. And that was just about the extent of the happiness he could muster. Everything else was a negative.

He hoped like hell that the captain could conjure

up the Night Runner—a *healthy* Night Runner. Without him, Friel would have a much bigger load to pull on this mission. Longer watches. Heavier packs. There would be less all-round security. Worst case was if Runner had survived as a zucchini or something. Then Friel would have to pull all his own burdens and most of the chief's too. Besides dragging his unconscious ass all over Montana.

POTTS WOULD RATHER have had the cap tell him to look for Night Runner than cargo. Over the course of a dozen missions together, he had come to respect the man as well as the warrior. More than once the Indian had saved his life, either indirectly by one of his instincts or by direct intervention in taking out a threat with one of his weapons. But beyond that, Night Runner had proved himself to be an ideal Marine. He never complained, no matter how tough the mission or how mundane the task. He always maintained a wry sense of humor when he did speak, never betraying that he had dropped out of Yale University half a semester short of graduation. Until Potts had checked into Night Runner's personnel jacket, he hadn't a clue that besides being fluent in English and the language of the Blackfeet, the man had mastered French and Spanish. When Potts had asked him about it, Night Runner had insisted that he was also capable of speaking Canadian. Potts smiled. He hoped Night Runner would get the opportunity to do so. And that someday, he'd be able to teach Night Runner how to speak Georgian.

"What are you doing in the military?" Potts had once asked him.

"Research. Maybe I'll own my own arms company someday, maybe get rich. Or maybe just write a book."

Potts knew better. Education or no, Night Runner relished the idea of being a warrior. Fact was, the Indian was the best all-round fighter Gunny had ever seen in the Marine Corps. He might not be the best shot in this Force Recon unit—that honor belonged hands-down to Friel. But he was first or second in almost every other category. And he had an almost supernatural ability to withstand pain. Wherever Night Runner was, Potts was confident that a mere blizzard and even the most grievous injury—hell, he probably could've survived the fall without a parachute—wasn't going to kill that Marine.

Satisfied that he had reasoned out Night Runner's fate, Potts turned his attention to the matter at hand.

First on the agenda was to keep Friel on track. He kept trying to stray. With such poor visibility, that could be fatal. Potts grabbed him by the shoulder and pulled him closer.

Homing on the PERLOBEs, they soon found the first snowmobile damaged beyond repair, much of it lost in the snow. Friel said, "Why don't you track down one of the other snowmobile transmitters, and I'll get the other. We can rally back here, then go looking for the captain."

"No," said Potts. "We stay together."

"But—"

Potts put his arm on Friel's shoulder and pulled him into a one-armed bear hug. In the smaller man's ear, he whispered, "We stay together."

"That's all I'm saying. Best thing is to hang like bats and shit upside down together. How many times do I have to preach that to you, Gunny?"

SWAYNE STUMBLED IN a circling sweep in the blinding snow, moving as quickly as he dared. It took no time at all for him to discover that the most advanced military technology in the world could be rendered useless in ten minutes of a Montana snowstorm. His high-tech rifle sight, with its low-light scope, would not work in this cold. Before he had walked even a hundred meters guiding himself with his digital compass, gauging the distance to within six inches, and his global location to within three meters, the digits had begun fluttering on the screen. The cold again. He tucked the device into his shirt pocket to rewarm it.

The topographical image that had literally frozen on the screen was telling him that he stood in the middle of a ravine with nearly vertical sides dropping into a stream bed nearly fifty meters below the level of the plateau. Yet, when he looked in any direction, as far as he could see—all of two meters—the ground was level. The question was: Should he trust his senses or a technological marvel that had taken leave of its own senses?

Answer: neither. He had to find Night Runner and fast. If they couldn't come up with him, the rest of the team would have to call in a secondary and get on with the primary mission.

He telescoped the stock of his rifle and probed the ground at his feet. Beneath a foot of snow, for as far as he could reach, the footing was solid. He probed and turned a complete circle. Solid in every direction. Orienting into the wind once more, he used the infrared binoculars, searching for the vaguest indication of a thermal image. There wasn't a pinpoint of heat in any direction. Night Runner must have fallen into a ravine. Or buried himself in a snowbank on impact.

Either way, he wouldn't survive long. At the ground level the snow swirled and ran like floodwaters. Even when Swayne was standing up, it kept blowing into his eyes and mouth. A man lying prone would suffocate in no time.

He put the binoculars away against his body again and stepped out, using his rifle as a probe once again. His next footstep was as solid as any he had taken today, but it was accompanied by a dull crackling that he felt more than heard. The earth shifted beneath him. He whirled and leapt away from the wind, in one motion tossing his weapon and grasping for a handhold, knowing that there would be nothing there. His attempt had no effect, for he was falling just as emphatically as when he had jumped from the Starlifter minutes ago.

His belly caught on a ledge. The global positioning readout had not been so far off after all. The blowing snow must have created a cornice at the edge of the cliff. Now, as his body began sliding downward, his grasping fingers unable to gain a purchase in the snowdrift, he knew he was going to find Night Runner after all. If not in this life, in the next.

His flailing feet found a toehold, but only a momentary one, as he felt rocks giving away. He kicked out to one side, then the other as his body continued sliding into an abyss that he had never seen, one that he might never see. To the left, something barked against his shin.

By now he had fallen to his armpits, and only by forming the numeral seven with his torso and arms could he stop the slide. He could not hold out for long, though. No matter how good his strenuous Marine conditioning, his arms were going to give out too soon. Reaching out with his left leg again, he realized that the solid irregular surface he hit was not stone, but a thick branch or root. Whatever it was, it became his only hope. The muscles in his shoulders, already overstressed from his desperate swim yesterday, had all but given in to the strain. No matter how hard he willed them, they began failing him, allowing him to slide, inch by inch, over the precipice.

Swayne wanted to cry out in anger, venting his frustration against his grandfather, not because he had anything to do with his predicament, but because the sonofabitch might be proven correct in predicting his failure at this mission. But he kept his silence, reserving valuable energy. Instead, he windmilled his right arm away from the cliff, reaching beneath him, grasping for the first hint of a solid handhold that he had encountered in this, his first trip to Montana.

The back of the right hand smashed into the face of the cliff and bounced away. His left hand lost its snow-grip, and Swayne slid into space grasping at air. His clutching fingers caught in a tangle of growth, a root the size of the handle of a baseball bat. The root held the cliff wall. And his grip held the root. Throwing his weight to the right, he drew himself up and grasped a second root, even as he realized the throbbing in his shoulder had turned to numbness.

Try as he might, Swayne could not see anything that could help him do more than hang on. The landscape in front of his eyes was no more than a swaying vertical gravel bed dusted over with the flying snow. In all his experience in mountain training and climbing, nothing like this situation had ever presented itself. Yes, he had free-climbed. And he had been made to navigate in a snowstorm using the most primitive devices, a map and a compass. But nobody had ever suggested that dry, fluffy snow blown into his face by winds of thirty knots could blind and suffocate him. Every breath in the whirling snow threatened to stuff his nose shut and choke off his throat.

And no matter how much he blinked, he could not clear his vision of the flying snow dust. He was going to have to climb back to the plateau blind and half-deprived of oxygen. One hand over the other, he worked himself an inch at a time upward. His hands and arms ached, as much from yesterday's bruises as from today's effort. But gradually he found his way over the edge. Reaching up with one hand and probing under the snow, he found a knot to grip halfway up the fingers of his right hand. It wasn't much, but it was enough. He probed again, this time with his left hand, and found a root the size and shape of a suitcase handle. Only at that moment did he dare to believe he had it made. He heaved himself up onto his belly.

Potts's voice crackled in his earpiece. "Any luck, Cap?"

Plenty of luck, thought Swayne, *all of it bad.* But he said, "Negative sighting on—"

Pellets began to pelt him. Odd pellets. Frozen red pellets. Hailstones of blood.

Swayne rolled away from the edge of the cliff so he could look upward. Finally, a tree came into focus, the tree that he had walked past by no more than six feet before stepping off into nothingness. More accurately, it was the skeleton of a tree—gray, stripped of all foliage and bark, turned a silver patina long ago. Swaying from that tree like a Christmas ornament was the body of a Marine suspended by the risers of his para-wing, floating in and out of sight in the breeze.

"Belay my last. I have a fix on Night Runner. He's hung up in a tree, dangling over a cliff. I can't determine his condition. Rally on my PERLOBE—

use extreme caution. Visibility is zero, and there is one helluva drop-off.''

LIKE EVERYTHING ELSE in Scenario 13 so far, lowering Night Runner from the tree was anything but ordinary in degree of difficulty. By the time Potts and Friel had homed on his PERLOBE, Swayne had shouted himself hoarse. To no effect. Night Runner's only response was to the weather, swaying in the Arctic-Express wind, icycles of blood dripping from his nose. Swayne decided to read that as a good sign. At least he had enough life left in him to bleed some of it out.

Swayne formulated a quick rescue. There was Night Runner's condition to consider. If he hung out much longer, he might freeze to death. And who knows when the tree might decide to topple? Because of those uncertainties, climbing the tree was out of the question. In the end, Swayne decided to keep the rescue operation simple. After all, there would be ample enough complications once they got him down and tried to get on with the mission.

After three attempts, Potts tossed a loop of a climbing rope around a sturdy branch twenty feet above their heads. Friel secured the loose end to one of the snowmobiles and idled away from the cliff until the rope was taut. Potts took two axes from the pioneer kit. He and Swayne took turns chopping at the base of the tree, Potts right-handed, Swayne swinging leftie, glad for once that he'd been born off-handed. In minutes, the tree began crackling,

and Swayne signaled Friel to put more tension on
the rope. He and Swayne stood back, doing a two-
step beneath the swinging Night Runner. The tree
gave way, smashing to the ground, its sound muffled
by the accumulated snow. Night Runner's unconscious body swung down in a gentle arc, into the
arms of the waiting Gunny Potts.

Swayne decided after checking his vital signs that
Night Runner could wait for a more thorough ex-
amination. More than anything else, they had to find
shelter from the storm and regroup. Before going on
with the mission, Swayne needed to know whether
he would have to accomplish it shorthanded. Already Potts had reported to him the loss of one of
the snowmobiles and a third of their equipment.

While Gunny Potts and Friel lashed Night Runner
to the cargo sled, Swayne extracted his all-purpose
electronics package, hoping that his body warmth
had coaxed it into operation in the last hour. It had.
He identified the position of the hunting cabin below
Black Butte, and charted a course that would take
them there. On the way, he couldn't help thinking
how dangerous it was to be driving blind, following
a compass heading. Even if they didn't drive into
another ravine, who knows when somebody might
take a low-hanging branch in the face, eliminating
one more member of the team?

The worst part was, every hundred meters or so,
he had to stop and recheck his GPS before going
on. Since the visibility hadn't improved at all, he
would make a radio call to Potts to make sure he

didn't drive up the back of Friel, riding behind Swayne. Another radio call would warn him that he had taken off.

After two iterations of this stop-go maneuver, an unfamiliar voice came over the radio.

"Spartan One," the voice said, "this is Mission Six-Alpha. If you like, I can give you directions so you don't have to keep stopping."

Swayne accepted the help of the duty radio operator at the OMCC without reservation, feeling slightly embarrassed that he had not thought of the solution on his own. Of course, the mission command center had instant and continuous access to his position as well the location of the cabin. And they were not hampered by the weather.

Now, if only he had a remote set of eyes that could warn him before he drove into a tree.

BLACK BUTTE, MONTANA—1247 HOURS LOCAL (1947 ZULU)

IN THE FIRST break of the mission, they found the cabin with only one hitch. Literally. Just as the voice from mission command warned him that he was within ten meters, Swayne saw the windscreen of the snowmobile passing underneath a horizontal pole.

"Duck!" he hollered for Friel's benefit, as well as for Potts, following closely. By the time his snowmobile had coasted to a stop, Swayne realized that the horizontal bar belonged to a hitching post used by hunters to secure their horses.

After they had cleared the cabin's perimeter, Potts carried Night Runner inside and laid him on the lower bunk. He began removing gear and outer clothing as Friel went to work starting a fire. Swayne looked around for clues—reminding himself that they were here on a mission, after all. By itself, finding the cabin did little toward accomplishing it.

Other than a four-foot-high snowdrift inside the open front door, he could see nothing amiss at first. He was struck by a moment of disappointment, thinking that the Commandant of the Marine Corps might have been captured without a fight. Then again, who wouldn't answer a knock in the mountains? And who wouldn't invite a band of armed men inside, thinking they were hunters? Especially if they talked about one of their number being lost or injured.

Yet even before his eyes had adjusted to the darkness, his nose told him that something was amiss. Once again he realized how much they were going to miss Night Runner's senses. He took out a penlight and swept its narrow beam around the one-room cabin.

He saw the door had been smashed in. That was proof enough the Commandant had been taken by force. Then his nose told him that the force had been deadly. He cast his beam around looking for the source of the blood smell.

Sprayed on the wall above the top bunk, he found ample evidence that there had been a violent struggle after all. Now, he wished that he had not doubted the combative instincts of the Commandant. As he looked closer and recognized what he was seeing, he prayed that these were not the Commandant's brains. The amount of blood pooled on the sleeping bag told him that whoever had suffered this wound could not have survived.

"A body," he told the others.

"The Commandant?" Potts asked.

"I can't tell. All I have is a bucket of blood and brains."

A second voice intruded in each of their headsets. "Find out. ASAP," Colonel Zavello ordered.

Swayne rogered, rolling his eyes. Even after four missions using the new high-technology communications apparatus, he couldn't get used to the long-distance eavesdropping and kibitzing.

Swayne's heart jumped in his chest as Potts tried wiping the bloody face clean. But the frozen blood obscured the features, so the Spartans could not tell whether this was the face of the man every Marine knew from the chain-of-command pictures in every orderly room in the Corps.

Friel, ever the pragmatic one, reached up and grabbed the corpse's hair, easily six inches long, thick, greasy, and black. That answered the question. This was no Marine, and likely never was.

Swayne made his report, and Zavello sounded relieved that Event Scenario 13 would be a rescue mission rather than a revenge operation against the Commandant's killers.

Potts stepped down from the bunk. "Well, would you look at this," he said.

Night Runner sat on the side of the cot, his head lowered, catching strings of blood running from his nose.

"Runner, are you all right?"

The Indian shook his head, streaming blood from left to right across the floor between his white Mickey-Mouse boots.

Not good. Swayne had never known the man to acknowledge anything amiss.

Potts grasped the Indian's head and lifted it. Runner's normally olive complexion was ghastly pale, his eyes gone blank and unfocused.

"Would you look at that," said Friel. "The chief has gone green."

Potts lifted his upper lip at Friel to shut him up. "Concussion," the gunnery sergeant concluded. "He must have hit the back of his head directly against the tree."

Night Runner mumbled something unintelligible.

Potts put his hand over his microphone and translated. "He says his back hurts, Cap. I found a spot. Off to the side above the kidney. Right here." He probed with his fingers, and Night Runner recoiled from the touch. "Cracked ribs at least. Maybe broken."

Swayne signaled that they should turn off their

transmitters, and Friel asked the very question on his own mind. "Can he make a go?"

Potts wagged his head doubtfully. Night Runner nodded his. Swayne bit his lip. Was it good news that Night Runner could comprehend the conversation? Or was he just nodding off? "Let's warm him up, and get something hot inside him." He rubbed his forehead, knowing they must act, for they had work to do.

Friel, went back to work at the fire. Potts helped Night Runner lie on his side. He took a handful of snow from the drift inside the door and washed his companion's face. Then he took another lump of snow and pressed it over Night Runner's nose and eyes. Runner mumbled.

"You're welcome," said Potts. "Hold that there until we can get the bleeding stopped. You need some time to get your eyes focused again."

Night Runner mumbled again, and Swayne recognized it as a protest against being left behind.

Swayne downloaded an electronic map to his PDA and handed it off to Potts. After a moment's study, Potts said, "Not too many ways out of here. Back to this highway, 287." He poked the screen with a huge fingertip.

Then Potts and Friel set about taking stock of equipment, provisions, and weapons. They brought in all they could of what had been recovered from the wrecked snowmobile. Occasionally, Potts would tend to Night Runner, replenishing his snow-pack, checking his vital signs, and keeping him from dozing off.

Zavello broke the calm inside the cabin with the first bit of good news of Event 13. "We just received a brief signal from the Commandant's PER-LOBE. I'll transmit the coordinates to you."

Within seconds, a blinking point appeared on Swayne's screen, indicating a spot where the route on the sketch map forked away from the main road, turning east toward Highway 287.

Zavello added, "The PERLOBE is six miles as the crow flies. Let me know when you make contact." Prodding them to get moving without saying so.

Swayne rogered and turned to his team. Potts raised his hands. "How do we pack, Boss? Three men or four?"

Night Runner grunted and held up one hand displaying four fingers without lifting his head from behind the snowball covering his face.

Friel looked up from the fire now starting to crackle. "Maybe it would be better if we didn't have to drag along any"—he threw a glance Night Runner's way and whispered—"dead weight."

Night Runner swung his feet to the floor and stood up, swaying. He took the snow mask from his face, looked around bleary-eyed to find his target, and pelted Friel with the bloody ice-ball. "Not dead weight," he mumbled, then flopped down on the cot, keeping his chin high, looking from man to man, daring somebody to contradict him.

"Pack for four," Swayne ordered.

LIKE EVERYTHING ELSE in their combat inventory that might look ordinary, their snowmobiles were not. Whereas the ordinary two-cycle engine might be heard for miles in the forest, theirs were electric, powered by motors that could achieve top speeds of forty miles an hour on flat, packed snow. The batteries were smaller than ordinary car batteries, but composed of elements developed in NASA's space program to make them last longer. They would not need recharging of their solar panels for thirty-six hours of continual operation. If the sun would ever show itself, the team could run on them indefinitely, and most importantly, silently.

Swayne decided that the lack of visibility allowed them as much stealth as a night approach. Later, he might reevaluate the situation and postpone hitting the terrorists until after dark. For now, he decided it was best to close on the PERLOBE signal. It bothered them that there had been a signal at all. Too convenient. Swayne suspected an ambush.

FOR THE FIRST time since he cared to remember, the team could not rely on Night Runner's almost supernatural ability to navigate. So Swayne drove the lead snowmobile, with Friel sitting behind.

He drove by responding to the course corrections given to him by the operator back at mission command, whose name he had learned was Winston.

They started slowly at first, with Private First Class Winston directing them to the road from the cabin. Gradually, as Swayne grew more confident about Winston's directions, they picked up speed.

He directed Friel to watch forward over his shoulder through the infrared imaging binoculars, looking for hot spots. Swayne reasoned that if the terrorists had been shut down by weather, they would continue to run their engines and give off exhaust signatures. Or else they might try to return to the cabin, and a head-on meeting might be avoided by picking up heat from an engine compartment.

About halfway to the PERLOBE location, Winston reported to Swayne that the Commandant's signal had vanished.

"Did it fade out?" Swayne asked. "As if the battery had died?"

Winston came back with: "It was a strong signal one second, and it disappeared the next."

Ambush, thought Swayne. Definitely an ambush.

Still, he did not dare slow down. Behind him, Potts drove the second snowmobile, with Night Runner lashed against his back, so he would not be lost if he should lose consciousness. The weight of both men, one of them Potts, plus the cargo sled proved to be too much in the soft snow. The snowmobile's skis could not plane to get up on top of the powder. So they had to drop the cargo sled and another third of their gear into a ravine before they had traveled a hundred meters from the cabin.

Both drivers had difficulty keeping on track. In

open areas, the wind blew the snow across their path, and they tended to drift with it. In the forested areas, the snow fell like a curtain. Swayne felt sorry for Potts, who had the more hazardous job of translating Winston's course corrections by adding a time lag.

Finally, they reached the trail fork. Winston warned them that they were within a mile of the final PERLOBE indication, and Swayne made a tight circle, turning on his headlights to alert Potts, and announcing a conference. They parked side-by-side, nose-to-tail.

Swayne said, "I don't want to stay on the road much longer. No more than half a mile. After that, we should move through the trees, on foot if we have to." He tossed his head, indicating the lump of humanity attached to Potts's back. "How is he doing?"

"Not much going on back there, right, Runner?"

The Marine's head came up, and after a long moment's fumbling for his microphone button—Potts had disabled the automatic-transmission feature—Night Runner's slurred voice mumbled. The content of the grunt indicated he was all right, but the quality contradicted him.

"We should have left him," said Friel.

"We don't leave one of our own." Potts lashed out with his left hand, and Swayne felt the impact on Friel against his back. He couldn't help feeling satisfied, even as he said, "Enough. Save that stuff for the bad guys. If we have to, we'll prop Night

Runner into a firing position and close in by ourselves.''

Friel grunted in assent, although not loud enough for the gunny to hear, and Swayne felt more than saw Potts's gaze questioning the wisdom of leaving a concussed man alone. Swayne hoped the decision would not have to be made, then rebuked himself for entertaining such an obvious denial of the possibility.

Moving the last half mile required all of an hour, as Swayne did not want to blunder into the ambush that seemed ever more inevitable.

Finally, his nerves could take it no longer, and he directed Potts off the road into a sheltered spot. They off-loaded Night Runner and continued down the road on graphite-frame snowshoes. Swayne knew it was risky to leave the man alone, that he might drift into a coma. But the mission and his other men were important too. More important, in fact. At least that was what the book said.

Another hour on foot took the team into a position where they would be within easy rifle range of the last signal, if they had been able to see anything.

Traveling the steep slopes had proved impossible in the ever-deepening snow. Deadfalls and thickets threatened to break a leg at any moment, and they made no progress at all. So Swayne, contrary to every rule of small-unit tactics, put himself and his undermanned team on the road. To compensate for the extraordinary risk, he ordered everybody to maintain intervals of fifty feet.

"So one hand grenade won't get us all," he said. Both men looked astonished—in this visibility, they could barely see ten feet.

"How are we going to see to keep our distance?" Friel asked.

Swayne answered by tying a length of cord around his waist and running out a length of ten arm spans before cutting it off and repeating the operation. Friel would be second, and Potts would bring up the trail, all of them strung together like pearls. They had used this daisy-chain technique often enough underwater. No reason it wouldn't work as well here, where the visibility was as bad as any underwater murk.

Ordinarily, Night Runner would have taken point. Since he was not available, Swayne led the march down the road, alternately warming his thermal binoculars under his parka and taking them out to look for hot spots.

At first he moved cautiously, perhaps too cautiously, tugging twice sharply on rope to signal Friel that he was stopping to search ahead with the binoculars, jerking once to tell them to move out again.

Soon the road switched back on itself, and he stopped to scan with his binoculars, looking for any kind of thermal alert. On his third sweep of the terrain, a splash of green painted the lenses of his binoculars. The thermal image fading in and out behind sheets of windswept snow took shape as a vehicle parked on the road ahead.

He jerked his umbilical cord three times and

dropped to his belly in the snow, practically suffocating himself in powder two feet deep, tangling his
snowshoes. As he cleared the suffocating snow and
repositioned his feet, he was glad for the poor visibility so his team could not see him struggling like
one of the Three Stooges. While waiting for Potts
and Friel to come up, he consulted his GPS to re-
fresh his mental map. That done, he resumed his
surveillance of the truck.

It did not appear to be stuck. That led him to
believe that there would be more vehicles farther
down the road. Or else this vehicle had been left as
a roadblock and rear security force. A series of gentle tugs on the cord around his waist told him Friel
was walking blindly toward him, reeling in the rope
hand over hand. All the technological tools at their
disposal, and they had had to resort to such a primitive expedient. That Montana's weather could reduce them to this was more awe-inspiring than all
the wizardry he had seen their electronic gadgetry
accomplish.

In minutes, Friel and Potts lay beside him in the
snow, Friel tangling himself in his snowshoes and
falling on his face, just as Swayne had done.
Swayne was glad for the cold-weather mask that hid
his smile.

As Friel spat and gasped and swore, Swayne un-
tied the cord from his waist. "I'll move up around
the bend. I'll put my hood down so you can get a
thermal image from my head. If I spot anybody I'll
let you know by radio. If I take fire, you scan around

with the binoculars until you can identify a source of the gunfire.''

''HOW CLOSE AM I to the truck?'' Swayne asked when he was certain he had gone too far. He could hardly believe it when Potts told him that he had closed to less than ten meters from the vehicle. Still, he couldn't see it. So this was what was like to be blind.

He inched forward and received the first tangible evidence that he was closing on the vehicle, not from his eyes but his nose. After he had traveled less than five meters, he smelled exhaust fumes wafted to him by the blizzard. A diesel engine.

A few seconds later he was on it, no more than an arm's length away before he saw patches of blackness in the covering of snow. It looked like a Dalmatian. Through the binoculars he had thought it might be a pickup with a topper over the bed. But no, it was a sport utility vehicle, a Dodge Durango.

Careful not to touch the truck, he looked inside and confirmed it was empty.

''All clear,'' he reported, and ordered the team forward. After they'd rallied, he took the binoculars from Potts.

Around the bend, a snowdrift fully twenty feet high had completely filled in the gap where the road cut into the ridge. The lead vehicle had burrowed into the drift. Apparently, the driver had run into it by accident. Or else he had tried to punch through it. In either case, the vehicle was stuck fast, covered beyond the windshield. The second vehicle in column had run into the back of the first. From the smells being circulated in the fickle breeze, it had punctured its radiator and lost its antifreeze. A third vehicle had nosed into the ditch to the right side against the hill. The fourth and fifth vehicles had run together. In each case, Swayne checked around and found no sign of fogged windows, except inside the second vehicle, probably from steam blown inside through the heater system. It had frozen on the windows.

Friel jerked a thumb at the truck and mimed pulling the door open to check inside.

Swayne vetoed the idea with the shake of his head, the risk of a booby trap too great. He directed Friel and Potts to retrieve Night Runner and the snowmobiles. He would continue snowshoeing downhill, as fast as he could tramp.

After they had gone, Swayne negotiated the huge snowdrift and moved out down the road, once again carrying the infrared binoculars. He vowed that he would never again complain about the weight of the cumbersome instrument. So far it had proved to be practically the only useful gadget in their high-tech inventory.

Twenty minutes later, while watching his back trail, Swayne picked out the thermal signatures of the snowmobiles approaching at fifty meters.

He stepped to the side of the road, not wanting to be in the way in case Potts could not slow down in time after he gave him the signal. Spotting a snow-covered log at just the right level on the bank, he lowered himself and leaned back.

The log felt soft. And it moved.

The drifting snow broke up and fell away from its resting place. Out of the white covering came a man, dressed in tropical camouflage, aiming a rifle up the road. He might have fallen asleep lying in ambush. Or else he was as blind as Swayne himself in this weather. No matter.

"What the hell are you doing?" the figure said. "Why don't you watch where the hell—"

Swayne brought the binoculars down across the man's head. Into his mike he called, "Ambush! Stop in position and get off the road. Don't drive off—it's a helluva drop."

Through the binoculars he watched them execute his command without hesitation, Potts lifting Night Runner from behind him and depositing him over the side of the slope.

"What's up, Cap?" said Potts, once they were out of sight downslope.

"Where's the ambush?" Friel asked.

Swayne almost laughed. "I'm sitting on it. I stepped off the road and landed right on one of the bad guys. Trust me, it's an ambush."

"What's our next step?" asked Potts.

Good question. Swayne had no idea where the remaining ambushers might be hidden. He concocted an expedient plan and briefed his men over the radio, directing them to his position using the IR binoculars and radio commands.

Once they were together, Swayne instructed everybody to huddle low over the body of the man he had knocked unconscious.

"Friel, try to revive him," Swayne ordered.

Friel was only too happy to oblige, pulling off the man's ski mask and rubbing snow in his face and on his neck. The ambusher did not respond, so Friel doubled his effort and within seconds, the man began to groan, awakening to find his pants full of snow.

Potts held a boot knife a foot away from the man's bleary eyes.

"Can you see what's in front of your face?" asked Swayne.

The man shuddered. "It's a knife. I'm freezing. I didn't fall asleep, Captain, honest."

Swayne exchange glances with Potts and Friel. *Captain?*

Swayne got it first. He turned his head away and cupped a hand over his own face. "He thinks he's talking to one of his own," he murmured into his mike. "I'm going to try to play it out."

Swayne turned back and growled into the man's face, "Are you aware of what could happen to the rest of our unit because you fell asleep at your post?"

"Yes, sir. Can I move? I'm freezing in my crotch." He tried to move a hand, but Potts held him, scraping the knife blade across to his face.

"I suppose you've forgotten your orders too."

"No, sir. I'm supposed to trigger the ambush.

The boys on the hill blow their Claymores, and everybody cuts loose, peppering the road.'' The man's eyes had begun to gain focus, staring at Swayne as if he were the stranger he actually was. He wasn't going to be able to pull this off for much longer.

"And where is the Commandant?"

The man blinked once, then twice, then lost control of his eyelids altogether, and they began fluttering. "Sir?"

"The Commandant? Don't you remember where we put him for safekeeping?"

"All due respect, sir. You're the Commandant, Captain."

Swayne dared not to look at Friel and Potts. He didn't understand the nonsense coming out of this fellow's mouth, but he couldn't afford to give up the charade just yet.

"All right, soldier. I'm the Commandant. Good, good. Just don't you forget it. Now, if you don't want to spend the rest of the night with your pants full of snow, you'd better start answering my questions as quick as you can. How many men are in our unit?"

Demand squinted at him. "Fourteen, sir. Don't you—"

"Silence. Point out their positions to me."

The squint left the man's eyes once and for all. "Hey, you're not the Commandant—" As he drew breath to shout, Swayne hit him flush on the jaw, and his eyes crossed again. He slumped back into the snow, bleeding at the mouth.

Potts turned the man's head downslope so he would not choke on his own blood.

"What's he talking about?" asked Potts. "The Commandant is setting up this ambush? It can't be *our* Commandant."

"Want me to finish him?" asked Friel.

Swayne shook his head. "No. We may need to wake him up later and ask a few more questions."

Swayne rubbed his forehead through the snow mask, trying to make sense of the information they had gotten before the man came to his senses.

Finally, a thought occurred to him. "Okay, I've got it. What do you do after you spring an ambush?"

Potts shrugged. "You kill as many as you can and then you get the hell out."

"But if you're not running from anything?"

Potts shrugged, giving the answer right out of the book. "You check out the kill zone. To see what damage you caused. Count bodies, collect intelligence, continue with the mission."

"Exactly. We stay put until the shooting stops. Then we try to locate the Commandant and deal with the rest of these goofy bastards."

He directed his men to take up positions that would allow all-round security.

"Anybody who spots the Commandant—*our* Commandant—and remember he's probably dressed in hunting clothes—sound off."

Once he had established that everyone was ready, Swayne flipped the safety off the man's M-16A1 rifle and started firing bursts into the road. It didn't take long. The hillside lit up on the left with flashes, the multiple explosions of Claymores that sent lethal steel pellets into the snow. After that came the rifle fire, at first intense, then weakening, then starting up again as the ambushers expended one magazine, reloaded, and started firing again. Then, as usual with ambushes, the shooting became sporadic. The men had been shooting blindly at first, filling the kill zone with bullets. Later they'd hesitated, waiting to see if anybody was returning fire. Finally, following the scenario of a typical ambush, the shooting stopped altogether. Swayne guessed that the command to cease fire would come next. In fact, he could hear the crackle of radio squelch and a voice calling out.

He rolled their captive over, and a walkie-talkie fell out of his jacket.

"Cease fire," a voice commanded. Another burst of automatic fire told Swayne this might not be an entirely professional group. "This is the Commandant, dammit. Cease fire, I said."

Swayne watched in wonder through his thermal binoculars as the greenish heat signatures of figures materialized on the road, men in dark camouflage moving out of the trees and standing in bunches. They were shrugging shoulders, talking, and even laughing. He recognized the aftermath of the adrenaline rush and the reaction of amateur soldiers to it.

How could these pretenders have kidnapped the Commandant?

"Private Eckert, where are you?" a voice in the handheld radio demanded. Swayne realized that the cluster of men on the road, thirteen in all, were staring his way.

"Everybody hold steady," he said into his own radio mike. "They're going to come looking for Private Eckert any minute. To chew his ass for setting off an ambush that turned out to be a false alarm. Has anybody seen the Commandant yet?"

Nobody had, they told him in turn, and Swayne began to wonder whether he'd lost that touch of his, the ability to calculate multiple scenarios in his head so that he could switch from one to another as circumstances demanded.

At the moment this circumstance was demanding quick action. All fourteen men of this force had been accounted for by Private Eckert, but no Commandant—except for the leader of the outfit, which was definitely not the Marine general nicknamed Bat Masterson.

Next, a pair of men broke away from the group on the road. While the rest of them remained standing in the open, lighting up cigarettes and milling around, at least half the eyes were focused in Swayne's direction. Suddenly, every way that this sequence could be forecast to play out had a bad outcome.

Swayne lowered his head and talked into his microphone without making a movement that could be picked up by the approaching men. They didn't seem too concerned. They had slung their weapons over their shoulders and were tramping across the snow as if they intended to drag the disgraced Eckert out of his hiding place and throw him at the feet of their commander.

Eckert's body lay between Swayne and Potts. Swayne murmured into his microphone, "Friel and Potts, try to take them without a struggle."

"Roger."

"Night Runner and I will cover the group on the road."

Night Runner did not respond except to slowly turn his body, bringing his rifle to bear unsteadily at Friel's back. Swayne could see he was far from being back. He gently pried Runner's fingers off the camouflaged white M-203X2, with all its electronic modifications, and handed it to Friel, who laid his 20-millimeter aside. Night Runner stood stock-still, his gloved fingers still crooked as if holding a rifle, unaware of what had just happened.

The moment the two soldiers were abreast of Gunny Potts, one called out.

"Eckert, you better have a bullet in the head or one helluva fine explanation for triggering the ambush."

The other man said, "The Commandant—"

He never finished. Potts swiped at the ambusher nearest him, hitting the side of his head with the butt of his camo-white rifle, a fatal blow crumbling his man into the knees of Friel's man. Both went down, and Friel held his man's face into the snow and struck out with his combat knife, driving into the left kidney. The intense pain and inability to breathe prevented the victim from crying out. The man went rigid, trembled, and stopped moving, his shriek trapped in the grip of his constricted throat muscles.

They would have to move fast now. Any military unit, terrorist or not, professional or otherwise, would have to be considered dangerous just by virtue of their willingness to be outdoors springing an ambush in this kind of weather.

As Friel cleaned the blade of his dagger by slashing it through the snow, Swayne pointed into a stand of timber less than ten meters away, but well hidden by the driving snow from the eleven remaining soldiers. From there, in his mind at least, the plan could play out. When they went at their ambushers, it would be from the ambushers' positions.

Swayne directed his men over the microphone, adding, "Don't kill them all. I need prisoners, especially if we can get their leader." Slipping down next to the road, the Force Recon Team took up positions behind trees close enough for them to see the outlines of the men in green camouflage.

Still watching through his IR binoculars, Swayne spoke into Private Eckert's radio. "Commandant. *Sir!* Eckert has shot himself in the foot. He says he wants to go home, and he's bawling like a baby."

Some of the men in the group burst out laughing.

One man stormed out of the bunch toward Eckert's position. The rest, not wanting to miss the ass-chewing of all time, fell in behind. When they were all moving, Swayne stepped out into the road and began counter-marching along the flank of their column. He looked over his shoulder and saw that the other Spartans had lined up behind him, stringing out parallel to the ambushers. Before springing his own ambush, he checked his enemy and saw that their weapons were pointing to no effect, half of the rifles still slung, the rest carried muzzle-down. The terrorists had not yet seen the Force Recon Team barely three meters away.

Swayne turned left and marched directly at the force until they came into view without the aid of binoculars. Then he hollered "*FBI!* Everybody freeze! Hands on your heads!"

The file stopped marching as if he were a drill instructor on the parade field.

By the way the men reacted to his warning, Swayne knew either they had been arrested before—or else they'd just watched too much television. A few dropped their weapons and put their hands to their heads. Two men tightened their grips on their weapons, but made no threatening moves. One man dropped to his knees, as if begging to be spared. All of them looked around to find the source of the commands. Swayne knew this was the critical instant, the moment in which a highly charged situation could go either way. In the one instance, the Force Recon Team would be able to disarm these men, find out where Commandant was being held, and get the hell out of Montana.

But in an elapsed time of only three seconds, he saw it was going south. The soldiers in camouflage dress were looking around for the source of the commands, unable to see the men in white standing in front of them, camouflaged by the blizzard.

Swayne pulled back his parka hood so the terrorists could see his head and recognize the danger they were in.

The move did not come off as he had anticipated. Eleven sets of eyes were now on him, and eleven minds seemed to realize that they were being held hostage by a single man, for they apparently did not see the other three of the Force Recon Team. And they did not feel threatened by a single FBI agent.

POTTS HAD MOVED around Swayne to stand at the cap's right shoulder. He didn't see what his leader saw, only the confusion in the eyes of the ambushers, confusion that switched to hostility in an instant. The two men who had dropped their rifles, bent to retrieve them. The others began to swing their weapons in the direction of Swayne, who yelled again for them to freeze. With no result. Potts mustered his self-discipline, forcing himself to wait for the cap to fire the first shot. Unless one of the enemy fired first. Since he was standing on the right, he would work on the most dangerous targets on the right side of the file. He gritted his teeth, waiting for the order, selecting the fastest rate of fire on his XM-80 Brat.

• • •

NIGHT RUNNER'S MIND was spending entirely too much time in Cuba. Not that he wanted to be there necessarily. Only that it was easier to remember what had happened in Cuba than in Montana. What was it, a week ago? He could bring his memory forward to the leap out of the plane and the difficulty with his jump goggles. There was that pain in the back—and, oh, yes, the brilliant display of fireworks inside his head. After that, nothing but daydreams. Thinking he had gone into the other-world of the Blackfeet, surprised to find it was so cold on the other side. Then awakening in a warm place with a fire—but not warm enough, for somebody kept washing his face with snow. Then an amazing trip into the whiteness again. A long period of loneliness that he tried to sleep through. And now this. Ghosts of men dressed in jungle camouflage carrying weapons. This might be another dream. Or it might be real. The men were raising their guns to shoot him. Could they do that in a dream? There came a shout from the man he admired, the man called Swayne. That was followed by another shout, by a man whom he did not like, the man called Friel.

FRIEL UNDERSTOOD EVERYTHING. He'd been in such shoot-outs before. In the streets of Boston. He could read the body language. The desperados could not see them—except for the captain, who had been shouting and had just thrown back his parka, exposing himself. All the eyes of the bad guys instantly focused on Swayne. *Excellente.* It was always *excellentamundo* when the shooting started that the bad guys were aiming at somebody else. Not that he wanted the captain to be Black and Deckered. Just that if anybody was going to get drilled, better somebody non-Friel. The Corps wasn't putting any kamikaze incentives into his pay envelope, and he wasn't all that crazy about giving his life for his God, country, and MTV. But he shouted anyway.

"He said *freeze,* you bastards. We got you surrounded." Friel liked to throw the first punch in a fight and apologize later. Shoot first and sort out the draftees from the women and children afterward. He could read this situation, and knew there would most affirmatively be shooting to be done.

SWAYNE WAS GRATEFUL for Friel's spontaneous shout, which injected just enough confusion into the situation to make the men in green hesitate. A peaceful resolution just might be pulled from the jaws of outright combat after all.

But no, the muzzles of two weapons, an M-16 and a sporting rifle, began to lift. If he waited any longer, like some twerp from the State Department hoping for a unilateral Iraqi cease-fire, he would be endangering his men.

When Swayne pulled the trigger, taking out the man with the M-16, it was as if he pulled the triggers on the weapons of both Potts and Friel as well.

• • •

FRIEL FIRED NIGHT Runner's rifle on semi-auto, as he always did. A true sniper, he was fond of saying, did not spray bullets like water out of a fire hose. Most days, he would be the DK, Designated Killer, and he prided himself on using a single round from his sniper rifle to take out an enemy soldier—one round per kill.

Today was no different. The man with the sporting rifle had drawn his attention the moment the muzzle began to come up in Swayne's direction. They had experienced situations like this, both in training and in reality. In a fast-developing situation, the man on the left took the most dangerous enemy on the left, the man in the center the most dangerous enemy in the center, and so on. So without ever saying so, Swayne would be expected to take out the M-16 shooter now pointing at his feet, now at his knees. Friel had visualized his first bullet striking the tab of cartilage at the base of the sternum before he had ever pulled the trigger. Visualizing it while pointing at it with the second knuckle of his trigger finger. Before he had fired, his eyes were on a search for the second most dangerous enemy. That would be the long-haired creepy bastard swinging an Uzi across his chest.

Four shots in maybe two seconds. Four men were down, dead before they bit the snowbanks. The first slug did indeed hit the sternum of its victim. It was Friel's favorite spot—the sweet spot, he called it because the impact to the solar plexus alone could be fatal. Behind that lay the heart and major arteries.

And behind that the spine. If a slug didn't kill the guy, he would be ditzed out by the pain of getting hit there anyhow. The second man, because he was shielding his sweet spot with the Uzi, had to be shot in the throat, the impact and subsequent tumble of the slug nearly taking his head off. The last two men took noggin shots in quick succession.

POTTS, HIS WEAPON on full automatic, did not allow himself the fine, artistic discretion of a sniper. He started at the right end of the line of targets, firing at the same instant as his cap, and swept the muzzle of his weapon from right to left, his eyes checking ahead of the line of fire so he might stop shooting if anybody gave an indication of surrender. None did. He kept shooting, tapping deeply into the 1500-round drum, the rate of fire so fast and the range so close, he was certain that, beneath their clothing, these men were being dismembered by the scythe of slugs.

SWAYNE HAD PUT down his man and shouted for a second one to surrender, although he doubted his voice could be heard over the clatter of Gunny's Brat. The second man, his eyes wild with the frenzy of the moment, was on his knees, praying. When the shooting began, he was sprayed with blood spatter. Instead of covering his head or throwing himself on the ground, he reached for his weapon, pointed it directly at Night Runner, and pulled the trigger.

• • •

NIGHT RUNNER MARVELED at his vision, the dream unfolding before his eyes. Against the white of the entire day there had been only the occasional monochromatic shades of gray. Even the dark green of the conifers and the camouflage of these dying men had seemed more black than green. And now black blood sprinkled and poured out of writhing bodies, coloring the snow. He did not miss having his own rifle to defend himself, for he did not believe it necessary. And he did not raise his pistol. For now he had been given a power that existed only in this new land, a power that he did not have on the previous side, a power that he did not own while he was in Cuba.

The men in black prepared to do him harm, but all of that was required of him in response was to raise his hands and ward off bullets. When he pointed his fingers at them, they died, their faces exploding, their bodies crumpling as if their spines had been broken. One man in particular, the man on his knees, might be spared. For he had the decency to kneel and pray. But then the evil crept into his heart, and he reached for his weapon on the ground, not knowing that it would be useless to him. The bore of the rifle became a perfect black circle, a single eye looking into Night Runner's eyes. Night Runner sighted down the forefinger of his right hand and commanded the man to die for his transgression. On his order, the man's head burst like a water balloon filled with blood, and the battle—lasting no more than five seconds—was over.

• • •

WITH A SWEEPING hand signal, Swayne directed Friel to check the bodies, and the sniper began moving down the line of corpses, starting with the men Swayne had shot and moving all the way to the right to those Potts had downed. Typical Friel arrogance, Swayne thought, to assume that anybody he shot was certain to be dead.

Meanwhile Swayne was surprised to see that Potts had let down his guard. While Friel checked the bodies, it was the job of the rest of them to make sure nobody popped out of the bushes or rolled over on the ground because he had not been finished.

Instead, Gunny Potts stared at Night Runner, who had not even raised his pistol. The Indian stood, his eyes closed, his arms spread over the carnage as if he were the Pope blessing the masses in St. Peter's Square.

"Runner, you gone squirrels?" said Potts. "It's a wonder you ain't dead. How come you ain't dead?"

"Because this dumb bastard forgot to reload his rifle after the first ambush," Friel said, holding up the 30-30 of the man who had tried to shoot Night Runner from his knees. He threw that rifle and all the other weapons over the embankment.

"Anybody alive?" asked Potts.

"Not a heartbeat in the whole herd of sorry bastards. Why the hell didn't they surrender when they had the chance?"

Before anybody could even speculate as to the

answer, a scream from the bushes sent Friel and Potts gliding into the snow at the edge of the road. Swayne saw that Night Runner had neither opened his eyes nor lowered his arms. He tackled the Indian, knocking him out of danger, regretting now that they had not left him at the cabin.

As they lay in the road, Runner wincing from the pain in his back, a figure materialized out of the snowy mist. Eckert. It must been horrifying for him to awaken and find himself buried under the two bodies of his comrades. As he reached the edge of the road, he could see the remainder of his mates, their blood oozing into red slush patches. He came to a standstill, his eyes wide open in shock. Potts and Friel came up beside him, each taking an arm. They led the man to Swayne, who helped Night Runner to his feet.

"Here's your survivor," Friel said, drawing his dagger playfully across the man's chest. "One Private Eckert. Let's see what kind of songbird we got here."

ECKERT SANG LIKE a meadowlark, the Montana state bird, but he knew nothing about the Commandant of the Marine Corps. The only commandant in his existence was one of the dead in the roadway.

An automobile mechanic from Miles City, he had come to these hills, telling his wife and boss that he was taking a two-week vacation to hunt elk. And he *had* hunted. But the real reason for his being here was the annual winter maneuvers of TMM, The

Montana Militia. When the surprise blizzard had struck, his unit had holed up in tents and cabins on the creek bottom, engaging in more traditional hunting activities—drinking whiskey and playing poker—as the storm raged on.

Until this morning. Somebody in the tents thought they heard snowmobile engines whining. At first nobody paid it any mind. Until the Sno-Cat started up and vanished into the whiteout.

The Montana Militia, having relaxed its guard, had been raided and cleaned out of all their winter transportation. Their commandant, a grocer from Lewistown, had ordered the unit into the field to set up ambushes in case the raiders returned.

Swayne shook his head. A few more parts of the puzzle had fallen into place. The terrorists, stranded by the blizzard, had happened upon a convenient source of transportation and taken advantage of it. He stepped out of the hearing of Private Eckert and made a report to Zavello.

Zavello reacted mildly, considering that thirteen semi-innocent wannabe soldiers had been slaughtered on the mountain. He told Swayne to give Private Eckert the impression that they truly were federal agents and to leave him alive to tell the story to the press, which wasn't going to believe him anyhow.

"Knowing what we now know," Zavello growled, "we're going to try to intercept the group by repositioning a second Force Recon Team on the north-south highway to your east. You and your team now have a change of mission: Avoid further contact with civilians or police authorities and extricate yourself from the mountains.'' He gave Swayne coordinates for a pickup point along the Madison River, and told him to get into position and wait for the storm to pass, when the Spartans would be extracted by helicopter.

It was a letdown for Swayne. All of today's killing and no good would come of it. The bloodiest of incidents had been little better than an accident. As he felt a sense of depression closing in on him, he struggled to fight free of it. Quite literally, they were not out of the woods yet. And there was Night Runner, whacked in the head and, for the first time since Swayne had known him, undependable. Not to mention that night was upon them at only a little past five o'clock, and the storm showed no signs of letting up.

He signed off with Zavello, and checked to see that the coordinates given him coincided with the pinpoint that had appeared on his GPS readout. For the first time in his Force Recon career, two consecutive missions had bombed.

Nevertheless, he went back to interrogating Eckert, and learned that a second ambush had been established east of the camp, on the road between this spot and the team's pickup point.

''Why would you do that? Once your transportation was stolen, why would you expect anybody to come back?''

''We thought the feds was trying to wait us out,

you know, like at Ruby Ridge. The Commandant brought us out here to catch you behind your own lines.''

Potts and Swayne exchanged glances and shook their heads. Grown men playing soldier. They should have stuck to their paintball games and Lazer Tag.

"How many radios are in your unit?"

Swayne saw something click in the man's eyes.

"I only have to give you my name, rank, and serial number," said Eckert, giving his best Clint Eastwood stare.

Swayne nodded to Friel. "We don't have time for this. If he doesn't want to tell us about the radios, put him to sleep with the others. If we're going to have another Waco on our hands, I don't want any witnesses testifying against the Bureau in federal court."

In one motion, Friel shoved Eckert and swept his feet from beneath him with a kick, sending him face-first into the snow-dusted pile of bodies.

Coming up with blood-drenched slush in his hands was all the pressure required for Eckert to reveal that each ambush patrol was equipped with two radios, and that a fifth, the base radio, was on the creek bottom.

Friel recovered Eckert's radio, and Potts, distaste registering, even in the dark, patted down the snow-covered corpses until he came up with the grocer's radio. Swayne smashed one of the radios. He turned up the volume on the second and put it into the breast pocket of his parka. He said to Potts, "Agent Brown, handcuff the suspect and read him his rights."

Potts was quick on the uptake. "I lost my cuffs in the scuffle."

"Then just prop him up against a tree and read him his Mirandas. Eckert, we're going down to arrest the rest of your people. Don't leave this spot for an hour. When you get out of here, turn yourself in and use my name—I'll put in a good word for you."

After making a fair attempt at reciting a television version of a defendant's rights, Potts helped Friel retrieve the snowmobiles. Having situated Night Runner behind Potts, Swayne started his machine and waited for Friel to snug up behind him.

The wannabe soldier, looking as though today's experience might persuade him to give up the life, came out of the darkness and touched Swayne's shoulder.

"What is it, Eckert? I'm getting a little tired of your crap."

"Your name."

"What about it?"

"You told me to use your name, but you didn't give it."

"Freeh. Louis B. Freeh."

SWAYNE FELT COMPLETELY defeated as he started down the mountain again. Behind him, Friel clung to his waist. Swayne could feel him chuckling, no doubt because he had given Eckert the name of the FBI Director. For himself, he was not amused, but tired. Not satisfied, but defeated. It was no achievement to kick the hell out of a bunch of pretend soldiers, only to find themselves relieved of their primary mission. And now, just to be extracted, they might have to fight their way through a second ambush.

A mile from where they had left Eckert, a voice crackled into the handheld radio in the breast pocket of his parka. "Bigfoot Six, this is base. Ambush Bravo requests permission to return to camp."

Swayne took the radio out of his pocket, trying to recollect the quality of the grocer's radio voice before he'd died. He growled into the handset, "Roger. Stand down."

"Roger. Base acknowledges Ambush Bravo has permission to stand down. Are you on the way in, Ted?"

"Roger. Out." Swayne threw the radio into the gloom, deciding that it was too risky to try maintaining the charade for even one word longer. Better to leave the rest of The Montana Militia in the dark about his whereabouts. He doubted anybody would try to go out on a night like this just because Bigfoot Six's voice sounded odd. More likely, they would chalk it up to interference caused by the storm.

After only twenty minutes of navigating blindly down the mountain, Zavello's voice rasped, "Spartan One, turn on your GPS screen."

Swayne did as he was told, and found that a new pinpoint had appeared.

"The Commandant's PERLOBE again?" Swayne said.

"Affirmative. The storm has kept us from getting into position to intercept the terrorists. Helicopter insertion is out of the question, even with night navigation instruments. The Highway Patrol has closed all the roads along the Madison River. That's perfect for us, except that we don't have any ground units capable of moving in. All commercial and military airports are closed. Stand by for another change in mission."

Where just moments ago Swayne had presumed that Event Scenario 13 had ended for the Spartans, he now could see hope that they might redeem themselves from the afternoon's fiasco.

A long pause followed. The only sound was that of a new form of precipitation. Ice pellets had begun rattling off the hood of his parka, clattering against the snowmobile's windshield.

A moment later, Zavello's voice came back, "Belay my last. Team 2400 is ordered to recover the Commandant."

THE MADISON RIVER VALLEY, MONTANA—1814 HOURS LOCAL (0114 ZULU)

"YOU'RE OFF THE mountain," Winston told Swayne triumphantly, after an hour more of blind driving, following voice instructions, snaking through the darkness. To Swayne, the difficulty did not matter. They were back on the mission. They were being given a second chance at redemption. "What can you tell me about the distance and heading to the last PERLOBE hit?" he asked the operator.

"It came from about a half mile off the main road to the highway. At a cattle ranch."

Swayne figured somebody at that ranch had probably had sudden, unwelcome company. A ranch would have trucks, probably with four-wheel-drive. Anybody needing transportation faster than a Sno-Cat could steal it. "Can you direct us there?"

Winston was guiding them down the road at thirty miles an hour when a new, welcome voice transmitted over the radio.

"Slow down."

"Night Runner," Swayne said, "what's up?"

"Barbed wire. Gates. Fences. Keeps the cows in."

Night Runner still sounded half-whacked, but the content of his warning could not be dismissed. Swayne shuddered to think about running into a barbed-wire gate at this speed.

"I can help," Winston said, tag-teaming onto Runner's transmission. "At 1-to-2,000 scale, the section lines show up on my screen—I can give you warning in time."

AT THE FIRST fence line, Night Runner piled off to check for wires. He found the fence with his feet, the wires laid on the ground.

"They drove over the fences with the Sno-Cat," he reported over the tactical frequency. "And that's not all."

Night Runner took off his heavy gloves and stuffed them into the pockets of his parka. Falling to his hands and knees, ignoring the stabbing pain in his back, he went across the road from side to side, allowing the snow story to be told him through the touch of his bare hands. He felt along the furrows left by tires, carefully handling the packed knots of snow that had been picked up by the tire-tread pattern and dispersed. He let his fingers wander up the sides of the furrows and across the snow, back and forth, finding the demarcations between undisturbed snow and that which had been traveled over. He entreated the snow to give up its story to his hands.

After he had learned all he could, he keyed the mike that the captain had shut off long ago and reported to the members of his team. "I have four vehicles—wheels, leaving the ranch, driving over the Sno-Cat tracks. Probably two pickups and two SUVs."

"Is there any way possible for you to tell how fast they were going?" Swayne asked.

"Yes. The knots of snow were scattered. The fresh snow was pushed aside like the bow wave of a boat. Fifteen, maybe twenty miles an hour."

"I know this is asking a lot, but is there any way you could possibly know how long ago they passed by?"

Swayne sounded so doubtful. "Wait one," Runner replied.

Night Runner took his seat behind Potts, held out his hands, palms up—this time with gloves on—and snickered to himself. No matter how well they knew him, these men always seemed too willing to doubt his ability. They would ask some technology geek to make his fingers fly across the keyboard and interpret invisible digital signals that would allow them to shoot artillery at an enemy only fifty meters away from themselves. That kind of magic they would trust. His ability, much simpler and obvious to anyone who would take the time to engage his senses, they always treated like voodoo. So be it. He had told himself a thousand times, if they wanted to treat him like a shaman, he would endure them.

Taking off his left glove, he probed with a bare finger to check the depth of the snow that had accumulated in the palm of his right in the last half minute. Extrapolating from what he had found in the bottom of the snow furrows, he said, "Twenty minutes, half hour, tops."

Friel chimed in. "Find a ranch. I can steal a truck and have us on the road in two minutes."

Swayne asked Winston for directions to the nearest ranch.

"Just ahead of you," he said. "A quarter of a mile away is the place they probably raided. The next-closest ranch is better than three miles away."

Night Runner said, "This is a big spread. They

probably have stock trucks. They would be best in the snow anyway.''

SWAYNE COULDN'T ARGUE with Night Runner's logic, and neither would anybody else. He gave the command to move out.

In only five minutes more, without bothering to stop for barbed-wire gates again, they approached a halo of light. In less than a minute more, the diffuse glow became a collection of individual blazing security lights that marked the headquarters of a cattle ranch.

Swayne could see the familiar shapes of buildings and other structures, quonsets, barns, silos, and corrals. Night Runner, apparently sensing Swayne's hesitation, directed him to a shop the size of an airplane hangar, with doors sixteen feet high. Of course, Swayne thought, any trucks on the property that could be put inside would be kept in there. He directed Potts and Night Runner to check out the farmhouse to see if anyone had survived the terrorists' raid. He didn't necessarily want to know the answer, but needed to gather whatever intelligence the group might have left behind. Even if they had slaughtered everybody on the premises, it would tell Swayne something—something about the ruthlessness of the group they were dealing with.

Friel grasped the doorknob of the quonset and shrugged his shoulders. The door was unlocked. As he stepped inside, Swayne thought that the Marine from Boston seemed more than a little disappointed that he would not be able to show off his abilities at breaking and entering. Inside, a pair of fluorescent lights barely illuminated the huge, heated interior of the building.

Swayne was dazzled at the clarity of snow-free air.

"So this is what it is like to be able to see stuff," Friel said. "Must be what X-ray vision feels like to Superman."

That sentiment expressed Swayne's thoughts exactly. For the first time since they had arrived in Montana, he had an unimpeded line of sight that extended beyond twenty feet.

And another pleasant sensation that he had been deprived of from the moment they had bailed out of the Starlifter. Warmth. He peeled back the hood of his parka and pulled off his snow mask. Four tractor trailers stood parked abreast on the concrete floor, all painted lavender with silver detailing. The signs on the doors read: "Madison River Valley Ranch—Registered Angus."

"After I retire, I want me a ranch too," said Friel. He was shaking his head. "But not in scrotum-shrinking Montana. Someplace decent. Maybe outside Hoboken."

Swayne tried to imagine the kind of cattle ranch somebody with Friel's personality would be able to run. He couldn't formulate an image out of the cognitive dissonance, and gave it up.

"Is this the smallest truck we're going to be able to get?" he asked, pointing at the tractors.

"We could ask the chief," Friel said. "But I'm pretty sure he would say we need the muscle."

Swayne detected a reticence in the normally cocky Friel. "What's the problem?"

Friel gave him an *aw-shit* grin. "Thing is, Captain, I never hot-wired something like these gargantuas."

"Check it out then."

A moment later, Friel stuck his head out of the cab. "Wouldn't you know it. The keys are still in it. What kind of hillbillies—?"

Swayne shook his head. "This isn't Boston—" The expression on Friel's face told him more than he wanted to know. The lance corporal had frozen in place, his eyes looking over Swayne's head toward the far wall.

"Turn around slow-like, you sonofabitch, and you can see for yourself you what kind of hillbillies we are."

When Swayne turned, he was, in a sense, grateful to be facing the double barrels of a 12-gauge shotgun and the bore of a big-game rifle. A man and a woman in their fifties, she with the rifle, he with the shotgun, stood glaring at him.

"You're alive," he said.

"You bet your ass, you sonofabitch," said the man whose weathered face might easily have come off a Marlboro billboard of two decades ago. "It wasn't enough you took three of my rolling stock. You had to come back for more."

Swayne went into his act. "We're federal marshals on the trail of maybe two dozen men. They're escapees. Kidnappers.''

The man lifted a corner of his narrow, wrinkled mouth. ''Bullshit.''

''Show us your identification,'' said the Marlboro woman beside him, lean and wiry as her husband, her body and face hardened by the daily rigors of outdoor life in Montana.

Swayne knew that federal law enforcement officials weren't automatically adored in Montana. So he played on a respect for fair play. ''Yes, I have identification, and I'm going to show it to you. First let me put down my weapon, so you won't feel threatened.'' He unslung his rifle and laid it on the cement floor. ''I admit, we came in here to see if we might borrow a vehicle to catch up with the people who took yours.''

The man snorted. ''Most people who borrow from us stop up to the house.''

''This is where I'm going to prove I'm being honest with you. I sent two men up to the house to check on you. It's a great relief to us to find you alive.''

''More bullshit,'' the man snapped.

The talk was tough, but Swayne could see a bare flicker of hope in the man's eyes, hope that he might actually be telling the truth.

''The people we're dealing with are desperate men. They killed a dozen men up in the mountains earlier today.''

The Marlboro man shook his head, still not daring to trust. "You trying to tell me that only two marshals is being sent out after a whole army of armed men? What are you, the Green Hornet or something?"

"I can understand your reluctance to believe me, but if I wanted to hurt you, I would have already. At this very moment, two of my men are standing behind you."

"You want me to start shooting and ask questions later?"

"One of my men is going to reach out very carefully right now and touch each of you on the shoulder. Gently. When you feel the touch, please lower the muzzles of your weapons."

Swayne nodded his head. "Night Runner?"

The Indian, who had walked out of the shadows behind the couple and moved more than a dozen feet across the concrete without creating even the blush of a sound, laid his hands on the shoulders of the Marlboro couple. Two sets of eyes widened.

Believers now, they lowered their weapons.

"Thank you," said Swayne. He picked up his CAR-15 and slung it over his left shoulder. Without even suggesting that his men disarm the couple, he formally asked them to borrow the truck. No longer concerned with credentials, the rancher assented to the loan of the truck, and offered a short stock trailer that would hold their equipment. While his men drove the truck outside to hook up the trailer and load their gear, Swayne introduced himself as U.S. Marshal Donatello, and learned that he was talking to Lester and Marcia Becker. He talked to the couple as the others worked, getting a telephone number so they might recover their vehicles later and be reimbursed for its use.

He asked about the men who had visited the ranch to steal. They told him they had finished up evening chores, tending the few remaining cattle that had not been sold off already and their sizable horse herd. That was when Becker had seen a convoy of snowmobiles and the Sno-Cat. Immediately, they had sensed trouble. A unit of twenty to thirty men—The Montana Militia—had been reported in the mountains. The Montana Militia had a bad reputation up this way. They trampled fences and scattered livestock in their so-called military maneuvers. They had been known to steal gas and diesel fuel, and when not poaching deer and elk, they sometimes butchered cattle. They had been careless in shooting off their weapons more than once, firing into the ranch buildings, and occasionally a cattle herd. So when the taillights had dispersed across their yard, the man and his wife had gone out the back door to hide in the cattle barns. Later, they had returned to the house and found the phone lines cut. Their plan was to drive one of the tractor trailers into Bozeman to notify authorities.

"Do you have any hired hands?"

Becker's face turned harder, his wife's softer. Tears came to her eyes. Swayne had his answer before Potts spoke up.

"We found a bunkhouse," the gunny said. "Three men dead."

Becker shook his head. "You're damned lucky we didn't shoot you the minute you walked into this quonset."

Swayne nodded. And what a fitting end that would have been to a mission comprised of one disaster after another. Killed by a pair of civilians. Decent people. "You shouldn't go out tonight," he said. "The people who stole your vehicles won't be back. I don't know where they're going, but they won't dare return here. Go back to the house. We'll notify the authorities by radio. I'm sorry for your loss."

With that, the Force Recon Team was off, Friel driving the semi, Potts and Night Runner crammed together into the sleeping compartment, resting.

Swayne finished his report to higher authorities, thanking Winston for today's help. Friel drove with headlights on and without radio guidance. It helped to be sitting high above the road, rather than virtually on it as they had been all day on the snowmobiles.

Lester Becker had insisted that they take the extra minutes to install chains on at least two of the driving wheels of the semi. "Whatever time you lose putting them on, you'll get back in the speed you'll be able to maintain," he said.

He had been right. Friel easily maintained a speed of thirty-five miles an hour. Traction was no problem, although visibility had not improved all that much. The farther the team drove eastward, away from the shelter of the mountains, the worse the problem became, as the wind swept a continual torrent of snow ahead of them on the secondary road.

They encountered places on the gravel roadway that were bare, and other places with snowdrifts so pristine that it was not apparent that three vehicles had passed by scarcely an hour earlier. Swayne worried that once they arrived at the juncture of the access road and the main highway, he might not be able to tell which direction to travel, either north or south.

That problem took care of itself. Zavello's voice crackled in his headset. "Another beacon signal. Moving north toward Interstate 90, which ties into I-15. They could be headed for Canada. Get after them."

Swayne intensified his stare out the windshield, as if that would help close the distance. For the first time since jumping out of the Starlifter, his mind began sorting calculations based on the certainty that they would close with the Commandant's kidnappers.

WOLF CREEK, MONTANA—1937 HOURS LOCAL (0237 ZULU)

THE FARTHER NORTH they traveled, the clearer the roadways became, permitting a four-minute stop to remove the tire chains. North of Helena on Interstate 15, much less snow had fallen. Although the wind continued to buffet them, it had switched, coming from the north rather than the west. And it was colder. Swayne couldn't believe the truck's digital readout of the exterior temperature, twenty-seven degrees below zero. So he rolled down the window and stuck his own thermometer into the howling wind. As he had suspected, the truck's indicator was wrong. The actual temperature was thirty below zero. Friel maintained a steady seventy miles an hour until Swayne caught his eyelids beginning to fail. Swayne took over driving, but did not fare much better. Eventually, he traded places with Potts, and although his mind wanted to keep on processing the myriad facts and experiences of this and the preceding mission, his body was having none of it.

FOUR CORNERS, MONTANA—2212 HOURS LOCAL (0512 ZULU)

SWAYNE DREAMED HE was being tossed about by that Cuban submarine again, but awakened to find Friel shaking him.

"What's up?" he mumbled, feeling his body coming back to life. And painfully.

Potts, at the wheel, said, "The storm is broke up. We're maybe fifteen miles south of the Canadian border. East off the interstate. The beacon reports keep on coming. We're closing in."

Swayne didn't understand. "The beacon reports? How come I didn't hear them in my headset?"

Potts smirked. "We turned off your radio. Since somebody had to stay awake to drive anyhow. It weren't necessary to have you keeping an ear open too."

"We're off the interstate just south of the border?'' Swayne repeated, thinking aloud. "That means they're probably going to sneak across the border somewhere nearby."

"That's what Colonel Zavello thinks."

Swayne checked the topo map on his PDA and spoke into his mike. "Winston, can you tell me how close we are catching up to these guys?"

"I'm putting up the last beacon signal right now. We got it not thirty seconds ago. The farther north, the more frequent the PERLOBE indications. I figure you're within three miles."

Potts, still pushing seventy miles an hour, suddenly yanked the steering wheel left as the road curved, and the pavement gave way to gravel. The semi fishtailed before Potts could regain control.

Potts slowed to fifty, which still seemed too fast, but the next radio report gave Swayne hope.

"Another beacon signal is coming up on your screen," Winston said. "It indicates a turn west, north of the mountain called Gold Butte. With your permission, I'll download a scale that will allow you to see every trail and fence line leading north into Canada."

"Download it then," said Swayne. He checked his screen. They had gained ground. They might yet catch the kidnappers before they could escape into Canada.

Time to start worrying, not about whether the terrorists would escape, but what to do when the team did make contact. Time to start thinking about shutting off the headlights and navigating in the dark.

Anticipating this as if he had been reading Swayne's mind, Potts said, "I'm ready to start running blackout."

"Kill the lights then and let Winston direct you by voice again."

Ten minutes later, they were running under full blackout conditions, maintaining thirty-five miles an hour. The scattered cloud cover let enough starlight pass for the wide-eyed group inside the cab to remain generally oriented.

The next PERLOBE transmission caused Potts to let up on the accelerator altogether, and the truck coasted to a stop.

Only a mile ahead and just off the road to the north, the beacon had showed itself as having moved only thirty feet in the last ten minutes.

"I'm thinking ambush," Swayne said.

"Maybe they just stopped to rest," Potts offered.

"Before crossing the border?" said Swayne. "No, either they want a fight—"

"Or they've left a rear guard."

"Right."

Night Runner's dark head snaked out of the sleeping compartment. "Then let's give them one. Let's get out there and kick some ass."

Swayne handed off the infrared binoculars to Potts, who rolled down his window glass and scanned all the way to the horizon in the direction of the last beacon hit. "I don't see anything."

Swayne wasn't surprised, remembering the experience in the mountains when the cold-weather clothing of his own man had proved to be so well insulated he could barely pick up an image less than a hundred meters away. "Switch to starlight mode."

Potts did and shook his head again. "I still don't see anything."

"That's a good sign," Friel offered. "If we can't see them, they sure as hell can't see us."

"What say we start unloading the gear?" said Night Runner, sounding to Swayne like his normal self.

As his men let down the rear loading ramp to get at the snowmobiles, Swayne began figuring an approach to the beacon. This was where the GPS locator proved its tactical worth. One of its most useful features was its line-of-sight/line-of-fire indicator. By selecting the coordinates of the beacon and activating the LOS/LOFI, the program would evaluate the topographical features and display a shaded area representing a visual shadow. Meaning that all the shaded areas were below line of sight and could not be seen—and by definition could not be fired into with direct-fire weapons.

By the time the snowmobiles were vibrating inside the cattle trailer, Swayne had calculated an approach path that would allow them to sneak up on the beacon without being seen.

He went off to cut through the barbed-wire fence to the left of the road at a spot where they would have access to a coulee running to the north.

Of course, being in the visual shadow did not guarantee that they would not encounter the enemy.

In fact, a smart tactical leader would calculate the visual shadow manually and position observation posts and indirect-fire weapons like mortars to cover those approaches. Swayne thought he might gamble on the lack of time for his enemy to prepare such defenses. And he repeated Friel's wisdom to himself as he walked back toward the rig. If he and his team hadn't been able to see the terrorists, they couldn't be seen—

Swayne couldn't decide whether he first felt or heard the missile fly by his left shoulder and hit the idling truck in the exhaust stack on the driver's side. All he knew for sure was that it was a missile. He hit the ground, rolling into the ditch, simply by reflex. Any damage that would have been done to him would have already been done. The fuel cell, part of the driver's step-up into the cab, had been punctured and ignited by shrapnel. Roiling flames and black smoke engulfed the cab, and a fireball swept back through the trailer, igniting and expelling a shower of burning straw through the slatted trailer sides.

He was swamped by a tidal wave of guilt and helplessness—he had survived the attack, leaving his men to be killed, and now he was facing the terrorist band without transportation and only a shoulder weapon. All the technology in the world wasn't going to—

Two electric snowmobiles, their riders in burning parkas, sailed out of the rear of the trailer and streaked down the road, trailing plumes of smoke, flames, and rooster-tails of snow. A third figure dived from the trailer and rolled in the road, extinguishing his parka, getting to his knees, and diving into the ditch.

Bent low, unslinging his rifle as he ran, Swayne reached the figure lying prone in the ditch. He rolled him over and looked into Night Runner's broadest grin.

"So much for Friel's theory about we-can't-see-them-they-can't-see-us," he said.

Swayne had to laugh with him. "Are you all right?"

"I've had better days, Captain. I dropped my weapon inside the trailer and had to go back for it. That's why I took so long getting out."

Flames lit up the landscape. Swayne punched Night Runner lightly on the chest, raising puffs of smoke from the now-brittle fabric. "Let's get away from here before we start taking sniper fire."

They ran—rather, stumbled in the calf-deep snow in the ditch, more than once falling down when a crusted snowdrift grasped and held onto their ankles. Once they had cleared a gentle rise and were below the radiance of the light spreading out from the fire, Swayne cut another hole in the fence.

The snowmobiles materialized within seconds. Swayne consulted his GPS screen and calculated a new route to approach the beacon. Of course, the element of surprise had been lost, along with a good deal of their supplies. And the enemy had risen yet another notch in his estimation. Now he knew they had missiles. Heat-seekers from the look of it. Possibly even one of a variety known to exist outside the arsenal of U.S. military forces that could be fired from over the horizon, propelled a hundred meters into the air by a charge of compressed gas, allowing it to acquire its target in the course of its falling trajectory, then igniting a rocket motor to propel it in for the kill.

He climbed on behind Friel, and Night Runner straddled the seat behind Potts. Even in the dim light he could see that the back of Friel's parka had been burned. He looked like Cruella DeVille, wearing a coat of Dalmatian skins.

In less than ten minutes, the team had navigated its way to Swayne's jump-off site without taking fire. Potts and Runner low-crawled to the crest of a knoll. Friel snapped open his carrying case and assembled his 20-millimeter smart gun.

As Friel crept up to join the others, Swayne made a quick report to Zavello. It bothered him that the beacon, which had been eluding them all day, had not moved in the last half hour. He couldn't believe that his enemy would try to dig in on this side of the border if their plan was to escape into Canada. It seemed logical enough that they would try to ambush the Force Recon Team once they had discovered them. But now that they had destroyed the semi and presumably its occupants, why weren't they moving out? Why stick around within a half mile of a flaming signal on the hillside? At any time now, a rancher would see the fire on the horizon and report it, if not investigate it personally.

Wondering whether his own GPS was defective, he asked Winston to confirm that the PERLOBE of General Masterson had not moved.

Instead Zavello came on the line. "We get the same readout as you. The thinking up here is that the group might be trying to make a last stand."

Swayne doubted his team would be so lucky, but kept his silence. He signed off and hustled to the top of the hill, slithering up beside Potts, who had his IR binoculars in hand. "What do you have?" he asked.

"I got four snowmobiles parked on the far side of the ravine. I got a clear sighting of three men, maybe four, hunkered down in the snow. I got a pickup truck half-buried in the ravine, its ass sticking up in the air. Three more men trying to dig it out." Then he answered the question that Swayne really wanted answered. "I got no visual on the Commandant. Got no idea where he could be, except maybe in that truck. Or maybe they took him out and walked him up the gully."

"You aren't looking out far enough." It was Night Runner. "I have a set of tire tracks. Headed off toward Canada."

Potts shook his head, wondering, *How the hell did Night Runner see so far in the dark without IR binoculars?*

Night Runner said, "I also got a platoon-size element maneuvering over the hill. Moving toward the road where we left the truck.''

Swayne took the binoculars and studied the well-armed force, maneuvering with M-60 machine guns, rifles, and rocket launchers. Somehow, the terrorist group had gotten into the supply channels of the United States military. The over-the-horizon heat-seeker that he had been worrying about was being carried by a weapons team. From the look of it, the group was moving tactically, leapfrogging in three maneuver units supported by at least one machine-gun squad and the missile team at all times. A basic military tactic, but difficult to bring off with the kind of precision he was seeing. So. They weren't dealing with a bunch of irregular forces like the TMM. He started running down the catalog of terrorists they had studied in the last year. Outside the Middle East, he didn't know of any group capable of mustering the numbers of men needed for such a maneuver as this and sneaking them into the United States undetected.

Friel spoke up. ''Want me to take out the missile crew and then the machine guns?''

''Roger,'' said Swayne. ''Use high-explosive heads set on proximity detonation. You laser the missile team, and I'll put a spot on the machine-gun team. After that, pick your own targets.''

Friel's gun was more than just a smart gun. It used the visible red laser dot like those in the action movies. But that could be defeated any number of ways once it had been spotted. In fact, one of the countermeasures was a computer that calculated the back azimuth to the laser and sent instructions to artillery computers so the big guns could lay down suppression.

Usually, though, the team sniper set his gun to project its spot on the infrared, invisible, range of the spectrum. The shooter looking through his infrared scope could see this spot. And the smart bullet that he fired would see it too.

The projectile carried miniature transistors and a microprocessor in its head. Once activated, it picked up the IR spot and locked on, maneuvering on the target that had been sketched out in its tiny computer memory. Each time the shooter fired and moved the laser dot to a subsequent target, a computer chip shifted the laser slightly on the IR spectrum to create a signature unreadable by the first projectile. Multiple lasers, like the one in Swayne's binoculars, could also designate secondary targets. A good shooter and his team might get off three or more rounds, all traveling at subsonic speeds to reduce the noise signature, and vanish behind cover before the first round had struck.

"I know it's asking a lot, Gunny," Swayne said, "but did you recover one of those portable ambush kits from the cargo sled?"

"Bits and pieces of one. I'll fire it up." Potts slid backward off the hill and ran to his snowmobile. In less than a minute he was back, unpacking and handing up articles for Swayne to arm and set up. While Night Runner and Friel watched, he and Potts put out devices, only enough to simulate a squad-minus, but it would have to do. As he worked, Swayne shared his plan in snatches of information.

Once everybody understood the plan, Swayne and Friel set off to fulfill their portion of it.

FRIEL, REMEMBERING THE fireball that had swept through the cattle trailer, was only too happy to position his laser dot directly on the man carrying a missile. This was the ginko who had given him the singed eyelashes and raspy throat, not to mention his now-air-conditioned parka. When he saw Swayne's laser dot appear on the breach of the M-60 machine gun, he touched off his first 20-millimeter missile, pulling the trigger, then sweeping the gun leftward in one motion, firing a second shot, sweeping again to cover fifty meters and light up a second machine-gun position to the rear of the maneuvering forces to fire a third time. He wished he had three more targets. The best he had ever done in practice was to touch off four rounds before the first one exploded. Tonight he was feeling quick. He would have liked to try for five, maybe even six.

Too late for obsessing over that now. The first round detonated, its fuse set to explode ten meters in front of the target as the returns hit its tiny radar receiver. It set off a secondary explosion of the missile warhead. Instantly a second and then a third explosion went off. Night Runner, the second best shot on the team, opened up on the lead maneuver-

ing team with automatic fire, one long burst, as
Swayne had directed, covering as much area as possible.

Potts, a good marksmen by Marine standards but
the worst of this team of Spartans, had been given
the targets among the work team and snowmobiles
at a much closer range. He fired off a Brat-burst in
their direction, and all four of them dived backward
off the hill at once. Total time of the engagement
so far, less than ten seconds. Swayne, who had not
done any shooting, activated the automatic ambush
timer.

As they ran downslope to their snowmobiles, a
computer chip, housed in a box no larger than a
package of cigarettes, took over fighting for them.
Miniature disposable rifle barrels positioned up and
down the line would go off at predetermined intervals, shooting intermittently, as Swayne had set
them, mimicking carefully aimed fire.

Swayne had selected a preset ambush option, one
that would give them the most intermittent fire, giving them time to maneuver. As they mounted the
snowmobiles, the return fire was heavy but disciplined—definitely professional soldiers. The kit
would spray real bullets from some of the devices,
but those had little chance of striking anything.
Their purpose was not to kill, but to deliver tracers
and specially designed rounds that made the sounds
of bullet ricochets. That would establish the reality
that the target was truly under fire and keep them
pinned down. Later in the sequence, some of the

devices would pivot and fire at a preselected avenue of approach, usually on the flank, anticipating a maneuver force coming at the position.

After the kit had expended itself, and the position had been overrun, there would be more surprises. As curious soldiers usually did, somebody would approach one of the devices, astounded that there were no bodies or conventional weapons. Eventually, somebody would pick up part of the kit to examine it. Once the computer detected the touch of a human hand, or if the one of the devices was merely moved more than twenty-four inches from the its original position, the entire package would blow up, creating the devastation of a booby trap a hundred feet long.

Swayne knew just exactly how big a risk the Spartans were taking in touching off hostilities with a force of terrorists this strong. Depending on how desperate the terrorists were or whether they were suicidal zealots, odds were better than even that they would kill the Commandant of the Marine Corps and themselves before surrendering.

But this was the war of the New Millennium, not combat steeped in the glory of Camelot. Your enemy was a sonofabitch, and by definition, somebody who want to hurt you in every way possible as badly as he could hurt you. These bastards had taken in the Commandant and hit three other military bases, killing indiscriminately. There would being no hostage-negotiating team trying to end a standoff. The press might not know it. The public might not appreciate it. But everybody in uniform, including ordinary soldiers, but especially special operations troops, understood that the only way to influence the action in a situation like this was with swift and deadly violence. That they had lost the element of surprise had been established when the missile destroyed the tractor trailer that had brought them all the way across Montana.

This was war, and by definition, hell. He didn't want the Commandant to die, and would do anything to prevent that. But now that the bullets had taken flight, combat, as it usually did, took on its own life.

For the moment, the ambush would reestablish an element of surprise. If the Force Recon Team could maneuver quickly enough around the north flank, keeping watch to the east, the only other probable escape route, they might come up on the part of the terrorist unit responsible for the custody of General Masterson. Their orders would be to kill the general, Swayne assumed—worst-case assumptions were the only assumptions he permitted himself in such circumstances.

The frigid night breeze swept past them, bringing tears to his eyes. This time he drove, as Friel had to manhandle his smart gun, a shade less than five feet long, a real load at 10.3 pounds without clips of ammo.

A late-rising moon had peeked out from its hiding place behind Gold Butte. It now cast long, eerie shadows across the rolling foothills of the buttes.

The snow sparkled, and he could see without using his infrared binoculars.

The first coulee that afforded a turn toward the east, he took. The sides of this depression were steep enough to keep them pinned in the bottom, and Swayne felt his heart hammering inside his chest, fearful that at any moment they would start taking fire from above. He had already calculated his only course of action should that happen. Keep on keeping on, at full speed. There was no defense or cover here below.

He consulted his snowmobile's GPS screen and saw that they were about to climb out of the coulee and cross a stretch of high ground—about a hundred meters before they could drop down again, out of the line of fire. The light of the moon, beautiful as it was, would expose them like moths on a lampshade. The snow dust they were generating would heighten the effect. But he had no choice other than to blast across the space. Holding his breath, bracing for the impact of a bullet, he cranked the throttle full-on.

With Friel clutching him from behind, the snowmobile soared out of the coulee, bounced once on the flat rise, throwing up sparkling crystals, and plunged across the open ground. It seemed like minutes, but seconds later they'd dived downward, flying out of the moonlight and into the night shade. Swayne exhaled, barely able to contain a shriek of elation. There had been no gunfire, and they were once again into protected defilade. It was a relief to hear Potts's voice, telling him a second later that they too had made it across the open area without incident.

That was when he was struck with a concern that had eluded him from the start. When they had first sighted the enemy platoon, the thought had nagged at him, but he had suppressed it. Now it came to him again. An entire platoon? How had a group that size been able to travel all this distance in only four vehicles? With all those weapons and snowmobiles?

Answer? There had been two units, one waiting here in the Sweet Grass Hills for a second, smaller snatch team to arrive. Reinforced, they could take the Commandant across the border. If necessary, after leaving a rear guard to prevent anybody from following.

Having calculated that, Swayne began to look around for some kind of base camp or other area where the second group might have been assembled, waiting.

His snowmobiles bumped across a set of tracks crossing the bottom of the next coulee. Immediately he threw on the brakes. "Night Runner. Check out those tracks." He bit his lip before making a seemingly impossible request. "Can you tell if it's one of the vehicles that came off the Becker Ranch?"

In a minute, he had his answer. "One vehicle, four-wheel-drive. I can't be positive, but I think it is a different tire pattern from those we first spotted down at the Madison."

"Direction?"

"Heading north."

To the border, barely four miles away, Swayne saw on his GPS screen. He turned north, following the vehicle track without a word to his companions. He might buy a few seconds if he kept his mouth shut.

But no, there was no avoiding interference from higher headquarters, which would have been tuned into his tactical radio frequency, eavesdropping. Naturally, Zavello would be keeping a close eye on their PERLOBEs as well. Before they had traveled a hundred meters, his voice blared in Swayne's headset.

"Where in hell are you going? The Commandant's PERLOBE beacon is behind you, it hasn't moved, and you're heading away from it."

"I'm following a set of tracks toward the border."

"I know that," Zavello barked. "I know *what* you are doing, dammit. What I want to know is *why*."

Swayne took a deep breath. "Worst-case. If this truck has the Commandant in it—that is, if the terrorists have discovered his PERLOBE and removed it from his person, they might be using the firefight to cover their escape into Canada. If I'm right, we may be able to intercept them before they cross to the border. I'm assuming here, again worst-case, that we are not allowed to cross the border without permission. If I'm wrong, we can go back to the PERLOBE." Swayne shut up, leaving his logic to hang in the air of the Operational Mission Command Center.

After a long pause, Zavello responded, "Roger. Continue."

Within minutes, Swayne had topped a rise. Below him, the land fell away into a long sloping plain. He could see by his GPS they were within half a mile of the international boundary. Using his binoculars in the starlight mode, he could see the tracks approaching the fence that acted as the demarcation. The fence had been laid down—or pushed down—and the tracks disappeared beyond the range of the binoculars to the north. He switched to IR mode, hoping against hope that he might be able to see a thermal image. If so, he might make a high-speed dash into Canada and overtake the truck. If they could grab the Commandant back and cross back into the United States, the possibilities of an international incident would be reduced to nothing.

But there was no thermal image anywhere on the northern horizon. He turned back to the south, retracing his track, reporting in the words what Zavello could see on his own screen. "No luck. We're headed back."

"Roger. What's your next intention?"

"Check out the beacon." He couldn't stifle the anger in his voice. If it was the terrorists' intention to kill the Commandant once a rescue had been launched, by now the deed was done.

ONCE THEY HAD circled completely, coming up to the spot where the platoon had been when they were first taken under fire, Swayne saw two men, one supporting the other, moving down the backside of the slope. They did not see him—and Swayne made a mental note to compliment the manufacturer of the electric snowmobile on its stealth capability. With a snap of the steering mechanism, he drove into them, hitting them at the knees, throwing them up and over the vehicle. He crossed the hill's crest, expecting to see the platoon still in the attack on the ambush kit, joined by the group from below, the group that had been digging out the buried truck.

His GPS screen told him that the PERLOBE beacon was still in that truck. His eyes, even in the tricky moonlight, kept trying to tell him that the platoon-minus of terrorists was deeply engaged in a firefight. But not with the ambush kit on the top of the hill, which by now had played itself out. Instead, they were fighting their way back down the hill, exchanging gunfire with the second group of terrorists gathered around their snowmobiles.

Stories about military operations from the earliest armed hostilities included instances by the hundreds of one military unit attacking another unit of its own side. Multiple firefights in Vietnam had been fought by a tank column snaking through the woods, turning back upon itself, and opening fire on the middle of its own forces. In the Gulf War of the nineties, more than one aircraft had taken Coalition Forces under fire—so-called *friendly fire,* though friendly was hardly the word for anything the size of a TOW or a thousand pounder deconstructing your head.

"What the hell is going on, Cap?" It was Potts,

joining him and Friel on the ground overlooking the battlefield, shielding his microphone.

"I don't know," Swayne said, as Night Runner found a spot and aimed his rifle.

Friel checked his smart gun. "I'm up," he said, scanning the battlefield with his designating scope. "Hardly any targets worth taking down. No more machine guns. No rocket launchers or missiles. I'll keep my eyes open for clusters of men, so I can take out two or three at a time."

"Fine," said Swayne, "but don't shoot until I say."

Friel looked up from his scope and scowled.

"I saw that," said Swayne.

Beside him, Potts chuckled. Swayne himself might have been amused, except that he doubted that it was possible for one part of this unit to be attacking another part of itself. The light wasn't that bad, and it did not seem likely that a unit so well equipped did not have radios. Even if one group had accidentally shot at the other, an organization professional enough to maneuver the way the platoon had demonstrated would certainly have recognized the mistake.

Before Swayne could give an order, the truck exploded. The pinpoint of light representing the Commandant's PERLOBE vanished from Swayne's GPS screen.

A second later, Zavello was demanding to know why.

Swayne reported the fire, and Zavello sputtered a

while, with nothing substantive to say, until he sputtered himself out.

Meanwhile, Swayne directed the team backward, out of sight behind the crest of the hill, and outlined a hasty plan. Friel was to remain up high, keeping the distance of more than a hundred meters that the smart gun needed to be effective. The other three would stay together, moving downslope, keeping covered.

"Sooner or later those people are going to realize they're shooting at their own. When they do, they're going to congregate and argue. If somebody is in charge, he'll be chewing ass on somebody else." He gave a second's reflection that every military unit had its Zavello. "That's when we make our move."

He said nothing about the Commandant. Didn't have to. Everybody had the eyes to see for themselves what had happened.

Swayne's calculations once again proved less than accurate. The maneuvering platoon took less than ten minutes to sweep down the slope and eliminate the cluster of men defending in the low ground behind the snowmobiles.

The platoon was taking no prisoners. What the hell was going on?

A quick check of the battlefield through his infrared binoculars told Swayne that he had more than the problem of trying to surprise the platoon. The group had left a detachment up on the hill, covering from the high ground where the ambush had originated. He decided not to worry about them. He directed Friel by radio to take the half-dozen men under fire with anti-personnel ammunition if they tried to get involved.

Friel rogered, his voice sounding more than happy to oblige.

Standing up and moving sideways to put the illumination of the burning truck at his back, Swayne approached the group. Knowing that he would be covered more than adequately by the automatic gunfire of Night Runner and Potts, and that Friel had loaded anti-personnel rounds capable of exploding and dispersing more than twice the shrapnel of a fragmentation grenade, he shouted, drawing on the charade that had been successful twice earlier today: "Don't anybody move! This is the FBI! Throw down your weapons and surrender!"

Nothing could have prepared him for the group's response. The lethal killing machine that had just maneuvered against the band of men in the bottom of the gully threw down their weapons and lifted their hands without hesitation.

"Don't shoot. My name is First Lieutenant John Carey. We're U.S. Army Rangers. Don't shoot, we're on the same side."

Swayne thought he might throw up, but he dared not give in to his illness. "Carey, get on the horn and tell those boys at the top of the hill to put down their weapons and march down here with their hands up. Under the Posse Comitatus Act of the United States, you're all under arrest."

"I tell you, we're Army Rangers—"

"And I'm telling you that you're surrounded by law-enforcement officers. If you don't get on the radio in the next three seconds, you may be taken under fire."

Carey did as he was told. Swayne had no time to sort through the astonishment he was feeling. His mind threw one possible explanation after another at him, until something plausible made its way to the top of all possibilities. "You were up here tracking down the guys who set off the bombs at the Ranger School in Georgia," he said.

The lieutenant nodded vigorously. "Exactly. These bastards—"

Swayne shouted, "You're the silly bastards. Don't you know we have laws prohibiting the military from performing law-enforcement operations inside the boundaries of the country."

The lieutenant nodded, his posture shrinking. "Yes, but—"

"But nothing. Chances are pretty damned good you and your bosses are going to be court-martialed for what has gone on here."

A chorus of protests and obscenities came up from the assembled group. Swayne thought he might turn their confusion to his advantage. "Unless you can help us clean up this mess you created."

The Army officer took a step toward him. "Anything. Tell us what to do, and we'll do it."

Swayne directed the men to begin throwing snow on the burning truck to put out the fire. By that time the group from above had joined them, and Swayne was hit again with a realization—he had directed a lethal counter-attack, not against terrorists, but against the Armed Forces of his own country. Talk about friendly fire.

Murmuring into his mike, he quickly briefed his team on the circumstances and told them to remain out of sight and in a position to react in case the soldiers decided they did not want to be arrested by the FBI after all. He asked Potts to deal with Zavello, giving a report on what had happened here, while he took care of the lieutenant.

His first concern was to make sure the Carey did not have a radio in his hands to make reports to his own headquarters. Once Swayne had all the radios under control, noticing that they were two generations old in terms of technology, he took the lieutenant aside.

"Carey, I don't know whether I can keep you boys from being thrown to the dogs, but I can try. If you will do something for me."

The lieutenant swelled up with relief. "How can I help?"

"Once we get that fire out, I'll have to check to see if there is a body inside. Somebody very high up in the military-industrial complex was kidnapped—I can't say who. It's close-hold material."

"Close-hold" the lieutenant understood. He asked no questions.

Swayne said, "My team—the other agents and I—might have to coordinate with Canadian authorities on the other side of the border, you understand?'' Carey nodded. He had turned into a regular yes-man. ''So we are going to leave you here are to clean up the mess you've made. Was that you who fired the heat-seeker into that semi on a road?''

Carry reluctantly admitted to it. ''Yes. We watched you get out of the truck with weapons. We knew you guys had to be the terrorists we're looking for.''

''And you didn't spot the men in this gully until they began shooting at you.''

''I don't know if I should tell you this.''

''Then I don't know if I can help you.''

''Okay, we had military intelligence from the scene of the bombing. We had a map found on one of the bodies. This was supposed to be a rally point for the terrorists. They pulled something on the Navy too—''

''I know all about that. So . . .'' Swayne hesitated to ask. ''How many men did you lose?''

''Seven killed so far. Another dozen wounded, three seriously.'' The lieutenant slumped. ''At last count. We haven't had time to fully consolidate yet. I don't know what the Army is going to tell those families.''

''I don't either, pal. I don't either.'' Swayne suppressed the swelling of grief in his chest. He couldn't afford compassion. Not now. It was a weakness he could not permit himself. ''You clean up the battlefield. Tell the Army to bring in an extraction chopper. You can use these few terrorists and their trucks as evidence that your mission was not a total loss. Do not let on to your superiors that you had a run-in with the FBI.''

The lieutenant came erect as it occurred him that he and his unit might recover their honor if they didn't have to report this surrender to authorities. They might be able to mop up this mess and vanish into the woodwork. ''Maybe our dead were lost in the bombing at Fort Benning,'' he said. ''Maybe our wounded came out of one of those barracks too.''

''Maybe they were,'' Swayne said without enthusiasm. ''Maybe they did at that.''

A shout came up at them from the gully, a report that the fire was out. Swayne and the lieutenant shuffled downslope in the knee-deep snow. The soldiers continued to throw handfuls of snow into the truck, sending billows of steam upward into the night sky.

''Is anybody in the truck?'' Swayne asked, holding his breath as he waited for an answer.

''No, sir,'' said one of the makeshift firefighters.

''No bodies?'' Swayne had to know.

''No bodies.''

Losing the Commandant wasn't much to be happy about, but Swayne felt buoyed by the news. At least he hadn't been toasted.

Swayne handed one of the obsolete radios back to the lieutenant, reminding him that there was to be no mention of federal authorities in the area. As far as the Army was concerned, their job was to clean up this mass, including the semi on the road, haul it off, and contact the Beckers, who would want to put in a claim against the government. They were to answer no questions and to avoid dealing with the press.

"That's the only way the Army is going to avoid the embarrassment of having broken the law. And you know damn well, Lieutenant, if the service gets embarrassed, somebody gets court-martialed. But never the generals. You understand that, don't you?"

"Max affirm."

"Do you boys have any vehicles?"

The lieutenant shook his head. "We air-dropped in. But we came across a pickup tipped over in a ravine. Maybe we could help you get it out and on the road again."

Carey led him to the next coulee over, but the all-too-familiar smell of antifreeze told Swayne this truck wasn't going anywhere.

Great, he thought. *How in hell are we going to get out of here without road transportation?* They might have to wait in these hills for days to avoid being detected and until the Marines could get a helicopter in to extract them. The Army certainly wasn't the only service subject to embarrassment. The second problem, of course, was far more serious. How was the Marine Corps going to coordinate with Canadian authorities to pursue the terrorists north of the border? That, however, was not his problem.

Or so he thought. He had assembled the team a mile to the west of the battlefield and made a full report to Zavello, as his men wolfed down rations warmed with chemical heat-bags, with Night Runner posted as a lookout. As Swayne listened to Zavello's new orders for the Spartans, he was too overcome by surprise to calculate how long it had been since he had eaten something himself.

After he had signed off with Zavello, Swayne signaled for their radio mikes to be shut off. He took the package of fruit offered to him by Potts and poked at it. Everybody in the group had overheard Zavello's instructions for them. They didn't seem fazed by the change in mission.

Friel's concern had to do with the battle they had just fought. "Wouldn't you know it? Our team gets into a firefight with a whole posse of Rangers and kicks their sorry asses all over Montana, but we can't even go home and be wolfing about it."

Swayne preferred not to think about it, couldn't stand having those deaths graphically imprinted on his mind. Better to leave the issue vague, the pictures in perpetual soft focus. In time his mental defenses would let him rationalize that the Spartans had killed no friendly forces intentionally, that all the casualties had been caused by the terrorists. Meanwhile, all he had to rely on was the thin excuse that it had all been a terrible, unavoidable accident brought on by the Rangers themselves when they fired that missile at his team.

He shook his head, wondering what he was doing

playing mind games on himself. Was this another symptom of the very weakness that his grandfather had accused him of? He didn't want to think about that either, and was grateful when Potts spoke up, spraying bits of his minced omelet.

"We been following that beacon indicator like the Pied Piper of Atlanta, thinking that the bad guys were trying to lead us into an ambush," said Potts. "Every time we hits a snag, the bad guys let up on the gas so's we can catch up. Then, when we slip up on them, they get away scot-clean. But they always leave a road map. Can that be an accidental accident? Every time?"

"Yeah," said Friel. "And why didn't they deep-six the PERLOBE? You telling me these guys didn't pat down a POW? A Marine, for chrissakes? Is that too stupid, or what?"

Not too stupid was what he meant, and Swayne agreed. But before he could speak up, Night Runner slid down the slope and hit him with a more immediate concern.

"Halides on the road," Runner said. "A vehicle stopping next to the tractor trailer."

Swayne detached Night Runner and Friel. "See if the driver has a cell phone, and don't let him call in an emergency report."

In minutes, Friel came back at him. "Number One, you'd better get over here right away." The tone in Friel's voice bothered him. He had something to tell Swayne that he didn't want to transmit on the radio for fear of it being overheard by

Zavello. Worse, there was a hint of *gotcha* in it.

When he and Potts had followed the snowmobile track to Friel's position, Friel approached, snipping two fingers at them. They shut off their microphones.

After they had isolated themselves electronically, Swayne said, "I thought I told you to get control of the guy so he couldn't make a report to the authorities."

Friel leaned into his face, "Me and the chief thought you should handle this."

"What the hell—?"

"This ain't no Farmer Jane."

"What the hell are you talking about?"

Swayne lifted his binoculars, putting them on maximum magnification to check out the figure examining the smoldering wreckage of the semi, lit up by the headlights of the vehicle.

There she stood, fully illuminated. Nina Chase.

"Ain't that the babe from the *Washington Promoter*?" Friel asked. "The one always trying to Hoover the goods out of you?"

Swayne felt a stab of alarm. Had this come about because of him? Had she literally been able to get this much mileage out of his hint about checking out the Commandant? That innocuous tidbit could lead her to the Sweet Grass Hills of Montana?

The amazing thing was that he had been using the technological resources and military intelligence of the most powerful country in the world. Somehow this civilian, with resources little better than gossip, had arrived here within a half hour of him. And without jumping from a plane and fighting her way across a winter wonderland of terror.

"Cap?" Potts called into his ear as he moved the snowmobile forward. "You aren't about to let a reporter narc us out, are you?"

Swayne didn't answer. She was up here because of him, and he had to know what she knew. If she was going to compromise this mission—and if he had been the one to allow her to compromise it, he had to know that, too. Talk about disgrace. He might well have allowed the Army Rangers to save face, but he couldn't see any way out for himself. He had blurted top-secret information to a news reporter. It could not possibly be a coincidence they were both trying to contact the terrorists.

He caught her at the driver's door, still unawares. As she reached for a cell phone on the seat, he grasped her left shoulder and turned her toward the front of the truck.

She yelped in surprise and shrank from him as he reached inside, grabbed the cell phone, and tossed it across the road, where it vanished into the fluff in the ditch.

By then she was over her initial surprise. She whirled him on him, an obscenity on her lips, her front teeth forming the letter F. But before she could speak her curse word, she caught sight of his face, rather his snow mask, and held her tongue. For all she knew, she had fallen into the hands of a terrorist-rapist.

Maybe he could scare her into telling him what she knew. He pulled his 9-millimeter and put its muzzle to the point of her chin.

She blinked twice and leaned into the pistol, studying his eyes. He narrowed them, summoning all the fury he could muster.

Her fear evolved into amusement, one side of her mouth lifting to form that smart-ass grin of hers. Usually he was taken by it. Not now. Now he was pissed.

"Jack? Is that you?"

"Dammit."

She tried to hug him, but he fended her off. "What are you doing here, Nina?"

"Looking for you, of course." She smiled at him, mischief dancing in her eyes. "I want to help you."

He shook his head, speechless. How could she possibly help him? He knew better. Now that he was not naked with her—in fact, now that they were both dressed in layers of winter clothing, his Marine-issue, hers Eddie Bauer—he could see how she had used him. No, that wasn't accurate. He was perfectly aware that he had allowed himself to be used.

He shook his head, talking more to himself than her. "I'm sorry I leaked that information about the Commandant. You have no idea how sorry I am."

"Forget that. I didn't even need what you told me."

He laughed bitterly.

"Could you take off that mask? You look like

something out of a cheap slasher movie.''

He shook his head. He wasn't about to reveal the extent of his humiliation to her.

''I know you don't believe that I didn't use your leak. But I can change your mind when I give you the facts.''

She raised an eyebrow at him, inviting an argument, but he did not give her one. In the back of his head, a clock was ticking. He was supposed to be on the track of the Commandant, following those tread marks in the snow. If the wind came up, the tracks would be blown away, and here he was, wasting time with a newspaper reporter that he shouldn't be talking to—that he should *never* have talked to, let alone jumped into bed with.

''Nina, I don't have time to play games. I'm supposed to be looking for—you know what I'm supposed to be doing, and I'm not telling you anything else. If you have something to say, say it. Then I'm going to disappear. Before I do, I'm going to disable your truck so you can't do something stupid, like follow us. So I hope you have enough gasoline to run the heater for a while.''

She pursed her lips. ''Jack, darling. You're not going to disable my truck.''

''Bet me.'' He waved an arm to bring Potts and the others out of hiding.

''Okay, maybe you will, and maybe you won't. Just hear me out before you do anything stupid. I *was* going to use what you told me. I *was* getting ready to go to the Pentagon and weasel my way inside with the little bit that I knew. Before I could, though, I got a telephone call. From one of the bad guys, Jack. The leader of these terrorists. His name is Pareto.''

"He told you his name?''

She nodded.

"All right, you have my attention.''

She put on her best smart-ass grin. "Take off the mask so we can talk like normal people.''

He tore it from his face. "Talk, dammit. Fast. I have to move.''

"I have a condition.''

"Condition? What is it with you?'' He turned his head and spat. "No conditions. I'm not making any deals. I must have been crazy—''

She held a hand over his lips. "Jack, I know where they're taking the Bat boy. And I know why. If you would just shut up and listen, I would tell you.''

"Ransom?''

She shook her head. "No more free information. Not until you give the your word that you'll meet my condition.''

"Just like that? You expect me to accept a condition in the blind? You must think I'm crazier than I really am.''

"Okay, one more tidbit. But only one. To persuade you that I know what I'm talking about. These terrorists are Canadian separatists.''

"Tell me something I don't know. We—''

She clamped her hand across his mouth. "Shut

up and listen, damn you. They want to do more than just separate themselves from the rest of Canada. They want to create an international incident, galvanizing Canada into a battle between those who are for the United States and those who are against. They think they can spark a crisis by enticing U.S. military forces into a battle, even if they lose it.''

Swayne laughed through her fingers and pulled her hand away. ''You're talking about a bunch of nuts. Canada isn't going to invade the United States, no matter what the provocation.''

''That's what you say, but I'm not talking about the legitimate armed forces. This guy tells me that they have a hundred thousand terrorist troops ready to come across the 49th parallel.''

''They wouldn't have a chance.''

''Of course not. They don't expect a chance. They're a bunch of zealots, people capable of giving their lives to a cause. What they want to do is shed some Canadian blood and turn the whole thing against the United States. First, the country divides itself between those who are pro-American and those who are anti. Then the separatists make their move to split away from the rest of Canada. In the past they've always tried a peaceful referendum. But they always fell flat on their faces. A hostile referendum just might do the trick for them. Then we would have two Canadas, one French-speaking, one English-speaking.''

''What does the Commandant have to do with it? Kidnapping the Commandant of the Marine Corps, bad as that is to us, is not exactly the kind of incident that's going to start a Canuck-American war.''

"Maybe not by itself. But add in the bombing at Fort Benning. The attack on the Minuteman III. The sinking of a Navy cruiser—"

"Still—"

She stamped her foot. "Is this a secret weapon? Talking people to death?''

He drew breath to come back at her, but held it.

"Okay, one more goody, but that's it. Then you have to give something.'' She raised an eyebrow at him.

He gave her nothing in return, not even a shrug.

As usual she interpreted it the way she wanted to. "Good, we have an agreement then.'' She hurried on before he could contradict her. "All those events, including taking Masterson, are just to show that they have a credible military capability. After all they have done, do you dare risk thinking they don't?''

He had to admit it was true. Their ability to evade both U.S. Army Rangers and his own Force Recon Team had proved they were capable of something more than the random car bomb. "Tell me more.''

"Nothing more. I'm not telling you another damned thing until you give me the ironclad guarantee I want. Meet my condition, and I'll tell you where you can get your precious Commandant.''

"Nina, you know I can't—'' She had begun shaking her head. "What?''

"I don't want information. I want more than just a scoop or an inside story."

It was his turn to be incredulous. "You want to come along? Out of the question."

"Your call. I have friends in low places. In the Navy?"

"No way."

"SEALs. They would be happy to take me."

"You must be dreaming. They wouldn't lift a finger to risk an international incident just to save the Commandant of the Marine Corps. They'd get a kick out of seeing him—"

"I wouldn't be telling them that they were rescuing Bat Masterson. I'd be telling them that I knew the location of the hideout of the people who sunk the *Thomas Jefferson* in San Diego Bay." She raised an eyebrow at him. "Saving the God of the Marines would be gravy. You think they wouldn't lord it over the Corps?"

She had struck a note, hitting him in a place where every Marine was most tender. He would not, could not, sacrifice the Commandant of the Marine Corps. Even worse, though, he could not allow the Commandant of the Marine Corps to be rescued by a special operations unit of the Navy. He decided he could lie. After all, he had done a hell of a lot worse today. Killing those Rangers, for instance.

"All right, I'll take you. Where we going?"

She burst into a bitter laugh. "Don't take me for an idiot. I know damned good and well that you'd leave me by the side of the road if I gave up all that

I have in advance—don't deny it. Hell, I would do it to you."

Swayne had nothing to say. His ears burned because, at this moment, she held more sway over him than his own commander. And because he was worried that Zavello was going to be on the air any moment demanding to know why he was not yet on the move. There was nothing to do but give her a nod of the head.

"Have your boys load up their little toys," she said. "We have quite a drive ahead of us."

Swayne and the team loaded their weapons, ammunition, and some rations. He was able to fit some explosives into the Ford, and his communications and electronic gear. They hoisted the two snowmobiles to the roof of the vehicle and strapped them down side-by-side, denting the roof. Nina protested the damage, but Swayne could not leave the vehicles behind. He couldn't allow valuable—valuable *incriminating*—technology to fall into the hands of either civilians or the enemy. Or worse, the Rangers.

They mounted up, Potts behind the wheel, she between him and Swayne. Potts started up and engaged the automatic transmission, but looked to her before moving out.

"Canada," she said. "We have to go into Canada. That's where they're hiding Masterson."

"That's your information?" said Swayne. "We already know they're going into Canada. We followed tire tracks up to the border. Canada is a big country. If you can't come up with something more specific than that, were going to drop you off at the nearest ranch house.''

"Don't pull righteous indignation on me. I invented righteous indignation, okay?''

Swayne stared out the windshield.

"We're going to do this one step at a time. First, you get us into Canada without being detected. As soon as you solve the first problem, I'll give you the next one. Eventually, we'll arrive at our destination and nobody will get left behind.''

Potts, embarrassed, gripped the steering wheel, waiting for Swayne's next move. In the backseat, Night Runner fidgeted, and Friel snickered.

"Move out,'' said Swayne.

EVENT SCENARIO 13—DAY 2

THREE HOURS LATER, they had begun climbing the western slopes of the Canadian Rockies, and Swayne had decided to end the mystery. "Nina, give me the location."

She shook her head.

"No more games," he said. "I have to know. Either it's too far for us to be able to do any good. Or else it's close enough that we need to formulate some kind of plan." He checked his watch. "If you give me the stiff-arm much longer, I'm not going to use the information at all. It's time for you to trust me."

Nina chewed her upper lip. "Okay," she said, "it's a place called The Fortress. It's a mountain lodging built on the top of a cliff. Before the war they called it Eagle's Nest, but after Hitler's retreat in Bavaria became known, they changed the name to Cougar's Lair.''

Swayne passed along the information, and Winston immediately responded, ''Hey, sir, I've got it. It will take me a minute to download to your screen.''

Swayne studied the photo-quality image downlinked to him by Winston, scrolling back and forth, up and down, across the landscape surrounding The Fortress. Cougar's Lair was an apt name. Situated at the edge of an alpine plateau, the two-hundred-room lodge had been built on a rocky promontory at the base of the Canadian Rockies overlooking a river valley to the east and a lake to the west. The effect was of a cul de sac of high ground that could be approached on land only through a small bottle-neck. A few good men with some heavy weapons could stand off a battalion of infantry.

He brought up an oblique view of the lodge, looking at it from below, at the base of the cliffs. The digital images had been created during the summer, showing vertical pillars of basalt shooting upward, sometimes leaning outward. He had been taught enough geology in his rock-climbing courses to know that the hexagonal formations could be extremely dangerous. You never knew when one of them would break away from the others.

Besides, at this time of the year, blowing snow would create dangerous cornices, hiding signs of broken and loose stone. So he dismissed the option of climbing to The Fortress from below. Even by day in the summertime, that would be a tricky proposition. At night, freezing temperatures and driving snow to complicate the icy fragile surfaces would make it impossible.

"Better check the map, Captain. By my odometer, we're within ten miles," said Potts.

Swayne brought up the topographical image on-screen and confirmed that Potts's dead-reckoning techniques had proved accurate. In this age of technological marvels, Swayne had always admired Gunny Potts for never allowing his old-fashioned navigation skills to atrophy.

"Does this mean you're not going to murder me?"

"Melodrama does not become you, Nina."

"You're not going to dump me out either?"

"I haven't decided what to do. Maybe I'll just leave you in the care of Lance Corporal Friel." At that prospect, both Nina and Friel groaned.

Swayne left on his GPS showing the topo map of the area so Potts could navigate. A thought struck him, and he asked Winston whether he could come up with a floor plan for the lodge.

"Working on it, sir. I'll get back to you."

The mood inside the sport utility vehicle grew somber, turning more tense as the glowing dot on the screen that represented their vehicle moved closer to the coordinates of The Fortress.

At about five miles from the lodge, Potts turned off the main highway. Immediately they found tracks in the snow, tracks that would lead them to

The Fortress. When they were within two miles, Potts slowed the Dodge to a crawl and asked, "What's our plan, Cap?"

Of course, Potts and the others would assume that he had a plan. Swayne himself was not so sure. The Fortress offered only two possible approach paths, and neither of them was militarily feasible. They could continue their approach on this road, but were certain to be opposed by an armed force at the bottleneck between the cliffs and the lake.

The alternative was to ride the snowmobiles in a circle to the west, crossing the frozen lake, keeping to the base of the western mountains in case they came under fire. Swayne did not want to approach the fortified position of the terrorists across the open ice for the last mile. Even at night it was a risky proposition. One set of vehicle headlights would be able to illuminate them. A single sharpshooter could pin down the team and eliminate them in detail. Before he could announce this was his choice as the lesser of evils, Winston spoke to him from Quantico.

"Hold your position, sir," said Winston, a sudden anxiety in his voice. "Now that the blizzard condition have stopped, I can help you out with some overhead observations. I have some thermal hits. Getting ready to download. There."

Swayne felt Nina pressing in on him to look at the screen. A collection of illuminated dots, sixteen in all, appeared on the screen.

"Northwest of the lodge," said Potts.

"On the lake," offered Night Runner. "An outpost?"

Swayne interpreted the screen. A series of dots and slashes of green imagery looked like a wash of watercolor that drifted to the southeast, dissipating as it went.

"Was that the heat signature of an airplane?" he asked.

Potts groaned. "An airdrop. Reinforcements?"

Friel snickered. "Probably just the media. Pictures at eleven."

Swayne doubted both conclusions. "No," he said, thinking aloud. "I have a bad feeling that this is an air drop of U.S. forces. It's too small for Rangers and too small again by half for the Air Force."

"More Marines?" said Nina.

"Way too many for Force Recon," said Potts. "If they were going to reinforce us, they might send one more team—four dots at most."

Swayne shook his head. "Colonel Zavello would not reinforce us without saying so, no matter how badly we had lost his confidence." He added, as much for his own sake as for the others, "And we haven't done anything to lose his confidence."

"SEALs."

Swayne nodded. "You're right, Night Runner."

Zavello came on the radio, and Swayne could tell that he was perturbed. "I have an update for you," he said. "I ran my question about other U.S. forces up the flagpole. I got nothing from SecDef, so I went directly to each of the services. The Navy denied it so fast that I knew the sons of bitches were lying."

Swayne cringed. If Zavello knew that he was baring the nastiness of interservice rivalries to a reporter for a national newspaper, he would court-martial Swayne on the spot. For that matter, if she should publish this story in any form, Zavello could identify the source. One detail, any detail, would give away Swayne and the team. The possibility of the Geneva Conventions Alternative applied to Nina occurred to him. As he tried to suppress the idea, Winston came on-line.

"I'm downloading a new series of thermal hits to you. I have three images on the road between you and The Fortress," said Winston.

Swayne shook his head. "Three defenders doesn't seem plausible. Is there any way to intensify a scan to look for others?"

"Roger. Wait."

Swayne covered his mike and spoke his team. "Seems too small for a credible reception committee."

"What if they're not waiting for you?" said Nina.

Friel groaned. Night Runner nodded. Potts shrugged.

"Makes sense," Swayne said. "A reception committee for the media. These three mutts hide out in the snow and let us pass. If we try to get out the same way, they might be able to hold us in for a while. But their real purpose is to meet the press. Literally. Escort them directly to the lodge, showing them the best camera shots. Pointing out the bodies of dead Americans. That kind of thing.'' Swayne had his fingers on the thermal dots scattered across the lake, dots that had begun to congregate and move directly toward the lodge. ''Including prisoners of war.''

''Hell,'' said Friel, ''the terrorists don't even need us anymore. They catch them squids out in the open and they'll have all the body count they need.''

''Cap?''

''What is it, Gunny?''

''Are we going to let the Navy rescue the Commandant's bacon while we just stand by and not even make toast and jam?''

Swayne didn't bother trying to interpret the mixed metaphor because he understood perfectly. ''I don't think the Navy is going to be rescuing anybody. They're going to be pretty damned lucky if they don't need some rescuing themselves.'' He swept his finger back and forth across the screen, tracing a stream of green thermal dots leaving the lodge. A collection of seven vehicles formed a convoy and strung out toward the lake. Swayne and the others watched as the vehicles stopped at intervals behind covered positions—he could see this by reading the topography of slopes and hillocks—overlooking the frozen landscape.

Potts let out the whisper of an obscenity.

The people on the lake were going to be taken under fire by a force of perhaps twice their number. A force situated behind cover. A force looking down from positions anywhere from ten to thirty meters above the ice. The SEALs, if that was who they were, were going to become the main course of Potts's breakfast analogy—toast.

Swayne finished outlining his plan to maneuver against the trio of men guarding the bottleneck into the promontory where The Fortress stood as Zavello broke the silence. "We've intercepted transmissions coming from the lodge. Phone calls to Canadian media outlets and the Canadian Armed Forces. By the time the sun comes up, those mountains are going to be swarming with television helicopters. Before the sun goes down," he observed dryly, "the Canadian Army might even manage to make it up there. That gives you about three hours to pull this off and get the hell out of there."

After a hesitation of perhaps ten seconds, Zavello came back at him speaking deliberately. "Your first mission is to rescue the Commandant and escape without leaving a trace. Your second mission, if you can't accomplish the first, is to execute the Geneva Conventions Alternative and get the hell out. There is no third choice. There will be no opportunity for the general being caught in a public spectacle making a confession of American wrongdoing."

"What's he talking about?" said Nina, sitting erect.

Swayne shushed her by pressing two fingers on her lips. "This is Spartan One," said Swayne in his most formal voice, knowing that this conversation would be recorded. "Request confirmation of the authority to execute the Geneva Alternative. Authenticate.''

They exchanged no more words. One computer interrogated the other until all the codes and acknowledgments had passed back and forth. Finally a clear-text message came up:

EXECUTE GENEVA CONVENTIONS ALTERNATIVE. SUBJECT—GENERAL HARLEY V. MASTERSON, COMMANDANT, UNITED STATES MARINE CORPS. BY THE AUTHORITY OF: GENERAL HARLEY V. MASTERSON, III, COMMANDANT, UNITED STATES MARINE CORPS. VOICE ACKNOWLEDGMENT: OPERATION NECESSITY KILLS.

Swayne couldn't believe his eyes, and apparently, neither could the other men. Nobody on the team was willing to look at the screen for any longer than it took to read the deadly message there. They turned away, each muttering his favorite obscenity under his breath.

"What?" said Nina.

Swayne keyed his microphone and shook the words loose from his craw. "I acknowledge Operation Necessity Kills.''

"Your acknowledgment is correct. Proceed. Maintain contact and report at your discretion. Mandatory report required upon the execution of Operation Necessity Kills.''

Nina gasped. "Let me get this straight,'' she said.

"If you can't save Masterson, you're supposed to kill him?"

"I'm not allowed to discuss it, neither to confirm nor deny."

Chase threw up her hands. "It doesn't matter whether you confirm or deny. I heard what I heard, and I can draw my own conclusions."

"You didn't hear anything, Nina."

"Don't be stupid—" Her mouth fell open. "Are you threatening me?"

Swayne grasped the front of her jacket, clutching it to her throat, pulling her face into his. "I can't threaten you. You're a civilian, and the radio traffic transmitted into this vehicle was military traffic for our ears only. If you did not hear it, I did not threaten you."

"Jack."

"Nina, you have no idea. Because of the message that I have heard in the last few minutes, I am no longer Jack. I am Captain John Joseph Swayne, United States Marine Corps. My first mission is to rescue my Commandant. If that is not successful, I have a second mission that I don't even want to think about. You don't want to think about it either. You don't want to talk about it. And you certainly don't want to write about it." He turned and looked over her shoulder into the backseat.

Friel leaned toward and spoke into her ear. "Miz Chase, the Captain is now going to ask each and every one of us if he has heard and understands his orders. Each of us is going to give him our answer, and you are going to give him yours."

Swayne asked the question. In turn, Potts, Night
Runner, and Friel answered, "I acknowledge Operation Necessity Kills and will comply."

All eyes turned to her. She looked Swayne full
in the face and said, "Who, me? I didn't hear a
thing. I won't say anything. No matter what."

Instead of releasing her, Swayne shook her by the
coat. "No evasions, dammit. Don't start talking like
a Washington politician to me."

She blinked rapidly. "All right, I won't write
anything either."

Swayne released her.

She shook her head. "You Marines are really the
limit. How could a man order his own assassination
as casually as if he were ordering tickets to the—"
She looked around the interior of the vehicle. All
four men stared at her. Her face went slack for a
moment. Then her eyes lit up. "Oh, when you say
don't talk about it, you mean don't talk about it."

"Night Runner and Friel," said Swayne. "Move
on the three men guarding the bottleneck. Let me
know when you've neutralized them."

"Roger. What about the SEALs?" asked Potts as
Night Runner and Friel vanished into the darkness,
sending up rooster-tails of snow behind their electric
snowmobile.

"They can be our frontal attack. We'll move by on
the flank and try to get into the lodge from the rear.
Maybe find the Commandant and get away with him
while the main battle is going on at the lake."

He looked to her.

"Nina, I need your help."

Her left eyebrow shot up to show she doubted the truth of that.

He tried a thrust she could not resist. "It's dangerous. It might get you killed. So if you don't want to get involved, just tell me and I'll find another way to do it."

She half-nodded, half-wagged her head. "Well, Captain Jack Swayne, you certainly have developed an unusual foreplay technique."

SWAYNE HELPED POTTS cover Nina's vehicle with snow. Afterward, he gave her the briefest of briefings. "Besides camouflage, this will defeat any thermal devices the Canadian Armed Forces might have." He brushed at the windshield, letting in the sparse starlight. "Watch through here."

He showed her how to operate a handheld radio and gave her final instructions. The others positioned the snowmobiles and busied themselves checking gear discreetly, giving him time alone with her.

The moment grew awkward. "Give me a call when you spot the Canadians. Then turn on your headlights and stand out in front of the truck with your hands up. They'll take care of you from there. Try to delay them." He shrugged, not knowing what else to do but thank her. He did, and she hugged him through the open window.

Swayne knew that the odds were better than even

that he would not see her again. If anything, the
SEALs attacking the lodge made his mission untenable, even impossible. He had a lot of respect for
the SEALs, but no force, no matter how good they
were, was going to be able to survive an ambush on
the naked surface of the lake. The terrorists were
going to be able to kill or capture all the proof they
needed of an American invasion.

And now that a new the level of desperation that
had been assigned to this mission—Operation Necessity Kills being the proof of it—he began to think
the unthinkable.

If Zavello's superiors were willing to authorize
the assassination of the Commandant, then what did
it matter that four other lowly Marines in the battle
zone might become casualties themselves?

Spurred by this urgent insight, Swayne peeled
Nina's arms from him and left her inside the truck
with a last assurance that he would call for her, hoping he sounded convincing enough.

Then he ran toward his snowmobile, and they
were off toward the lodge.

TRACER RICOCHETS STREAKING up into the night
told Swayne the firefight on the lake had begun. The
team raced toward The Fortress at top speed, keeping to the edge of the woods as much as possible.
Finally the woods gave out, and Potts and Friel
drove across an open area not far from the edge of
the cliff toward the shadow of the lodge, a shadow
irregularly cast by searchlights and explosions on

the lake. In minutes they reached more substantial shadows on the grounds of The Fortress.

The images transmitted by Winston had showed a building surrounded by landscaped grounds, green foliage, and flower gardens. The light of day, coupled with the backdrop of the mountains, had created a setting of majestic tranquillity. Now the building loomed up into the night sky, black, Gothic, foreboding. The windows had been covered for the winter by sheets of plywood.

The snowmobiles skidded to a halt beside a fountain below the northeast corner of the lodge. The team dismounted and hid among the statuary. Friel and Night Runner took up firing positions among the family of bronze grizzly bears, the sow standing seven feet high on her hind legs clawing at the air over Night Runner. Potts hid beneath a waterfall of bronze. Swayne worked his way among a flight of Canada geese—three times normal size and lifting out of the water, taking off before the bears.

"Search the perimeter?" Potts asked. "Find an entrance?"

"No good," said Swayne. "No matter how much of their force is out there on the lake, they wouldn't leave the entrances undefended—probably have bunkered machine guns."

Potts stared upward into the blackness where the building became one with the sky. "We could scale the drainpipes. Come in from the top."

Swayne shook his head. "Too obvious. They would be thinking helicopters. They would have somebody in the stairwells, probably on the roof too, also in bunkers.''

Potts began nodding. ''I wouldn't be surprised if they were eyeballing us now.''

''Same here,'' said Swayne.

Friel grunted in the negative. ''Creeps me out, too, but I checked the roofline with infrared and night vision. I don't see anything.''

''They don't need another firefight. They already have the Navy doing what they wanted *us* to do. When the Canadian military comes up the road behind us, we'll be cut off. If they spread a couple battalions of paratroopers across the lake to the road, we're caught red-handed. About the only way out of here is for us to free-fall over the cliff.''

''Captain Swayne, I've got something.'' It was Winston.

Swayne liked the tone of optimism in the young voice. ''Give it to me.''

''Check your GPS, screen 107.''

Swayne took the computer from his parka and brought up the cached image that Winston had downlinked to him.

''It's the floor plan you wanted,'' Winston said triumphantly. ''Not exactly an architect's blueprint. I got it off a Web page for the hospitality chain that owns the Cougar's Lair lodge. This one has the floor layouts for the areas open to the public. I'm sorry I couldn't locate anything for the basement or administrative areas—they just leave those things blank in their publicity material. I'll keep checking around some historical Web pages to see what I can come up with.''

''Roger, you've done fine. We can use this. Appreciate your effort. Out.''

Swayne tapped the screen with a fingertip, drawing Potts's attention to the layout. ''Suppose we went up to one of the middle floors and pulled the plywood off one of those windows beside the drainpipe. They might guard the roof and all the entrances, but they wouldn't be expecting us to come at them from the middle floors.''

''Let's do it,'' said Potts. ''Night Runner?''

NIGHT RUNNER REPLIED by dashing through the snow to the base of The Fortress. He worked along the base of the building to where a buttress of river stone projected from the lodge. In the right angle between the buttress and the wall, a six-inch drainpipe ran up to the roof.

By the time he heard Swayne and the others dashing to the base of the building in turn, Night Runner had already climbed the pipe past the first floor.

He decided to go in on the third floor. It was a lucky number for him, his number on the team, the lucky number that he had taken from his sometimes-Christian upbringing, representative of the three Christian gods that he could never quite combine into the single deity, as the Dominicans had demanded.

He fastened a rope above one of the pipe brackets and threw down the running end of the line. Then he inched along a decorative ledge no more than four inches wide, gripping the mortar grooves with his strong fingertips, grateful the stone niches had not been filled with ice.

Full sheets of plywood, four feet by eight feet, had been laid horizontally to cover the windows. Runner was glad to find that the plywood had not been bolted down, but was held with wing nuts.

Balancing on his left foot and holding himself by a claw-like grip with his left hand, he reached down and pulled an eight-inch knife from his boot. By rapping on one wing of each nut, he found the first two came loose right away, and he was able to spin them off by hand.

He pulled the plywood's left side, and found that he could get a gap large enough to slip his fingers inside for a handhold. The next part would be the toughest. Half kneeling, half holding himself with a left-handed grip, he inclined himself sideways to stretch and release two more wing nuts on the bottom of the plywood. Behind him, he heard the panting of one of his fellows scaling the rope to the same ledge that he was now clinging to.

"Damn, Runner," said Potts. "How'd you finger-climb that pipe?"

To Night Runner, it was no big deal. He had once rappelled like some action-movie hero from beneath the Highway 2 bridge a hundred feet above the Two Medicine River in Montana. Trouble was, his rope had only been twenty feet long. More than a negligible engineering miscalculation. Even at thirteen, he was adept at getting himself out of tight situations—usually involving the tribal police. He had swung on the rope until he came close enough to the cliff wall to grab onto the rocks, release the rope, and free-climb to safety. In that instance, as in many other instances since, the stones in the cliff wall had not been mortared together. And he'd had no trustworthy plywood handholds to afford him the leverage he needed. This, by comparison, was taking the escalator.

Once the lower wing nuts had been sent spinning into the night, the plywood in his left hand could be pulled away another four inches. Carefully, he regained his feet and began working on the upper fasteners. Behind him he heard the labored breathing of Friel. He knew it was not the effort of climbing that had left the Bostonian breathless. Friel had never been fond of heights, and the rapid breathing betrayed his stress.

Once the upper wing nuts were off, Night Runner could pull the plywood back far enough to slip his body between the window and the covering. He shrugged out of his backpack and held it out to Potts, who took it reluctantly because it meant releasing one of his handholds. Night Runner pushed into the gap between the window and the plywood, letting it press in on him, supporting him from behind. From that point, it was simply a matter of replacing his gloves and punching a hole in the glass so he could unlock the window sash. He slid it up, stepped inside, and pulled the curtains off the walls so they could not impede the others. He flashed a penlight around the room, and saw that the furniture had been covered with drop cloths. Unveiling a ladder-back chair, he shoved the plywood sheet outward and propped the chair between it and the wall to keep the gap open. Then one by one, he took the weapons and packs of his teammates and guided them into the room.

Once they were all inside, they wasted no time in discussing tactics. For they had practiced moving through buildings of all kinds, both in training and on previous live exercises.

Swayne showed his GPS Screen to Night Runner, and pointed out the nearest stairwell on the floor plan. "To the Bat Cave," was all he had to say, and they were on the way to the basement.

As usual, Night Runner led the formation as the Spartans cleared the hallway and maneuvered to the stairwell. In the first place, he had the most advanced technological devices for running the point. Clamped to his head was a miniature television monitor that was suspended on the boom in front of his right eye. The two-inch screen was fed by cable to a modified night-vision scope on his rifle. In a combat situation, he could point the muzzle of his XM-16A4 around cover without exposing his body. The camera would show whether the way was clear, and if it was not, a bright spot on the image before his eye indicated the sighting point. All he had to do was pull the trigger, and his bullet would strike wherever that spot rested, for whatever range he had zeroed. The Force Recon Marines had asked for and received a modification to this electronic periscope. A separate cable could be detached from the scope, a device borrowed from big-city cops, providing a lens less than a quarter inch in diameter. In situations demanding exceptional stealth, Night Runner could look around corners without exposing so much as the tips of his fingers.

Before going into a hallway, Runner extended his stealth lens beneath the door and manipulated it to look both ways down the hall. Satisfied that the coast was clear, he slipped into the hall, turning right and keeping right, toward the stairwell. Friel crossed the hallway, taking cover in the alcove of the door opposite. Potts followed Night Runner, maintaining an interval of ten feet. Friel, a right-hander, and Swayne, a left-hander, extended their weapons from their respective alcoves to provide cover.

Friel and Swayne waited for the other two to secure the stairwell before moving out. The Spartans did not use an overlapping technique, except when they had been spotted and taken under fire. That was because Night Runner's warrior instincts usually surpassed the capabilities of their fancy technological tools. It wasn't only that he had superior senses. His vision was so keen that he could pick out irregularities in foliage, identifying the outline of a stationary bird in the trees that others could not see even when it had been pointed out with a laser spot. He had ears seemingly capable of detecting tones above and below the range of normal hearing as well as unusual sounds at a distance.

Inside the stairwell, Friel and Potts pointed their weapons downward, while Swayne and Night Runner focused their attention upward. The men knew to hold their breath and to minimize movement as Night Runner swiveled his head upward and downward, over the banister and up into the shaft of space that ran from the roof to the basement between the staircases, listening.

Only when Night Runner gave the thumbs-up did they dare to breathe. Then Swayne put down his own rifle and took out one of the special tools from the urban combat kit in Potts's pack. The tool was little more than a twelve-inch handle and a set of ratcheting jaws. It came with a packet of carbide tool bits with chiseled points at opposite ends. Swayne inserted one of the bits into the jaws of the ratchet and placed the carbide tip between the stairwell door in its metal frame. A quick jerk downward forced one bit into the edge of the door and the other bit into the steel frame, effectively locking it.

By this time, Night Runner had moved up to the next landing, looking around corners with his low-light scope and listening with his bat's hearing. Night Runner continued moving upward, keeping to three landings ahead of Swayne. When Swayne reached the door to the roof, he found that Night Runner had already slipped the lock and opened the door far enough to allow a peek around the roof with his stealth lens.

After Night Runner had closed the door and stepped aside so Swayne could lock it, he said, "Three men. One huddled against a steam pipe keeping warm. Two others behind the ramparts watching the fight on the lake."

Swayne double-locked the door with his bits, hesitated, then triple-locked it. Together they hustled downward.

SWAYNE WAITED AS Night Runner peeked beneath the basement door. "Not much but vertical pillars and a boiler room," he said. He turned the monitor away from his eye so Swayne could see the cavernous room. "Odds and ends, storage, some junk furniture and a work area, maybe for the handyman."

"Let's go," said Swayne. "We'll split up and work around both sides of the room."

Night Runner and Potts went left, working clockwise around the basement. Swayne first used his locking bits, then went right with Friel. In less than a minute they had cleared the room, meeting at a set of oversized double doors, the most likely way into the heart of the lodge. After Night Runner checked beneath these doors, he looked up, shaking his head. "No sign of life. Looks like the laundry and maids' work area."

They let themselves into the laundry and worked around it as before, finding that it had not been used or occupied recently.

Ahead of them, another set doors led into an

atrium at the bottom of a double staircase. Beyond that were more doors.

Swayne felt his anxiety rising. He knew that the battle outside was not going to last very long because of the vulnerability of the forces on the ice. He checked his watch. They had burned nearly ten minutes of the time available and still had not located the Commandant. By even the most optimistic estimate, they had little more than two hours left. Maybe less.

A lot less. Zavello came on, speaking calmly into his ear to tell him that the Canadian Armed Forces had launched a pair of reconnaissance flights from Edmonton and that military garrisons both in Calgary, Alberta, and Vancouver, B.C., had been mustered.

"The one in Vancouver is a parachute battalion," Zavello advised. "They are boarding planes right now. The unit out of Calgary is mechanized infantry. They are already on the road. Expect a parachute drop at first light and a mechanized attack soon after. What is your progress?"

Swayne gave him an update, forcing himself to admit that they had made little progress beyond getting into the lodge undetected. Zavello rogered his report without comment. The flat, resigned tone of his voice prompted Swayne to ask about the possibility of getting a fleet of troop helicopters into the mountains so they might extract themselves, the Commandant, and the dead and dying among the fighting force on the lake, which he still presumed to be SEALs.

Zavello rogered again. "We have already been working on that, and a flight of three has already departed Malmstrom Air Force Base. They will sneak across the border on your word and be ready to pick you up. Be prepared to mark a landing site."

Swayne heard the flatness in his own voice when he responded with "Roger" and signed off. The charade from mission control did not fool anybody.

"He's lying," said Friel. "There aren't any helicopters coming out of Montana. They're going to leave us here."

"That can't be," said Potts.

Swayne wanted to assure the gunny, but he shook his head. "I'm going to level with you boys. I agree with Friel. If they do launch anything out of Malmstrom, it'll be a missile. I don't know of any other way they could expect to clean up this mess without leaving people alive to testify against the Administration. But that doesn't change our mission."

"The Commandant," said Night Runner.

Swayne nodded vigorously. "He's our top priority. If—"

Night Runner waved frantically, signaling for him to be quiet. "General Masterson," he said in a stage whisper, pointing toward the doors. "He's out there."

Night Runner swiveled the tiny television monitor away from his eye so the others could see it. Three men descended the staircase. Two of them had rifles slung over their shoulders. They were both supporting the third, unquestionably a captive, unquestionably General Masterson, Commandant of the Marine Corps. The general stumbled once, as if he was drunk or injured.

The Spartans allowed themselves only a glance at the screen. Then they moved quickly and silently, putting their backs against the walls flanking the doors leading into the laundry room.

With a shake of his head, Night Runner indicated that the men were not bringing Masterson in this direction. After a moment he sat up, withdrawing the stealth lens and replacing it on the scope.

Night Runner waited for the other three heads to come close to him, then whispered, "They took him through the opposite door. I got a peek inside. A pantry. Big one. I saw a light come on under the door and then go out."

Swayne understood. "They went into a room beyond that. Maybe a kitchen?"

"Walk-ins," said Potts. "I used to sling hash browns. Walk-in coolers make good jail cells. We used to play practical tricks, lock each other up."

Swayne checked his watch. "If we can't snatch the Commandant and get out of here in an hour, I doubt we'll be getting out at all."

Swayne and Friel went to the staircase, keeping out of sight from above. Night Runner came up, listened, and pointed his rifle's television lens up the stairs by extending his arms and not standing behind it. Once he gave the all-clear, Swayne and Friel stayed behind to secure the stairwell, and Potts and Night Runner entered the pantry. Friel, then Swayne went inside, and Swayne used a pair of his bits to reinforce the pantry-door lock, creating an obstacle behind them. The opposite door, about thirty feet away, let in a splash of light underneath. By the time Swayne had the first door secured, Night Runner had peeked into the next room with his stealth lens.

"I have four men, two sleeping on cots, two guarding a cooler door," Night Runner reported, murmuring into his radio microphone.

"And I suppose this door is locked," said Swayne.

Night Runner adjusted his lens so he could keep watch on the sentries, and tested the handle. He pressed his lips together and nodded.

"Kick it, you think?" asked Potts.

Swayne had already run the options through his mental calculator. Even in this age of high-tech, sometimes the best method for getting things done was to kick a door and bust some heads and asses.

Swayne and Friel took an extra ten seconds to affix silencers to their 9-millimeters. Then they stood shoulder-to-shoulder, pointing their pistols at the door, looking to Night Runner's television monitor to get a rough idea of where the sentries would be once Potts went through the door.

They had practiced the drill before. "Try not to kill everybody," Swayne directed in a low whisper. This admonishment was for Friel, who could be entirely too efficient when it came to gunplay. If possible, Swayne wanted one of the terrorists alive so he to get some information.

Swayne and Friel pointed the muzzles of their pistols to the right and left respectively, so their aim would be nearly dead-on when the door came open. Potts and Night Runner backed up a dozen feet or so.

When Swayne dipped his head, Potts ran at the door, launching himself like a hockey player taking an opponent into the boards, hitting the door high and knocking it off the hinges in one motion. The door clattered to the floor and skidded, Potts on top of it, his weapon at the ready.

The guards, sitting in chairs on either side of the cooler, were transfixed in the first instant by the sight of a giant man sledding toward them. In the next instant, they realized what it meant. The instant after that, they were both dead, both head-shot. They slumped back into their chairs, their rifles rattling against the concrete floor.

By then, Night Runner had charged into the room at full speed, his weapons at the ready, bayonet fixed. Before the other two terrorists could sit up on their cots, one was staring into the Cyclops eye of Potts's weapon, and the other's eyes were cross-focused on the tip of a bayonet resting on his nose.

Swayne and Friel, seeing that the kitchen was secure, returned to the pantry door next to the stairwell and listened. Swayne tried to recall the magnitude of the sound Potts had made going through door and hitting the floor. He remembered the splintering of wood as the hinges pulled free. He recalled the slap of Potts's toboggan against the floor. Noise enough, but not too much, apparently.

Hearing no footsteps coming down the double staircase, he left Friel for security and went back into the kitchen.

Potts held his weapon on one of the groggy sentries still alive. In the other hand he yanked at a heavy combination padlock on the handle of the walk-in cooler.

Swayne sized up the situation, glancing at his watch. An hour and fifty-two minutes remaining before he estimated the first Canadians would be arriving on site.

"Do either of you speak English?" he demanded.

Neither man answered. In fact, neither paid attention. They were both transfixed by the weapons pointing at them, looking as though they were still trying to determine whether this was part of their dreams or one horrible reality. One looked over at his dead compatriots, blood pooling on the floor behind their chairs, and the look on his face showed the dawning realization that this was no dream.

"Night Runner, try French."

"Parlez-vous Français?"

Their eyes twitched, but neither said anything.

"Translate, Night Runner."

"Oui."

"Give me the combination to this lock, or I will kill you," Swayne said in English. As he spoke, Night Runner picked up the translation immediately, as though Swayne's thoughts were channeling into his mind and spilling out of his mouth. "I have tools that will let me break the lock. That will cause me some delay, but you must believe that I can do it." He waved at the carnage of the pair next to the door of the cooler. "If you do not help me, you will sleep with them." No reaction.

At least at first. One of the terrorists glanced at the other, and their expressions hardened. Of course, Swayne realized, he would not have been the first to have threatened these two. He doubted that any verbal threat that he could make would compare to a terrorist leader desperate enough to pull off what had been accomplished by these bastards in the last two days.

Swayne pulled his pistol and fired it for a second time into the head of a terrorist. The man flopped backward on his cot, blood spattering on the stainless-steel cabinets behind him. Swayne turned the gun on the fourth terrorist. He no longer needed a translator. The man, his eyes wide in terror, blurted the combination so quickly and so repeatedly that Night Runner had to shut him up and demand he speak it more slowly, translating to Potts as he did so.

The man that Swayne had shot sat up, cradling his left ear in his hands, blood running down his forearm and dripping off his elbow. He might be hard of hearing for a while, but the slash on his cheek and hole in his ear would eventually heal, leaving him one hell of a war story to tell the ladies.

Potts turned the dial as Night Runner directed him. With a quick jerk the lock came open.

Swayne never took his eyes off the terrorists as Potts threw down the lock and grasped the heavy chrome handle of the cooler door. Was it going to be this easy getting to the Commandant? *No!*

"Gunny, wait!" he barked.

Potts jerked his hand away from the door handle as if it had scorched him. "What's up, Cap?" he asked. "Booby-trapped?"

"I can't say. All I know is this goofball flinched when you grabbed the cooler handle." He waved the pistol under the man's nose. "Night Runner, ask him if it's booby-trapped."

Night Runner asked, and the man shook his head, muttering a response.

"What did he say?"

Night Runner shrugged. "He's talking crazy now. Suddenly he's got courage. First he said it wasn't booby-trapped. Then he called us a bunch of goddamned dogs."

Swayne look at his watch. "Stand back. Night Runner, tell him to stand up and open the cooler door."

The men of the team found cover behind pillars and metal cabinets. Swayne kept watch on the man's behavior as he sidled toward the cooler door, prodded by Night Runner's bayonet. He took a deep breath and reached for the handle with such certainty that either there were no explosive

charges wired, or else he must be willing to die for
his cause.

Night Runner must have felt the same way, for
he ducked behind a stainless-steel table.

The wiry terrorist grasped the handle with both
hands and hauled the door open all the way, pulling
it to his chest and backing around in an arc until his
back was to the wall.

Swayne saw he was using the door as a shield
and pulled back himself, expecting a blast in his
face. But there was no explosion. Instead, he heard
scratching on the floor, and when he looked around
his pillar again, he realized the terrorist had been all
too accurate with his report. A huge Rottweiler,
broad as a torpedo across the chest, came rushing at
him, teeth first. Swayne jumped back just as the animal' s jaws snapped shut on the air where his elbow
had been. The animal belly-rolled in the air, whipping its body around to land sideways, losing its
grip and skidding on the floor. Even so, it scratched
at the concrete with all fours—Swayne could see
the white marks of those scratches. He fired off two
quick shots. Without so much as a yelp, the dog
dropped, its back broken, but still determined to get
at him, its front feet windmilling against the floor,
still making those white marks.

Swayne heard another set of dog claws scratching
the floor and the breathy cursing of Potts, who was
trying to keep a second, even larger Rottweiler at
bay by poking at it with the point of his fixed bayonet. Swayne knew how much Potts disliked dogs,

and he marveled at the gunny's discipline in not shooting the animal outright with the unsilenced weapon.

"What are you waiting for, Cap?" Potts demanded.

As with the first dog and the uncooperative terrorist before that, Swayne did not want to kill. But in his head the mental clock kept ticking away, now at less than an hour and fifty minutes. Two more quick shots finished both dogs.

He became aware of the sound of yet another set of claws, this time more rhythmic. A third dog lay at Night Runner's feet on its side. The Blackfeet Indian scratched its ribs, and the animal's hind legs whirled as if it were riding a bicycle. The dog's head lolled back, and its tongue hung out the side of its fearsome jaws.

"Someday you're going to have to teach me how you do shit like that," said Potts, moving toward the cooler. He flipped on a light switch as Swayne joined him, and they both went inside.

"Place is bigger than the house I grew up in," Potts whispered.

Swayne pointed. "There, in the back."

A length of chain-link fencing had been strung across the cooler, partitioning it. Behind the fence, palettes had been laid on the floor, and a mattress had been thrown on top of them. The figure on the mattress stirred and tried to sit up. Swayne recognized General Harley Masterson, whose photograph was posted with the rest of the chain of command in every orderly room in the Marine Corps.

The Commandant's eyes would not focus on them. His chin fell on his chest, and the general collapsed on the mattress. Swayne saw that his left wrist had been handcuffed. The other cuff was fastened to a chain padlocked to an iron ring attached to the wall. The general lay in a pool of vomit, perhaps a reaction to the drugs given him.

Potts cursed as he pulled the fence down. Swayne glanced at his watch. So. It wasn't going to be so easy after all.

"Get Friel in here to pick the lock on these bracelets." He followed Potts out of the cooler and looked to Night Runner, now making the sweep of the kitchen, the dog following at his heel.

"Night Runner, have you got anything in the medical kit that might neutralize a tranquilizer?"

Night Runner grimaced. "Amphetamines. Dangerous thing, trying to cancel out a tranq."

Swayne shook his head free of the notion. A manic general might be worse than a dopey one.

Friel leaned down to work on handcuffs, but recoiled.

"What's the problem?" Potts asked, alarm in his voice.

"The man reeks like yesterday's cabbage, Gunny. How am I supposed to do my job when I can't even breathe around him?"

"A little respect, Lance Corporal. You're talking about the Commandant of the Corps."

Friel's face screwed up in a grimace. "I don't care if he's the Archangel Gabriel, Gunny. Man stinks like he been eating out of a two-holer."

Potts raised one eyebrow less than a millimeter, and Friel looked as if he'd been clubbed by a meaty noncom fist. He held his breath and bent to his task.

As Potts and Friel came back into the kitchen, a sudden ringing startled them all. A wall telephone next to the cooler door captured their eyes. On the second ring, Swayne noticed a wrinkling of toes sticking out from beneath the cooler door.

"Night Runner, translate," he said, and went on without pausing. "You there, behind the cooler door, answer the telephone in the normal way. Give the normal report without any deviation, and I will spare your life. If anyone comes down because you have alerted them, I'll kill you. Do you doubt it?"

The door came away from the wall, and the man walked to the telephone, widening his eyes and shaking his head to answer the last part of Swayne's question as it was translated to him. Night Runner moved in close to overhear the conversation, and Swayne directed Friel and Potts into the cooler to prepare the general for travel. "Make sure he has some boots. If you can't find his, take a pair off one of these guys. And get some warm clothes for him. We have to get out of here."

Friel seemed only too happy to be dressing the general in clothes not covered in vomit.

Swayne glanced at his watch again, not liking it

that mentally he had lost more time than he'd realized.

The terrorist cupped his hand to the telephone and spoke to Swayne in French.

"They want to talk to Henri," Night Runner translated. "But Henri came down with a terminal migraine when we busted in."

Swayne said, "Tell them the man's taking a crap. He'll call back."

Night Runner translated, and the terrorist passed the message along. Swayne could tell by the tone of the conversation that the caller had grown insistent. Finally, the wiry terrorist cupped his hand over the telephone, shaking his head, and Swayne knew they weren't buying. He raised his eyebrows at Night Runner, whose eyes widened in disbelief.

"You want me to be Henri?"

"What else? Time is running out, and stalling isn't going to get us anywhere. Act like you have the stomach cramps or something."

Swayne could hear a thin shouting coming out of the earpiece of the telephone. Night Runner reached for it, but Swayne held up his hand. "Have our buddy tell them you're on the way, running."

The man did as he was told. He handed over the telephone to Night Runner as Potts and Swayne dragged the limp body of the Commandant out of the cooler. They laid the general on the cot, his feet dangling. Swayne put the two surviving terrorists inside the cooler. Before he shut the door, he pointed a finger between one of the men's eyes and

said, "Behave. Or else—" He pointed to the Rottweiler sitting at Night Runner's left knee, then back
at the men. The threat required no translation. Both
men's heads bobbed up and down. Swayne closed
the door and inserted the padlock into the handle.

Night Runner was in the middle of groaning and
gasping, wheezing and whispering instead of talking
into the phone. It was good acting, and Swayne
hoped that the boys upstairs would buy it.

Night Runner wrapped up his little act, whining into
the telephone, *"Oui, oui, oui,"* before hanging up.

Friel, engaged in lashing an oversized boot to
General Masterson's left foot, his head turned aside
to breathe unfouled air, asked, "What are you, one
of the Three Little Pigs?"

Potts laughed. Night Runner didn't get it. "They
bought the Henri bit, but they want us upstairs in
two minutes with the Commandant. They're sending
a squad to meet us in the lobby and take him into
the other wing."

"That tells us something. They're situated in the
wing closest to the lake. Not only that, but they
expect people to be moving around. So they won't
get suspicious if they see *us* people—at least, from
a distance."

"They told me and Antoine to bring up the general. They won't be expecting four of us."

That was no problem to Swayne. He gave them
a quick rundown on his scheme to get the general
out of the lodge. Afterward, he watched Friel and
Runner pick up the least bloody of the two dead

men. He led them back through the pantry, removed his locking bit, and sent them on their way, the corpse's feet dragging.

"This is a kitchen," he told Potts, "a basement kitchen. That means—"

Potts was ahead of him. "Service elevators. Or maybe a dumbwaiter."

Swayne decided against the elevators. Too noisy. The dumbwaiter, apparently, had been the original means of delivering food to the main floor restaurant. It was large enough for at least three service carts. Potts loaded the general inside and braced himself against one of the walls, his head forced down to his knees. Swayne packed himself inside on the opposite wall, crooking his legs over the general's limp body. As Potts began hauling on the rope, hand-over-hand, Swayne inserted a fresh clip into his 9-millimeter and unscrewed the silencer. Much as he detested Friel's demeanor, the smell of the general revolted him as well, especially in such a cramped space.

When they reached a set of doors marked on the inside with a large M, Potts slowed their progress to crawl, keeping as quiet as he could. Even at that, the ropes knocked against the shaft, and pulleys squeaked somewhere high above them.

Swayne heard heavy footsteps—too heavy and too many footsteps to be Friel and Night Runner. It had to be half a dozen men, supremely confident that they were in command of the lodge, to be making all that racket. He reached out a hand to stop

Potts from pulling them up entirely into the doorway. He tried to peer out of a crack, but all he could see was a partition. He slid open the doors of the dumbwaiter, finding himself at eye-level with the floor in a service nook of the hotel's main dining room. Eager to get to the fresh air, he slithered out of the dumbwaiter and to the edge of the partition in time to see eight men in all, heavily armed, striding past the dining room with its tables shoved into a corner, the chairs stacked into a pyramid.

After the men had gone by, he motioned Potts out of the dumbwaiter. "Leave the general," he whispered. "We're going to have to fight our way out of here."

He and Potts lay against the half-wall near the doorway leading into the restaurant. He glanced around a column easily six feet in diameter to get his bearings. The column was the trunk of a tree eighty feet high, towering from this floor to the roof of the center of the lodge. He remembered this feature from the floor plan downlinked to him. Beyond this was the majestic great room of the lodge, with entrances to the north and south, hallways at least thirty feet wide, the openness rising five stories high. Diagonally across the lobby was a gift shop, its walls decorated like a museum of the Plains Indians with skins, beaded skirts, bows, arrows, and lances. To his right were the front desk and lobby. Directly across from the restaurant he could see the centerpiece of the building, a fireplace larger than most storefronts, its opening gaping as large as a garage door.

Shots came from Swayne's left down the hallway. He recognized Night Runner's weapon on automatic, followed by the deliberate *pop-pop-pop* of Friel's handgun. Swayne estimated that five or more of the eight terrorists that had gone past were down and dead.

Boot steps, again heavy but now fewer in number and running in panic, retreated up the hallway. A burst of fire cut short the boot steps, followed by the sound of a body crashing to the stone-tile floor. Swayne could hear distinctly now—two more sets of running feet. Men running and shouting for help, and for the first time, returning fire. One set of footsteps ran by the dining room, and Swayne lifted his pistol and fired in one motion, hitting the man in the neck just below his right ear.

Potts, he saw, felt confident enough in Friel and Night Runner to know that eight terrorists were no match for them. He had turned his attention the opposite way down the hall to watch for reinforcements, which would surely react to the gunfire.

Especially now that the final set of footsteps had stopped running. Swayne peeked over the dining room half-wall and saw the lame effort of one man reaching around a corner with an AK-50 carbine, wildly spraying automatic fire at Runner and Friel.

Just as Swayne took aim, the man saw him and sprayed just as wildly in his direction, stitching up the far wall of the dining room and splashing bits of glass from the enormous chandelier that dominated the center of the room.

One shot to the throat from Swayne's pistol put an end to the terrorist's terror.

"Want me to get the general?" asked Potts.

"Go ahead. I'll see if I can gather up the rest of the team before the bad guys send in the cavalry."

Swayne stood up and stuck his left arm into hallway, giving a thumbs-up signal, indicating to Night Runner and Friel that he had neutralized the last of the eight terrorists. It was no ad-lib signal, but one of dozens that they had practiced since working together. He closed his fist and pumped the arm twice, indicating that they should come on at the double time.

FRIEL WAS DISAPPOINTED that Swayne and Potts had finished off the last two terrorists just as he was about to. Once when he'd been aiming in the center of the fleeing man's back, and again when he'd had a sight picture of the two arms flapping up and down around the corner, shooting off the AK-50. Then again, he knew he shouldn't worry about not getting all the kills. He had no doubt there would be more fighting to come.

He signaled Night Runner to go first, holstering his pistol and unslinging his 20-millimeter, checking the preset fuses for the third time in the last hour to make sure they were set on proximity so they would explode before striking the target, scattering fragmentation, keeping an enemy's head down.

And sure enough, as Night Runner hurdled bodies on his way down hallway, four men ran out about halfway down the wing farthest from the central lobby. They spread out across the passageway, taking up firing positions, their legs spread, their weapons coming up. Friel barely took aim at all, just pointed at the center of mass of one of the four and fired well clear of the left shoulder of the running Night Runner. He knew his teammate would not even flinch at the sound of the 20-millimeter round slashing past him. Everybody on his team, and anybody in the Marine Corps who knew him, knew Friel could shoot between your arm and your body and put the eye out of an enemy three hundred yards beyond.

The explosive head detonated three meters before it reached its target's chest, blowing lethal fragments to a radius of ten meters or more, and the four men were thrown back, three of them dead before they hit the floor, the survivor screaming in agony, scratching at his face.

By then, Night Runner had leapt out of sight over the partial wall. And Friel too was up and running, his bulky gun held horizontally, waiting for another group of victims to show themselves. He painted the visible red dot on the far wall of the west wing as he ran. He kept the spot steady to within a one-meter circle, a skill he had practiced over and over again. His eyes were doing all the movement as he made his dash, darting from one doorway to another.

• • •

BEFORE FRIEL COULD make it to the dining room,
Swayne had already decided it would be too dangerous to cross the hallway to get to the back of the
hotel grounds. Running down the east hallway was
out of the question—too far with a direct line of fire
from the west wing.

That meant they would have to go out the front
of the lodge. By now, he could visualize terrorist
squads bailing out the west doors, splitting up and
running around the building to cover all the exits.

Any second now, the Spartans were going to be
trapped inside The Fortress. The terrorists would not
even have to attack them, only keep them pinned
inside, waiting for the media and the Canadian
Armed Forces to arrive and take over the battle. If
that wasn't urgency enough, the dining room was
vulnerable to an attack from almost any of the floors
above the gift shop. At least two dozen terraces extended out into the vast open space of the great
room above them, allowing clear sight lines.

The instant Night Runner dived to safety in the
dining room, Swayne shouted to him, ''The medical
kit. See if you can revive the general. We're going
to make a run for it, and he's going to have to help
himself, even if he's a little manic.''

Swayne checked his watch. An hour and ten
minutes. A thought flashed through his mind: What
if he was wrong about being sacrificed for the
political sake of the Administration? With their
firepower, they might be able to hold off an enemy
like the terrorists indefinitely. When the Canadian

Armed Forces came up to take over the battle,
Swayne thought he might strike a truce, if he could
somehow get their trust. It would be a way to insure
the survival of the Commandant. Let the Administration secure its own survival.

He heard Friel's footsteps running down the hallway. He stuck his head and rifle out to provide fire
support, and saw the red laser spot nailed to the far
end of the hallway. Once again he marveled that a
man could run at full speed and still keep his
weapon that steady. Friel was nothing if not a highly
evolved killing machine.

Swayne also saw that he was not the only one to
hear the footsteps. Three rifle barrels and two heads
poked out of a set of rooms and began firing down
the hall. Before Swayne could fire, the red laser dot
shifted to the nearest target, a pair of arms spraying
an AK-47 on full automatic. A second later, the
arms evaporated, and the AK-47 spun away harm-
lessly, sliding off down the hallway. Likewise, one
of the heads burst into a spray, and the farthest man
was flung backward against the doorway before he
crumpled to the floor.

Friel vaulted the half-wall into the dining room,
the left leg of his camouflaged trousers drenched in
blood below the left knee.

"You're hit," Swayne advised. Not to prove his
mastery of the obvious. Sometimes the adrenaline
pumped so hard a man could not tell he had been
wounded.

"Nah, it's from that creep we hauled upstairs."

Swayne sagged in relief. "Get ready to blow out of here," he shouted to his team. "Night Runner, how is the general?"

Night Runner lay on the floor, leaning down into the shaft of the dumbwaiter, ministering to the Commandant.

He tossed a syringe aside and called out, "Coming around. But slowly."

"Potts, Friel," said Swayne. "Lob a couple boomers down each hallway so they'll keep their heads down."

While the two men went for the compartments in their packs that held their concussion grenades, Swayne made time for a quick report. Whatever happened, he wanted Zavello to know that he had the general in hand, alive and well.

Zavello sounded less than jubilant, and Swayne knew that he had been right to believe that a missile might soon be on its way. *And how did it get to be ten minutes later already?*

"Confirm that you have not resorted to the Necessity Kills alternative," said Zavello, his voice flat.

The lack of affect in Zavello's voice chilled him to his core. Somebody in Washington had condemned them to death, and Zavello, too much of a Marine to betray the betrayal by the politicians, was giving it away with his lack of enthusiasm that Team 2400 had accomplished the first part of its mission to snatch the Commandant. The colonel's tone was full of defeatism, and Swayne wanted no part of it. So he signed off, fighting back the urge to tell Zavello what he suspected—and maybe give himself the ultimate satisfaction of having the last word in telling Zavello what a sonofabitch he was. But he did none of these things. Instead he signed off as a professional, the way he would want to be remembered. For his part, Zavello played it to the hilt, demanding a full report once they had gotten clear of the lodge and were evading in the wilderness. "I'll be sending search and rescue helicopters to pick you up once the snowdust has settled," Zavello said. "That's a promise."

More than anything else, this promise, unsolicited and excessively earnest, unsettled Swayne.

"Boomers up," said Potts, cradling two of the devices in the palm of one hand like a pair of jumbo Easter eggs.

"On my command," Swayne said.

Like everything else they carried, the space-age hand grenades had been designed for maximum effect and minimum hassle for the Force Recon Marines. The explosives were half as heavy and twice as lethal as normal compositions. For ease in carrying, each device was split along its longitudinal axis and hinged so the flat side could be carried against the body—a man could carry two in his shirt pocket beneath a sport coat, barely raising a noticeable lump or wrinkle. To use it, all a Marine had to do was set the digital timer—from three seconds to twelve hours—close the two halves on their hinge, and chuck the device. Magnets kept it closed and in the shape of an egg for throwing by hand.

Another way to achieve its default three-second interval was to close the egg-grenade, slip it onto the point of a bayonet, and sling it in the direction of the enemy. The bayonet tip armed the grenade, and the extra leverage gained by using a bayonet as a throwing lever improved a man's range anywhere from ten to twenty meters.

Night Runner had helped the general to his feet inside the shaft of the dumbwaiter. The general stood swaying, cursing at the Indian. "He thinks Night Runner is one of the bad guys," said Friel.

"We're Marines, sir," said Night Runner, averting his nose. "Force Recon Marines. We're here to get you the hell out of this place."

The general came to attention, almost falling over, and started spouting his name, rank, and service number. Night Runner looked back at Swayne over his shoulder.

"Potts, after you toss the boomers, take over the Commandant. Night Runner, lead the way out. Potts follow. Friel and I will cover your six until you give the word. We'll meet you outside."

"Which direction do you want to go once we get out there?"

"Good question—"

A blast of gunfire made everybody crouch closer to the floor. Emboldened by the lack of activity by the team, the terrorists had begun to shoot into the dining room. Their fire was not well aimed, their apparent target another chandelier.

"Good question, Gunny. Let's see how the situation develops when we get there. Maybe we can make it to the snowmobiles and get the general into the woods. E and E from there. Boomers out. Friel down the south corridor, Potts down the west. Now!"

The four concussion grenades, built for blast and noise with very little shrapnel, were airborne, at once. Night Runner grabbed the general and hauled him out of the dumbwaiter shaft, clasping his hands over Masterson's ears. Everybody else hit the floor, shielding their faces, protecting their ear canals. Swayne worried momentarily that Night Runner's sacrifice for the sake of the Commandant might deafen him. But he didn't have much time for thinking about it. In a split second, his body felt as if he were being worked over by wet towels soaked in saltwater to add sting.

When the last blast had gone off, he was on his feet, diving over the half-wall, taking up a position behind one of the columns in the great hall, looking for targets amid the black smoke billowing their way from each wing. He was not surprised there were no targets. Every door within thirty feet of those grenades had been blown in, the concussion causing such sudden and violent changes in the atmospheric pressure that eardrums and maybe even eyeballs would burst. Anybody in a room with the door open would have been immobilized, perhaps cut to ribbons by flying glass and splinters of wood. Out to fifty feet an unprepared, unprotected man would be stunned, probably for up to half an hour. Even beyond that, the effects of those grenades could be devastating—the damned things were practically too dangerous to throw unless you had a decathlete's arm or used the bayonet for throwing leverage.

Swayne checked behind him. Night Runner had reached the huge triple set of doors, twelve feet high, at the entrance to the lodge. He pushed through to the outside and knelt behind one of the stone pillars supporting the porch roof. Potts was half-carrying, half-dragging the Commandant, his left arm hugging the general around the chest. The general was still bitching at the Marines he believed to be his captors, still spouting his name, rank, and serial number—which Swayne realized had too many numbers in it to be true. Not a good situation. If the Commandant hadn't gained his senses by the time they reached the snowmobiles—*if* they reached the snowmobiles—Potts might have to thump him on the watermelon and strap him to his back to get him out of harm's way. What a picture that would be. What a story back at the officers' mess—if they ever made it back to tell it.

Night Runner waved them on, and Swayne cursed himself for allowing his mind to wander into fantasyland at a time like this. He directed Friel out ahead of him because he had his sniper gun, which improved their chances against any heavy weapons outside. Swayne kept a watch behind him as he ran, turning often to cover the central hall of the lodge with his weapons. But they were not challenged from behind. The boomers had done their jobs.

Outside, the cold hit him, and he remembered the least yielding of their enemies, the weather.

All the excitement inside, the stress, and the fighting had raised a sweat. The exposed skin on his face and hands felt as if it had crystallized.

"Do we make a run for it, Cap?" said Potts.

"You sonsabitches will pay for this," the Commandant growled, his speech slurred.

"I'm loving this fresh air," said Friel. "Anybody out there?" He fumbled with his night-vision goggles.

Night Runner adjusted the monitor on his night-vision gunsight and swept the scene to the west. Swayne set his binoculars to thermal detection and full power and brought them up as Night Runner groaned. "They're out there, all right. In big numbers. Standing in the open."

"In the open?" Potts asked.

"Just wait till the Marines get their hooks in your asses," the general growled.

"Christ almighty," murmured Friel. "Cap, I ain't never punched the lights out of a general before, but if you get tired of listening to or smelling the Batman, I'll be first to volunteer for—"

"Quiet, Henry." Swayne scanned right along the horizon from the corner of the lodge to his left, counting thirty to forty thermal hits in one sweep. The ones that interested him most were perhaps eight men standing in a group at the middle of this formation, walking toward the lodge. Whereas all the other images indicated heads and faces sticking up from behind cover, these eight were standing, casting full-line images of the human body.

"They're naked," Night Runner said. "The bastards have stripped some of the POWs. They won't last a half hour out there."

"What the hell are they trying to prove?" said Friel.

"They're Navy," said Night Runner. "On full magnification, I can see their tattoos—anchors and shit."

Swayne knew that Night Runner's scope had an optical magnification of 20-power and a digital magnification capability of 200x. But—

Potts asked the question on the Swayne's mind. "How can they be SEALs?"

"Trust me," Night Runner insisted, "they're SEALs."

"No way, buddy. No way could they get that many SEALs to surrender in the pink."

Swayne was thinking the same thing. A man on his own might experience a weak moment and give up. But anybody who suggested a surrender in a group that size would be shouted down. A SEAL who actually tried it would end up like Castro's crab bait, shot in the back.

"They didn't give up," said Night Runner. "Check out the Frogs guarding them. See those cases they're packing around on their hips?"

Swayne switched his binoculars from thermal to

night-vision capability. And there it was, the evidence that the SEALs had not disgraced themselves. The guards were carrying gas masks. Somehow the terrorists, wanting prisoners more than a body count, had disabled the Navy men with gas and picked them up off the ice like the beached SEALs that they were.

"What the hell is going on?" the Commandant demanded.

Potts put hand on his shoulder. "General Masterson, we're Marines. Force Recon Marines. Do you understand me?"

"That's right, you bastard," the general slurred. "Force Recon Marines are going to drop in here and kick your asses."

"He's out of it, Captain."

"Do we make a run for the snowmobiles?" asked Friel.

Before Swayne could answer, it became apparent there might be no more decisions left to the initiative of the Force Recon Team. From behind cover near the lake, a white searchlight hit the front of the lodge, blowing their night vision and neutralizing their NVG scopes instantly.

Instinctively, everybody crouched, keeping their eyes shut against the brilliance of the searchlight.

A loudspeaker crackled. "You must surrender like your comrades. You cannot escape." Spoken with a French accent.

Without waiting for a response to the surrender demand, the terrorists launched one of the "mad minutes'' that the conventional military loved to use in firepower demonstrations. Automatic guns, heavy machine guns among them, opened up, shattering all the glass in the doorways behind them, singing off the granite lodge in a cacophony of ricochets as if the Spartans were being attacked by killer bees. Swayne realized that he had not seen all the enemy firepower in his first glance around with the thermal binoculars. Now shots were being fired from enough additional positions to indicate an additional twenty or so more guns than he had first thought. For a full thirty seconds, the shooting was so intense that he dared not even asked Night Runner to peek around the corner of his stone shelter with his stealth lens— too much danger that one of his fingertips might be shot off.

In the middle of it all, the general piped up. ''I told you, you sonsabitches. Now you're going to get it.'' He crowed, ''The Marines have landed, you bastards.''

''I hope we get out of this alive,'' Friel muttered in a lull of the gunfire. ''Think of the story we're going to be able to tell on the Commandant of the Marine Corps. We risk our asses to save his, and all he can do is diss us and breathe in our faces.''

Swayne shook his head. Friel. Cool as a cadaver. Smart-ass as always.

Gradually the shooting died down to a few sporadic shots like the last kernels to explode in a pan of popcorn. Swayne asked Night Runner if he could get a clear shot at the searchlight by holding his rifle and scope around a corner and shooting by remote.

Night Runner tried it, and Swayne had his answer by watching the tiny monitor hanging before the Indian's eyes.

"Total washout," Night Runner said, scratching the Rottweiler behind the ears. "Can't see the laser dot. Can't see anything but white."

"Maybe I can pop up and get off a quick round with a proximity fuse," said Friel. "The shrapnel might blow it out." His face tensed as the firing picked up again.

Swayne shook his head. The terrorists had reloaded and begun a second mad minute. "Let me look. Maybe I can take it with a burst of fire using manual sights."

"Manual sights," said Friel. "What's this world coming to?"

Swayne debated. Pop up first and take a look? No, he might have only a second or two of visibility before he was dazzled. Better to use that brief time looking through his sights and squeezing off a burst. Besides, sticking his head up into that hail of fire was safer done once than twice.

When he came up, Swayne found that the scene was just as much a whiteout as yesterday's blizzard. He blinked rapidly, thinking that somehow his own vision had suffered the same effect as the television monitor. But no, the scene had gone white for another reason. He ducked back down without shooting.

"Why you looking so snakebit, Cap?" said Potts.

Friel shook his head in disbelief. "Why didn't you shoot?"

Swayne answered with the one word that could mobilize even the most poorly trained soldier into instantaneous action. *"Gas!"*

"Like I said, you sonsabitches are done for."

Swayne looked at the general, wondering if he ought to strike the Commandant, who for most Marines stood higher on the chain of command than even God. After all, it didn't look as if there were going to be any survivors to court-martial.

"Back inside," he ordered. "All at once. They're shooting in the blind through the cloud of smoke. If we lay down a base of fire, all we're going to do is give them a sound to shoot at. If you do get hit, it won't be because they're good but because they're lucky."

"Swell," said Friel, putting on a Mona Lisa grin. "Guess that means it won't hurt as much, eh, Captain?"

Swayne laughed.

Potts did not. "Henry," he murmured, and Friel collapsed against the stone.

"Let's go," Swayne ordered.

They ran for the doorway as a group, Swayne lending a hand to Potts to drag the reluctant general inside, their boots clumping on the glass, scratching, squealing, and tinkling as they ran across the stone floor.

"Into the basement?" Night Runner shouted.

"No, find a stairwell. We'll go up." Swayne figured the cold air might keep the cloud closer to ground. Even if it didn't, the stairwell would provide them with the least amount of air circulation until the wind dissipated the cloud. He knew there were terrorists on the roof, but better that than—

A rattling of gunfire came at them from above. The terraces. Not everybody from the terrorists had gone outside. Some had gone up to take commanding firing positions.

Friel answered the gunfire first, throwing up the muzzle of his sniper gun and shooting from the hip. The explosion gave Potts enough time to duck around the corner into the west stairwell, from which the enemy had first come at them.

Night Runner and Swayne sprayed the upper floors with automatic fire, not so much at selected targets, but to disrupt the ability of the terrorists to aim their fire. Night Runner went to one knee, and for a second, Swayne thought he had been hit. But no. He was taking careful aim. He had found a target. Swayne saw an ear. Night Runner fired at the small disk, and the great hall filled with the shriek of a man flopping on a third-floor terrace. A second shot stopped the screaming.

Swayne reached the stairwell and heard both the unnaturally light step of the bulky Potts and the irregular, stumbling steps of the dazed general going up ahead. This was a dangerous situation, for at any moment one of the doors in the stairwell above could be thrown open, and a squad of terrorists could take out the Commandant and Potts, the rock on whom he was leaning, such a stalwart fighting man that he'd been the only one unfazed by the general's stench.

Next came Night Runner, recognizing the danger, running past Swayne to cover Potts's move upward, the huge, broad dog at his heels.

"Come on, Friel," said Swayne, checking his watch. They had just under an hour to get out of the lodge alive. He looked toward the entryway—ten seconds, if that cloud got here before the friendly fire of an ICBM.

He began counting down, readying himself to grab Friel by the nape of the neck and drag him inside the stairwell if necessary. At five, Swayne stepped to the door of the stairwell, a concussion grenade attached to the tip of his bayonet. He gave a great heave, and the grenade sailed upward into the darkness.

"Fire in the hole!" he hollered.

Friel dashed past him and said, "Let's go, Captain," straining the words through his teeth. He started up the stairs.

Swayne was close behind, catching up to and passing Friel on the second landing. *Now, how could that be?* He and Friel nearly always tied for second behind Night Runner in physical-training dashes. He looked down toward the sound of Friel's sloshing footsteps, and realized that he had been shot in the leg after all. Each of his right boot prints on the steps was stenciled in blood.

Before he could make a comment about it, the

concussion grenade blew, throwing them both up against wall.

Swayne slowed a step, supporting Friel, pushing him past. Friel shrugged him off.

"Don't wait on me, Captain. If you wait on me, you'll be backing up."

Swayne saw the strain on Friel's face, the pain in the eyes and the paleness indicating an excessive loss of blood, the initial symptoms of shock. "I'm not waiting on you," he said. "I'm just doing your job is all. Somebody has to watch our six."

The building shook from a second explosion.

"What now?" said Friel, beginning to struggle in the climb up the stairs, pulling himself up by the banister. "Artillery, you think?"

A second and then a third explosion followed, coming nearer. Swayne shook his head. "I don't get it."

Potts and Night Runner met them on the fourth-floor landing. They were struggling with the Commandant, who kept trying to pull away to go for the door. Potts finally grasped the old man from behind, squeezing him in a bear hug, lifting his feet off the ground. "I'm going to get court-martialed for this," he muttered.

"And a maximum sentence, you bastards. The penalty for kidnapping under the Uniform Code of Military Justice is death."

Night Runner shook his head. "He's still out of it."

Swayne patted the Commandant's cheeks. "No,

he's coming around. He knows that terrorists wouldn't be subject to the UCMJ. He knows we're Marines. At least he wants to court-martial us.''

"The Commandant wants to court-martial us, and that's a good thing," said Runner with a wry grin.

"You bet your ass, mister. You're all going to swing for this.''

Another explosion struck, sending a shock wave into their stairwell.

"What the hell *is* that?" said Friel, just reaching the landing and gasping for breath.

"You're hit," said Night Runner.

Friel shook his head. "Nah, I'm aces.''

Finally, Swayne understood. "We'd better get the hell out of here," he said. "They're clearing the stairwells with grenades, trying to drive us down to the ground floor and into the gas. Let's get the general and Friel up to the roof before—''

Above them a door opened, and a metallic clanging sounded on the fifth-floor stairs. The team traded glances. They damned well knew the sound from their experiences in urban-combat training and in at least one combat operation somewhere around Event Scenario Nine.

A hand grenade.

With three seconds left until detonation. *Three seconds tops.*

The tendency was to go down, but that was where they would be exposed to that cloud.

Two seconds.

Night Runner grabbed the door, and Potts dived

through it into the hallway of fourth floor, twisting his body so he would not land on general. As he rolled on the floor, Night Runner dived in after, clearing the hallway with the muzzle of his rifle, his newfound canine combat partner exposing his fangs as if eager for a fight. The impact of hitting the floor jarred his injured ribs, taking his breath away.

One second.

Friel leaned more than dived out of the stairwell. Until he was hit from behind by Swayne and thrown to the carpet.

The next thing through the doorway was black smoke and shrapnel. Lots of shrapnel.

All Swayne could hear was a fuzzy clanging in his ears. All he could feel was a vicious stinging up the backs of his legs. Even so, he looked around, assessing the damage to the others. The general sat up, pinching his nose. Potts shouted at him, blood streaming down the left side of his face into his mouth, bleeding and talking in slow motion. Swayne was fascinated by the sight of the huge bear of a Marine calling to him soundlessly, his words punctuated by red spray and bubbles of bloody spit.

Friel had not picked up any new wounds. Night Runner had escaped unscathed.

Swayne focused on Potts's lips, and shook his head to answer that he had not been hit.

Night Runner moved back into the stairwell, as always, putting his superior faculties to work listening. How he could hear at all was a mystery. Swayne saw him pick at both ears and realized that, once again, the warrior had been smarter than the rest of them. He had been wearing earplugs, probably since back in the dining room when Swayne had ordered the use of boomers. A good Marine and a smart one too. Swayne wished he'd had the same foresight.

He rapped himself on the side of his head, giving himself an attitude adjustment and a renewed focus. He checked his wristwatch. Less than forty-five minutes—no, the concussion had stopped his watch. How long ago did that grenade go off anyhow? He demanded that his mental clock start to work on its own as he began calculating their alternatives.

What options did they have?

Not many. Night Runner stepped out of the stairwell, pulling the door to, wincing. He pointed downward, then moved two fingers like the legs of a running man. Then he held up all the fingers of one hand. Message: five terrorists lurking below.

But why? It didn't make sense. They no longer had to kill or capture the team. They already had their prisoners, the Navy SEALs.

"Do we go up to the roof?" said Night Runner. Swayne could barely hear him, but made out the message by watching his lips and reading the thumbs-up signal.

"No," Swayne said, realizing he was shouting. But he was not the only one. The general was at it again, holding his nose and pointing to Swayne. Rather than becoming more lucid, he seemed to be getting worse all the time. Doing what? Telling him that *they* stank? The grenade must have ruined his sense of smell if—

No! That wasn't what he was saying. Swayne cupped his hand behind an ear. "What?"

The general stopped pinching his nose and took his hand away from his face, so Swayne could finally read his lips. "Pinch your nose and blow gently. It will open your ears, Marine."

Two things, both good. The general was back, realizing that he was among his own kind. And when Swayne did as the general suggested, his eardrums, which seemed to the been packed into the center of his head by the concussion in the stairwell, cleared.

"Give me a weapon," the Commandant ordered. "It's payback time for these bastards."

"We don't have time, General," said Swayne. "We have to get out of the lodge. Maybe out the back. Night Runner, check one of the stairwells toward the west."

"Belay that," said the Commandant, stopping Night Runner in his tracks. "Why do we have to get out of the lodge?"

Swayne gritted his teeth. "General, with all due respect—"

"Bullshit. Anytime a Marine says with all due respect, that's exactly the opposite what he means. Say what's on your mind."

"General you may be the Commandant of the Corps, but on this mission, I'm in charge. We have to get you out of here alive, and that means getting out of the lodge.''

"Why?''

"We're in Canada. Did you know that?''

The general shook his head. "They've kept me on drugs. I thought we were still in Montana.'' A kind of dawning began to show on the general's face. He sniffed at his hands. "Good God! Has anybody noticed the bad smell of me?''

"General,'' said Friel, "has anybody *not* noticed?''

Potts had had enough. He raised a hand to cuff the wounded man.

"No,'' said Masterson. "He's right, by God.''

Friel gazed upon his Commandant with a renewed admiration.

Swayne consulted his mental watch. "By my calculations, the Canadian Armed Forces will make an airdrop on this area very shortly. I have it on good word that there's a mechanized force moving up the mountain. They can't be permitted to catch us anywhere inside the country. It would—''

The Commandant finished Swayne's sentence for him. "It would embarrass the Administration.'' The general began nodding as full understanding dawned. "The implications are—'' The general's head came up, and his eyes, blue-black as a gun barrel, pinned Swayne. "By chance were you ordered to apply the Geneva Conventions Alternative on me?''

Swayne bit his lip.

"Be quick about it, son."

"Affirmative, sir. But we snatched you. So it didn't come to pass. But now I think it will turn into an even more radical—"

"You bet your ass it will. They're perfectly capable of applying the Alternative as a collective measure to the whole bunch of us. Are there any other American forces around?"

"Navy SEALs."

"What the hell is the Navy doing—never mind that."

"Right," said Swayne. "We have to get out of here."

"No, we don't."

"General, don't pull rank on me now. I'm responsible for your safety and—"

"Forget rank, son. Are any of you wearing personal locator beacons? The PERLOBE things?"

The Spartans looked at each other and shrugged. *What did this have to do with anything?*

Then it hit Swayne, causing his jaw to drop. The PERLOBEs, of course. They could do more than track a unit's position. Under circumstances of pinpoint bombing, it wouldn't be necessary to take out the lodge, merely *hoping* to bury the Spartans and all evidence of their existence. Anybody with a receiver could pinpoint the teams—every one of them by his unique digital code—and send a smart bomb straight down the chute and right into their individual hip pockets—more accurately, their shirt pockets, where most of his men carried them.

Swayne's PERLOBE was on his wrist, attached to his now-useless watch. He stripped it off, threw to the floor, and prepared to stomp it.

"Don't!" said the general. "They'll just launch immediately at the last known location if they suspect you purposely sabotaged the signal—I was part of the panel that approved the procedures."

By then the other men had produced their personal beacons. Potts and Night Runner used a type disguised as a pen, although Runner's had not functioned since his hard landing against the tree during the blizzard. Friel's was a dummy rifle cartridge.

"What?" Friel said. "Throw them out the window?"

Swayne shook his head. "Not far enough."

The general was shaking his own bristled head. "They'll be using heavy ordnance, thousand-pounders at least."

Potts, his blood drying and crackling on his face, muttered, "On their own troops? On the Commandant of the—?"

Friel said, "A direct hit by a thousand-pound bomb would—"

Again, the general finished the sentence left hanging. "Vaporize any evidence that we are Americans, including dental structure. As far as anybody would know, the Commandant never set foot into Canada."

Swayne put his mind into overdrive, determined to come up with a calculation that would get them out of this impossible situation. He needed an option now as he had never before needed one. "What do we have?" he asked aloud. "With all this high-tech equipment, what do we have that could throw these things far enough to give us a safe standoff distance?"

Potts took out his bayonet, which gave extra leverage as a launching device for the boomers.

Swayne shook his head. "Even an extra ten meters wouldn't be enough."

Friel, his breathing now grown ragged, pointed to the Rottweiler. The dog snarled at the pointing finger, and Friel jerked his arm back. "What about him? Could we tie the PERLOBEs to his collar and scare him away?"

"No," barked Night Runner.

"He's just a dog—"

Night Runner threw a shoulder into the doorway to the stairwell and was gone, taking each landing in two leaps, the dog at his heels.

"What?" Friel gasped. "Did I say something anti-dog or something?"

As NIGHT RUNNER bounded down the last flight of stairs, he saw a fog seeping under the door to form a cloud near the floor of the stairwell. He stopped and showed the palm of his hand to the dog.

"Stay," he ordered in a stage whisper, both in English and French. The dog's claws clattered on the tile as he backpedaled, came to a stop, and sat on the lowest landing. The animal cocked its huge, cubical head, raising its tan eyebrows as if to ask: *Anything else, little brother?*

Runner turned toward the door and listened for any sound of the five men he'd glimpsed earlier.

Nothing.

He'd have felt better if there'd been a sound. That way, he'd know the extent and direction of the danger. His enemy might be on guard in the lobby. Or he might be gone. Nothing to do but gamble.

He summoned his guardian angel and namesake, Heavy Runner, to help him in his quest. In his mind he pictured Heavy Runner riding across the sea of the prairie, armed with only a coup stick. Into the guns of a ragged band of cavalry out to avenge the losing side in the Battle of the Greasy Grass, where Custer had died in disgrace. Slapping the stick across the skull of a terrified soldier who'd thrown down his rifle and run.

He propped his rifle against the wall, checked his pistol, drew a huge breath, and descended into the waist-deep cloud.

In the lobby, the cloud enveloped him, giving him comfort that he could evade his enemy like the very ghost of Heavy Runner. He called on every power in the spirit world to guide him toward the gift shop.

On the way back to the stairwell more than a minute later, Night Runner felt the very confidence of his namesake's spirit after counting coup. He'd not met the enemy, but he had gotten what he wanted from the gift shop. The cloud in the stairwell had climbed to the first landing. The Rottweiler still sat erect, the gas up to his shoulders.

Runner released enough breath to order the dog out of danger. "Go on," he said, and waved at the beast. The dog stood up and began to make his way up the stairs.

Until the moment he bent over to retrieve his rifle, Night Runner did not sense danger. Perhaps, if he'd not been holding his breath, he would have smelled it. If his ears had not been ringing with his pulse, he would have heard.

What he did hear was the scratching of dog claws. Urgent scratching. He looked up to see a black and tan body hurtle past him into the cloud.

Night Runner whirled, bringing up his pistol in time to see the Rottweiler smash into a soldier dressed in a gas mask. The animal tore at the face protector, and the soldier squealed.

Runner fired four times into the cloud at belly-button level, and two mask-muffled cries answered his pistol shots.

Then he was off, running up the stairwell, drawing clean air into his lungs, pausing at the next landing to call back for the dog. He heard growling and more cries, but soon all the sounds died out, and he knew the gas was having its effect on the animal that had saved his skin. But he could not go back to recover the dog.

A part of his brain, the part that revered the spiritual side of his heritage, spoke to him. It told him he must thank the dog that had lent its life for his.

It told him that the ultimate act of sacrifice could only have been managed by a guardian spirit. And that he should name the Rottweiler.

So he did, even as he ran up the stairs to rejoin his companions. And with a sad heart, he called the animal Heavy Runner.

BY THE TIME Night Runner yanked open the stairwell door and returned to the hallway, Swayne had collected his injured team members and the general at farthest stairwell in the west wing, leaving the PERLOBEs together in the hallway. Night Runner gathered up the three devices and ran toward the others.

"What the hell are you doing, Marine?" said the general. "Is this about that damned dog?"

Friel murmured weakly, "I'm sorry about saying we should tie the beacons to the dog, okay?"

Night Runner ignored the apology.

Swayne understood that Night Runner's intentions had nothing to do with the dog. They had everything to do with what the warrior had retrieved from the gift shop in the lobby—a bow and arrows.

He leaned Friel against the wall and went to the windows at the end of the hall. He picked up a chair and broke out the glass, then kept pounding against the plywood until it tore free and sailed off, spinning into the blackness that had begun to turn a shade toward dawn.

As Night Runner produced duct tape and began strapping the PERLOBEs to the shafts of his arrows,

Swayne thought of the Navy SEALs. Would it be right for them to be sacrificed to the Geneva Conventions Alternative while Force Recon team survived?

He ran back to Friel and picked up his sniper gun.

"The selector," Friel murmured, on the verge of unconsciousness. "It's still set on the visible reticle dot."

Friel could barely keep his head erect. He began sliding down the wall. The general grabbed him and lowered him to his side. "I'll bind up his leg," the Commandant said. "You go help that other Marine down there."

As he ran toward Night Runner, Swayne turned on the laser designator, and the red dot danced on the wall ahead of him. He tried keeping it steady, as he had seen Friel do so many times. No luck. He hoped the Boston Kid would not slip into a state of shock.

Night Runner lifted the first arrow high, pointing toward the lake. "Shoot well over the SEALs," Swayne said. "I'll take care of the guards."

Night Runner was already on the second arrow by the time Swayne had brought the sniper gun to his shoulder and picked out the dazed SEALs stumbling toward The Fortress. Only half a dozen of them were standing under their own power, helping the others. The others had succumbed to the effects of the gas and the biting cold.

Night Runner was notching his third arrow, when

he said, "You know that Friel has those fuses set to proximity, don't you?"

"Affirmative."

Swayne picked out the SEALs in his scope, hoping that they had not fallen too far into shock from the cold to recognize what was happening. He played the reticle dot across one man's chest. No reaction. Next he caused the dot to dance from chest to chest, bouncing up to hit faces. Nothing. It wasn't going to happen. The men were going to die, and although he had been in conflict with Navy units both professionally and jealousy-wise all his career, he did not want them to be killed.

Finally, one of the men reacted, jumping as though he had been stung by an insect. He alone among the SEALs had noticed the visible laser dot. In the next moment, all the SEALs dived to the ground, recognizing what it meant.

Only then did Swayne fire the sniper gun, calmly shifting the spot to the left shoulder of one of a pair of guards, who were startled by the reaction of the SEALs. He squeezed off two fire-and-forget 20-millimeter rounds and ducked back inside. He and Night Runner began a sprint down the hallway, Swayne shouting for the others to dive into the stairwell.

Potts, himself unsteady, was barely able to drag the now-unconscious Friel into the stairwell, helped by the general, before the world outside the lodge erupted, first with the explosions of the puny 20-millimeter rounds, then with two enormous blasts.

• • •

THE STEALTH BOMBER pilot had put out two thousand-pound smart bombs, one set to a frequency in the cluster of beacons. This was a true fire-and-forget mission with no need to worry about a laser designator. The bombs would home on the beacons as surely as if they were dropped down a laundry chute. Before the first blinding explosion behind him, he had already begun his turn back toward the south, confident that his bombs had homed in on those beacons, accurate to within one meter. Those people would never know what hit them. Why he was bombing inside Canada, he did not asked himself. Who the enemy was, he was not told and did not need to know. Most especially, he did not want to know.

He put his craft into an invisible racetrack holding pattern over Waterton-Glacier International Peace Park, awaiting further orders.

NIGHT RUNNER AND Swayne never reached the stairwell leading to the roof. The force of a blast coming through the same window from which they had launched arrows and the 20-millimeter rounds now poured in, lifting them off their feet and throwing them thirty feet down the hallway. They hit and rolled another twenty feet. All Swayne remembered were the points of impact on his knees, elbows, shoulders, and face as he cartwheeled down the hallway. *Rug burns,* he thought. *I'm going to be covered with rug burns.*

It was a ridiculous thing to be worried about, he told himself, especially since he wouldn't be living much longer to feel the pain. But before he could even dismiss such a negative thought, he blacked out.

POTTS LAY ON the roof, dazed, and listened to the sounds of many boot steps. He looked around for a weapon before he realized he and Friel and the general were surrounded by faces in the growing dawn. Lots of faces. French-Canadians. An exceedingly white race of people, he thought. And naked bodies—the SEALs.

The general pointed to the sky. Potts recognized the blossoms forming in the air.

"Paratroopers."

From the northeast came the sound of motorized vehicles. And above all in the distance, a helicopter droned.

"Dammit," said Potts. "How in the hell are we going to get out of this?"

"Good question," said a strange voice.

A chunk of a man dressed in cammies and pointing an Uzi at them stepped out from behind the SEALs. He gave a signal, and three other soldiers, all armed with AK-47 rifles, stepped into the clear, disarming Potts and the dazed Friel.

"Pareto," the Commandant growled. He looked to Potts. "I don't remember much, but this is the bastard in charge of these terrorists."

"And you are my prisoners. You are on Canadian

soil unlawfully. What you have done constitutes an invasion of Canada. Expect the worst when our military arrives.'' Pareto looked toward the eastern horizon. ''Better yet, when the Canadian media comes on scene.'' On cue, as if he had directed it himself, a brightly colored news helicopter came over the horizon at them, its rotor blades flashing the morning sun their way. ''Canada,'' said Friel. ''I hate goddamn Canada.''

Speaking in French, Pareto directed his men to herd the general and the other Americans back inside the building.

SWAYNE CAME TO his senses in the hallway at the sound of heavy footsteps in the stairwell. He opened his eyes and peered through the slit under the door in time to see the nude SEALs, the Commandant, and Potts carrying Friel all come down the stairwell, escorted to the basement by armed guards. This contingent was followed by a blocky figure barking orders in French and talking to a younger vulture of a man at his side.

Swayne guessed this was the terrorist leader, and wished he had developed some language facility other than Spanish and Farsi.

As the talking heads disappeared out of sight, he pulled his pistol and unsteadily found his feet, thinking he might dash into the stairwell to have his final shoot-out. He'd run out of a thinking man's options. All that seemed left to him was a suicidal attack. All he thought he might salvage of the operation was to kill the leader of these terrorists.

As he took hold of the doorknob, a hand grasped his ankle. He looked down to see Night Runner shaking his head.

"Get a weapon, Runner. We're going into the stairwell."

"No."

The refusal from such a dependable noncom stunned Swayne every bit as much as the bomb blast.

"I mean, *nossir*!"

Swayne never dreamed Runner would ever balk at an order. His astonishment must have showed itself to his most fearsome warrior.

"The elevator," Runner explained.

Swayne blinked. The bomb blast must have shaken the sergeant's equilibrium.

"Not us," said Runner. "Them. The guy told the guards to take the POWs down the stairs to the walk-in coolers. He and his XO are taking the elevator."

Swayne got it. He sprinted down the hallway to the elevator doors, not hearing Runner behind him. But once Swayne was there, the sergeant was at his shoulder. Together they pried open the doors and stepped inside.

When the car doors opened two floors below, Pareto and his exec entered the car.

Above them, two sets of eyes watched through the ceiling grate, and two sets of ears listened to the soft conversation in French.

Although Swayne could not translate, he could see the little Napoleon type preening. A cocky little turd, he thought, getting ready to hand over American special operations forces to the Canadian government.

Swayne braced himself for a stop when the floor-button panel lit up the letter *B*. The XO pushed two buttons at once, the *B* and the *5*. He and Night Runner exchanged glances as the elevator continued dropping into the shaft below the basement. It had traveled easily as far as from the upstairs to the basement before it finally stopped. Swayne figured they had dropped fifty to sixty feet below the ground when the doors opened and the two terrorist leaders stepped out into a lobby. The leader threw his parka over a chair, and the XO leaned back inside to shut off the car's power, keeping the doors open in the below-ground shaft.

Swayne looked to Night Runner, and the sergeant told him what he wanted to know.

"The fat guy is Pareto. He calls himself a general. He's changing into a dress uniform before going out to meet the Canadian Armed Forces like some goddamned conquering hero."

Swayne nodded and pulled up the grate. "You stay here."

Night Runner cocked his head.

Swayne pulled the palm-sized PDA from his pocket and manipulated a series of keystrokes.

"Are you calling this in?" Night Runner asked incredulously. "What good will that—"

Swayne shook his head.

Runner nodded. "Are we going to take them out down here?"

"No." Swayne grasped the elevator cable to lower himself into the car, but pulled his hand away and wiped off a fistful of black grease that had come off the pulley. "Cover me. I'm going to have a look around."

NIGHT RUNNER WATCHED the captain swing down and drop into the car. As best he could, he shifted himself to provide covering fire, if it were going to be needed. *Impossible,* he decided. There was no way to aim his fire—he'd have as much chance of hitting the captain as the terrorists. If the shit broke loose down there, he would have to hop down and shoot from inside the car. *What the hell was Swayne doing?* Some things about the white man—even the best of them—he would never understand.

WHEN THE ORDER came to restrike, the Stealth bomber pilot had to arouse himself from daydreaming mode, gazing at the occasional hole in the clouds that let in a spectacular view of the spectacular Rockies. Now and then he'd let his mind absorb the fuel calculations his navigator gave him. From the look of it, they'd be tracing loops in the sky for hours.

But no. They were given a course, a mission, and a frequency. His senses took life. He braced himself, turned out of the racetrack pattern, and began an immediate checklist rundown on their second bombing run.

SWAYNE CLAMBERED INTO the space above the elevator car seconds after Pareto barked a command in French to his XO. Night Runner had barely hauled him to safety and replaced the grate before the exec had restarted the current to the car.

Swayne lay still, the pulley whirring beside his head. He felt a tap on his shoulder. He looked up as Night Runner pointed his pistol downward and mimed a recoil.

Swayne shook his head. Like the sergeant, he wished he could just shoot the sonsabitches and take his chances on getting away from the Canadians with the Commandant. But they might not have time with all those forces closing in on The Fortress. He needed to pull off something more dramatic, something that would buy them a good half hour.

The car stopped on the main floor. Pareto and his XO covered their faces with gas masks and stepped out into the lobby. Pareto gave an order, and the exec took off his mask and tested the air. When he did not pass out, Pareto tossed his mask away, and reluctantly, so did his aide.

When they were out of hearing, Swayne said, "There's a command center down there, stocked with communications and provisions for a battalion for a month. Must have been the hotel's original wine cellar. Or maybe a bomb shelter built in the fifties."

Night Runner stared into his captain's eyes with a look of: *Thanks for the tour, but so what?* But he asked politely, "What are we going to do about Pareto and the Commandant?"

Swayne sighed and crossed his fingers. "Give me your PDA."

He worked the tiny computer's controls until he could transmit on voice mode like any handheld radio.

"Nina," he said. "Come in."

Swayne's heart pounded. If he transmitted too long a burst, he might be in trouble. If he did not transmit at all, she might be killed.

"Where the hell have you been?"

A grin lined Swayne's face. He wanted to tell her so many things that it surprised him. The revelation in that was that he cared more for her than he'd ever let himself imagine. But he could say only one short thing: "I had my radio off. Get your head down and keep it down."

"Not so easy to do, pal—"

Before she could finish the sentence, Swayne knew why. He could hear the rumble of rotor blades in the transmission of her message: "I'm in News Chopper 32, Alberta's finest outlet for the CBC."

The adrenaline hit him like a medicine ball to the chest. No matter if it did expose him and Runner to danger, he had to tell her. "Get the pilot to hide behind the lodge—drop down over the cliff if you have to."

"What the hell are you talking about?"

"Get over the side, right now." If she wouldn't listen to that, he'd just have to appeal to her greed. "Meet me on the roof in five minutes, and I'll give you the biggest story of your life."

"If you don't, you bastard—"

Swayne didn't wait for the rest. He shut off the PDA and dropped into the elevator car. Runner was right beside him, hitting the floor soundlessly. *How did he do that?*

They stood looking out the bullet-spattered lobby from behind one of the tree-trunk columns.

Outside, Pareto had mounted himself inside an open truck. He stood on the seat, his hands on the windshield looking out to the front, as his XO drove him onto the lake toward a line of vehicles and paratroopers advancing a mile away in formation. Behind Pareto's parade vehicle, the remainder of his troops marched in column.

"The triumphant victory march," Swayne murmured.

Runner stirred. "Want me to run up and get one of the sniper guns or something? Maybe take out as many as we can?"

"Nah," said Swayne. "Let's watch. Then we'll go down and take our Navy friends out of the cooler and get out of here with the Commandant." He smiled at Night Runner, who looked at him as if his boss had gone mad.

"Watch."

PARETO ADJUSTED HIS uniform, pulling at his kid-

skin gloves and patting the wrinkles out of his
parka. Puzzled, he stuck his hand into one pocket
and pulled out a camouflaged plastic case little
larger than a packet of Players cigarettes. He
frowned at a spot of black grease that had gotten
onto the white of his glove leather.

He opened the box, and saw it was a tiny computer with an array of keys. He had seen computers
like this before. They were the kind of gadget the
Americans gave to their special operations soldiers.
For a moment, he thought it might be General Masterson's, the one in his possession when he had been
taken from the hunting cabin.

But no, that one had been destroyed in the truck
fire in the Sweet Grass Hills, along with the Personal Locator Beacon, the—

The PERLOBE!

A message blinked on the screen of this device:

TRANSMITTING PERLOBE SIGNAL 240001.

It occurred to Pareto that such a signal might give
away his location to American rescue forces. He
chuckled. Too late for that. There were the Canadians less than a mile away, advancing cautiously
to meet the man who might one day become prime
minister of a separate—and very French—North
American country. He might soon be the father of
his very own nation.

His lips formed around a French obscenity for all
people who spoke English.

Just as the point of a smart bomb hit him in the face, vaporizing him, his exec, and his vehicle, dropping their last remains through a gigantic hole in the ice.

Dead fish floated up to the surface, even as a second bomb struck, vaporizing the vapor.

SWAYNE AND Night Runner saw the first flash, and bolted for the stairwell before the blasts hit the lodge in tandem, toppling its facade.

They never saw the Canadian regulars withdraw across the lake and open fire on the smoke, a secondary gaseous vapor that was all that remained of Pareto and his troops—the remainder had sunk beneath the water.

Swayne was intent on getting the Commandant out of The Fortress before the Canadians recovered from their shock and advanced again. He led the way into the kitchen, diving as Potts had done earlier, sliding on his belly, firing into the torso of first one terrorist sentry, then the other. In the doorway behind him, he heard the report of Night Runner's pistol, and two more guards dropped.

In the seconds after he unlocked the door, captives began pouring out of the cooler. Swayne found the SEAL leader and sent the detachment into the elevator, briefing the men on the way about how to manipulate the button panel to give them access to the wine cellar.

"Stay in the cellar until after the next blizzard," said Swayne. "Keep up on your operational freqs until you get the word that it's clear. Then keep your eyes peeled on the lake day and night for your extraction.''

The Navy officer, a wide-eyed, still-naked lieutenant, rogered and put his men to the task of gathering clothes from dead terrorists.

Swayne didn't wait around. He herded the Commandant up the stairs, with Potts carrying the now-unconscious Friel over his shoulder.

They reached the rooftop just as the helicopter landed. Swayne put the Commandant, Potts, and Friel aboard.

Nina pinched her nose. ''What the hell have you boys been eating? Carrion?''

Swayne felt a moment of embarrassment for the Commandant, who harbored no such sentiments of his own. He merely pointed to the unconscious Friel. ''It's him,'' he said.

Swayne and Night Runner laughed. ''Drop the Commandant in Montana,'' Swayne ordered Nina, knowing full well she could get the news chopper pilot to do anything she demanded. ''Leave him off in the mountains near where he was when this whole thing began. These other two boys need some medical attention. Take them to Malmstrom Air Force Base.''

''What about you?''

''Night Runner and I will find our own way out. On the snowmobiles. It will be the first time I've had a vacation in years.''

''See you back in Virginia.''

"You can't write this, Nina."

"You said—"

"I meant it too. It's the biggest story of your life that you'll never be able to write about."

She gazed at him a long, soulful moment, then smiled.

He looked at the pilot.

"Don't worry about him," she said. "I'll see he doesn't write anything either."

"Nina," he shouted over the noise of the turbine.

"Yeah, Jack," she said, her eyes bright with emotion.

"Don't be too nice to him."

She never spoke a word. The single tear that streaked its way down her cheek revealed all that needed to be said.

EPILOGUE

THE COMMANDANT OF the Marine Corps, once feared lost, walked out of the mountains and into the arms of a civilian search and rescue crew, no worse for wear. The cabin at Black Butte had been cleansed by fire, and long before the spring melt, the USMC's lost battle equipment had been recovered, leaving no trace of the events that had gone on in the mountains of Montana. Once back inside the Pentagon, General Masterson launched an immediate top-secret investigation searching for a mole who would have had access to classified information as to his whereabouts and the PERLOBE technology he'd carried the night of his kidnapping.

THE CANADIAN ARMED Forces concluded that a power struggle among forces of the militia had led to a fatal clash, in which all members of the forces had been destroyed. They surmised that a truck bomb had been intended to destroy Canadian Armed

Forces as well, but somehow it had gone off prematurely, destroying the suicidal terrorists. Anonymity, the worst fate of terrorists, had been Pareto's end.

SWAYNE AND NIGHT Runner enjoyed their vacation traveling through the mountains, Night Runner acting as guide and survival instructor as the two men lived off the land on their week-long odyssey back into Montana. On the second day of sunlessness, the snowmobiles had to be abandoned for lack of power, so they fashioned snowshoes and walked out. Rather than being upset by it, Swayne appreciated the respite from high-tech weapons and gadgets. Only when safely inside Montana did he contact headquarters, and only then by pay phone. Calling Colonel Zavello collect gave him a great deal of satisfaction.

THE NAVY SEALs were extracted without incident two weeks later without ever having been discovered in the wine cellar. Sometime in the first hours after an early February blizzard let up, a military plane equipped with skids landed on the lake and took off the embarrassed and half-clad but well-fed SEALs, who had adopted a new team member, a 105-pound Rottweiler.

A SUBSEQUENT UNDERWATER reconnaissance mission located a Cuban submarine sunk in the spot where Event Scenario 12 had ended for the Spartans. Intelligence experts surmised that the boat had sustained damage to its conning tower hatches and had taken on too much of the sea before the vessel could recover and regain the surface.

THE GENEVA CONVENTIONS Alternative, as well as an entire string of operational contingencies known under the code name Necessity Kills, were themselves killed in a top-secret Compartmented-Information session of a Senate Armed Services subcommittee chaired by one Senator Jamison Swayne, Rep.-S.C.

FORCE RECON TEAM 2400 was reunited and put on extended R&R, pending assignment to Event Scenario 14. Marine Corps policies and procedures were amended so no more Force Recon Teams would be assigned a mission with the number 13.